CROOKED ANTLERS

J.G. MARTIN

For Mom and Dad.

VELOX BOOKS
Published by arrangement with the author.

Crooked Antlers copyright © 2022
by J.G. Martin.

CONTENTS

THE LEGEND OF COLD ROCK KEEP

The island was nothing without the lighthouse.

It was the defining feature. A stone monolith, rising out of the earth like a haunted spire, sweeping its glowing gaze out across the rage of the Atlantic ocean. Cold Rock Keep was different from other lighthouses, though. Cold Rock Keep had a body count.

Ever since anybody could remember, the island had been a haunted affair. A cursed place where ships went to die. The legend went that once upon a time, way back when the town was first erected in god-knows-when, there lived a coven of witches upon Cold Rock. They practiced their craft there because they thought the ocean would keep them safe.

And it did. For a time.

But like any old story, the players eventually disappear, and so too was the case with the witches. They died off, or were killed. Who can say? History has a funny way of forgetting itself. Whatever the case was, the shipwrecks didn't let up, and so a lighthouse was built on the island to warn ships away from its serrated shores.

That lighthouse, though, didn't seem to help matters one bit. In fact, after it was built the deaths just went up and up, and soon the jagged coastline of Cold Rock was filled with the corpses of shattered vessels. It didn't take long for the townsfolk to come to an agreement that the island was cursed, and the lighthouse had somehow become a conduit for evil.

After that, folks started avoiding Cold Rock. Local folks, at least. They knew better, because their mothers and fathers knew better, and their mothers and fathers had known better before them. They passed down the warnings in bedtime stories, or cautionary tales before trips to the sea.

"Don't drift too close to the lighthouse," they'd say, "unless you want the ocean to gobble you up."

My brother often told me the same.

A fisherman by trade, George was the captain of a small ship called the Trout's Kiss. It didn't belong to him, it belonged to the company he worked for, but it really should have—he could drive that boat through a hurricane and make it out the other side. Everybody knew it. He wasn't afraid of anything in all the ocean, save for that damn lighthouse, and he'd tell you the same. "I'd sooner row a skiff through a storm," he'd say, a pint of beer in his hand, "than drift the Trout's Kiss past Cold Rock!"

That was then, though. He died three days after my ninth birthday.

Capsized.

His boat tossed him and his first-mate overboard and the Trout's Kiss smashed into a thousand pieces against the Cold Rock coast.

I went to bed and my brother was alive. When I woke up, he was dead. No goodbyes. No last words. Just gone. It was the moment I realized the legend of Cold Rock Keep wasn't just a myth. It was the moment I realized it was the truest story ever spoken.

See, my brother was a superstitious man. A good sailor. There was no way he'd find himself near those rocks if not for some darkness pulling him there, and maybe that same darkness had then begun pulling me, or maybe it was just my childhood grief, but not a week after his funeral I went down to the docks and untied his skiff. Then I rowed it out into the harbour.

I rowed it out toward Cold Rock Keep.

Too long, I decided, had that towering mausoleum lorded itself over our gentle town. Too long had it stolen our loved ones and filled them with the sea. It was time somebody did something about it and in that moment, on that brisk summer night, I decided that somebody would be me.

So I set off toward the sweeping beacon that haunted the ocean like a ghost in the dark. I rowed and rowed until I got close enough that rowing didn't do much anymore, because the ocean became all rolling waves and riptide currents. I remember feeling panicked, like I'd make a grave mistake, an impulsive decision that I was now going to sorely regret, as I tossed and churned in the soup of the sea. First, I lost one oar, then the other.

Then the boat tipped over like a rubber duck in the bath, and the looming figure of the lighthouse vanished. Darkness took me. Frigid, wet darkness.

When I came to, I spat out a river of seawater. Trembling and disoriented, I gathered my bearings. Surrounding me was a mess of wood—the remnants of my little skiff, or some other sorry vessel. Not ten feet away, great waves thundered against razor-blade rocks, jutting out of the coastline like the jaws of a shark while their sea-spray washed over me, reminding me where I was.

I rolled onto my back. There, towering above like a titan of myth, loomed Cold Rock Keep. Its spiral architecture reached up into the moonlit clouds while its yellow light swept in a hypnotizing circle, humming an electric tune. It felt like it was calling to me. Beckoning me toward its heavy doors.

I pulled myself to my feet and realized I'd come all this way without much of a plan. In retrospect, I wondered if I ever truly *meant* to make it there at all. Perhaps I had been so sick with grief that I was hoping that the ocean would simply swallow me up in the same place it'd swallowed George, and then it would let us be together again. Perhaps I just wanted an end to my misery.

Whatever the case, I didn't have anywhere to go but forward now, and so I walked toward the lighthouse. As I did, I passed stone columns. Gravestones, I realized, carved with effigies for men whose stories I knew better than any nursery rhyme.

Rupert Dougee, 1892.
Fell from the lighthouse
while effecting repairs
to the roof.

Body inexplicably found thirty feet from the structure, torso split in half on the rocks, seagulls nesting in his ribcage.

Howard Newton, 1903
Died peacefully
in his slumber.

Haunted by vicious voices. Took a liter of whisky just to get himself to sleep every night. Found dead in his bed, partially decomposed, with his open journal in his hands. His last entry? *I fear the ocean not half as much as I fear the malice in these walls.*

The lighthouse had always been monstrous, that much wasn't up for debate. Whether it smashed you on the rocks or drove you mad once you washed ashore, Cold Rock Keep would take what it wanted and leave the world more miserable for it.

Now, I meant to change that. Little nine-year-old me, with nothing to defend himself but a sturdy rock and his brother's hand-me-down pocket knife. What choice did I have? At that moment, none. I was there, and there was no going back. Only forward.

So I ascended the steps to Cold Rock Keep.

When I opened the doors, I found old beer cans and nudie mags. The walls inside were dressed in graffiti, and the tables and chairs were chipped and carved with names and memories. A steel spiral staircase wound upwards, clutching the narrowing walls of the lighthouse. At the very top sat a hatch leading into the upper-most room.

Something tugged at me then. Something pulled me toward it, and I knew then that it was the room the light spun in lazy circles, tempting souls to their deaths. It was the source of all this misery.

Heart thrumming, I took the stairs two at a time.

When I reached the top, I found the hatch sealed shut. An old padlock hung off of it that read Maintenance Key #1. While I didn't have the maintenance key, I did have a rock, and so I bashed the padlock clean off the hatch and pulled it open.

Light blinded me. Vicious, vibrant light spilled out like an un-corked supernova. My ears filled with the whirring drone of whatever mechanism drove the artificial sun. Shielding my eyes, I clambered up the ladder leading into the hatch, one step, two step, until I was in the room proper.

And then something strange happened.

Things became dim. I opened my eyes and found the blister-ing light gone. In its place was a faint glow, and even that was quickly fading, receding back into some great void until it was only a firefly speck in the distance.

Then that, too, vanished.

Darkness enveloped me. Not turn-off-the-lights-it's-bedtime darkness, but *true* darkness. The sort of darkness you find yourself in when you're six feet under, buried beneath the worms and the dirt. The sort of darkness that's so thick the pressure of it is almost suffocating.

My hands scrambled across the surface, looking for the hatch I'd come through, but it was nowhere. Gone. I shouted and I hollered, cursing the lighthouse, cursing myself for being foolish enough to stroll onto Satan's doorstep with nothing but a rock and an old pocket knife, but predictably that didn't solve my problem either.

Eventually, out of options, I sat down in the void and cried.

I cried for my mother, who would wake up tomorrow worried sick, wondering where I was, calling me in as missing to the sheriff. They'd search and search and never find me and she'd just tell them to search some more because there would be no way, no possible way, that she could go on living if she knew both of her babies were gone.

I cried for my father, who was out of town on business and would no doubt blame himself for him always being away or abroad, and then maybe one day he'd get so fed up with all the guilt that he'd turn it around on my mother and tell her she should have been watching me better.

Most of all, though, I cried for my brother. I cried for George because he had always told me to steer clear of Cold Rock Keep, and then he died to teach me that lesson. I decided I knew better than he did though, even though he was the fisherman and I was the stupid little brother, and I came out here looking for revenge and all I managed to do was make things so much worse.

"Look at this one," a nasally voice said. "He hasn't any light."

I wheeled around, terror jolting through me. "Who's there?"

"He will join the others."

"The others?" I shouted. "You mean my brother?"

"Give him time, Agatha," came another voice, this one more shrill.

"Time?" the first voice snapped. "He is here for violence! He is angry, desperate and murderous and would see us killed and our home burned to ashes. Don't you see? He has no light, Beatrice, and therefore the cretin has no *time*."

I scrambled backwards on instinct. It was difficult to pinpoint which direction the voices were coming from, but I was certain there were two of them.

"Don't be so dramatic, Aggie," the second voice said. "Can't you see the source of that anger? It's his brother. He's been hollowed out by grief and filled up with pain, poor thing."

"You're them—" I stammered, my mouth too dry to properly speak. "You're the witches, aren't you?"

Agatha's nasally voice snickered. "Oh, look how perceptive the child is, sister. I hardly think the world will miss a lightless dunce such as he. Let me do it now. I'll be quick about it."

"Hush, Beatrice. Child, I sense a haunting in your soul, a longing for your brother. Do you miss him?"

The question made me furious. It was proof, I realized, that the witches knew about the murders they were committing, knew about the pain they were causing, and yet still chose to reap our community again and again. Tears welled in my eyes.

"Yes," I said, lips trembling. "Yes, of course I miss him! Do you have any idea how many innocent folks you've gone and killed?"

"Do you have any idea how many we've *saved?*"

Agatha's words caught me off-guard. I tried to voice a response to her then, something well thought-out and appropriately accusatory, but all I managed to do was stand there slack-jawed.

"See, Agatha? Look there—near his chest."

"*Please*, that's hardly anything. Still well-worth a purge."

"It's proof the child's got some light in him, that's what it is."

"Just about anybody's got *some* light in them, you bleeding heart!"

The situation was the most bizarre and unsettling thing I'd ever encountered. "What do you mean 'people you've saved?' "

"What we mean," Agatha began, somewhat impatiently, "is that Beatrice and I lived peacefully on Cold Rock island for many, many years. We practiced the magic of the land. Grew our crops. Caught our fish. We didn't hurt anybody, but one night a vessel goes and lands on our shores, ties us up in the middle of the night and burns our bodies in a pit. A pit! They drink for hours and hours after that, a real revel, exchanging high-fives and how-do-ya-dos—"

Beatrice sighed. "They slept in our ashes."

"Not terribly hygienic, were they?" Agatha said. "Course, we had seen their ship on the horizon already. Saw it getting loaded on the docks for some time, and so we knew what was coming our way. Took precautions."

"*I* took precautions," Beatrice said. "*You* tried to beat them with a club."

"Must you *always* interrupt? I'm being kind enough to give this little cretin some context before we Snip him. The least you could do is pipe down for his bedtime story."

Agatha took a moment, and I could sense the two witches glaring at one another in the darkness. "Anyway, dunce boy, where was I? Ah yes, we made damn sure our murderers met an end that suited them. Sent them all into a rage, didn't we? Made 'em chop each other up. Ha! Poetic justice, you might say. Beattie and I figured we'd just go ahead and get rid of that bad lot before they infected anybody else with all that hatred.

"Then, wouldn't you know it? We found out that once you're dead, you're much more in tune with the spirits of the living! Learned we could measure the worth of a man from a thousand yards based on the size of his glow. And often we did. We used our magic to lure the worst souls into the rocks. Mangled 'em up good, and saved folks the grief of dealin' with 'em."

I shook my head, stunned. "So many ships crashed on those rocks. So many. You're telling me that everybody, all those sailors, were evil?"

"Not in the least, sweet little fool," Agatha said. "We only killed the bad eggs. The rest of the folks washed up on shore and somebody came around for them... eventually. Same goes for those lighthouse keepers—most of 'em, anyhow. There was that one doing work on the roof before a storm. Poor sod got blown halfway across the island before making a mess on the rocks."

"Oh," Beatrice added. "And there was Howie. The sweet man who liked to journal—I did so like him. Awfully handsome."

"Howie... you mean Howard?" Agatha let loose a snort of laughter. "Poor lad was a smidge clairvoyant and never knew it. Said he heard voices, and I suspect he did! Overheard me and Aggie arguing 'til the break of dawn like a couple of braying donkeys. It's no wonder he drank himself to death."

"A shame!"

"Yes, a shame. The man had a great taste in whisky."

The void, once pitch-black, grew brighter. It became bright enough that I could make out shapes flitting around me, formless, like laundry in the wind.

"Oh," Agatha said, somewhat shocked. "He can see us now, can he?"

"Course he can, look at him. He's glowing, isn't he?"

A question lingered in my mind. "Why is it that your magic became more powerful after the lighthouse was built?"

"More powerful?" Beatrice said, confusion lacing her words. "Whatever do you mean?"

"It's just that the folks back in town always said there were more deaths after the lighthouse was built. Did it… did it help you kill folks?"

"Ha!" Agatha laughed. "The child's stupidity is beginning to grow on me, Beattie. I'll give you that. No, you toad-brained fool, the lighthouse didn't make us any stronger or smarter or more devilishly beautiful than we already were. All it did was convince folks to come sailing into the harbor, since they figured what could it hurt with the lighthouse guiding them away from all that ails 'em? More sinners, more shipwrecks. Easy as that."

"Oh," I said, and another thought crossed my mind. As it did, the shapes slowly faded from view. My glow, I realized, was dimming and the void was beginning to grow suffocating all over again. "And my brother? Why did you kill him?"

"Oh," Beatrice said, pausing. "Well, we didn't kill your brother."

Tears formed in my eyes, and I quickly dabbed them with my sleeve. "What do you mean you didn't kill him? He died out there on those rocks! His boat capsized not a hundred yards away."

"Well," Beatrice said, slowly. "We had only ever intended for… Oh, heavens. Who was it?"

"Reed Vallas," Agatha offered.

"Reed Vallas, of course. Yes. We had only intended for that fellow—he was the first-mate on the boat your brother captained. That man was an urchin. A rapist. A murderer. He was a stain on this town, and frankly the world is much better off without him."

I sucked in a breath. A sort of weepy, deep breath, the kind you take when you're beginning to calm down, but you're not quite ready to be done with being upset. "Then why did you kill George?"

"Dunce, child!" Agatha said. "Weren't you even listening? We just told you that we didn't—"

"Aggie!" Beatrice snapped. "Look at him. The boy is glowing again! Faint as it is, we should really be nurturing that light."

Agatha mumbled something, sounding equal parts impatient and frustrated.

"Your brother *was* meant to wash safely ashore, child. Honest. Reed panicked after the Trout's Kiss capsized, and not wearing a life vest, grabbed onto your brother to save his own skin, and ended up drowning the both of them."

The words washed over me like a winter tide. Cold. Painful. "And you let Reed pull him down? You didn't try to help?"

"How to explain this?" Agatha said with a sigh. "Our magic is less of a scalpel and more of a sledgehammer. Small incisions in destiny, like pulling your brother free from Reed, proved impossible for us."

"Then can you bring him back?" I said, desperate and heartbroken. "Since he wasn't meant to die? I never even got a chance to say goodbye and—"

"No," Agatha said. "We can't."

It was exactly what I expected to hear, and yet it still hurt like the day he died.

"Are there many moments like that?" I muttered, the light radiating from me flickering in the dark. Off and on. Off and on. It was as though it couldn't decide whether it wanted to stay or go. "Do many innocent people die because of the things you do?"

Silence filled the void. If the darkness had been thick and suffocating, then this silence was like the bottom of the ocean. It felt heavy. Crushing.

"Sometimes," Beatrice said. "Sometimes I suppose that innocent folks *do* get washed away."

"Is that okay?" I asked, my tiny voice cracking under the weight of the question. It didn't feel okay to me. Why did innocent folks have to die so bad people could be punished? "Should you really be doing that?"

"I..." Beatrice began. "I'm not sure."

"Beattie," Agatha said, and her voice was hushed. "You're glowing."

"Oh," Beatrice said, and the formless shape of windy laundry sort of bent down, as though examining itself. "It appears that I am. I'd almost forgotten what that felt like… Why! Look at you, too, Aggie!" She giggled. "I can almost see your icy heart with all that light."

True to Beatrice's words, the both of them were beginning to radiate a faint glow. The shapes danced upward, bickering with one another in words I couldn't quite understand. They swirled and snapped and whipped above my head, until eventually they stopped and floated back down, now bright things.

"We've had it out, Aggie and I, and we've decided you're right."

"I am?" I said.

"Course you are, dunce boy," Agatha said. "We got so wrapped up in keeping busy and trying to do good, that we forgot to nurture the most important light of all—our own."

Beatrice snickered. "Oh, look at you, Aggie. First you wanted to purge the poor child and now you're doting on him."

"Well, that was before he started glowing like a candlestick, wasn't it?"

"She's right, child. And so are you. It's become clear to us that we can't rightly keep helping other people if *we're* out of sorts. So we're going to focus on us. Get back our light."

"You are?" I said, feeling joy for the first time since George had died. The light surged inside of me. "That means you won't hurt anybody else?"

"Mhmm," Beatrice said.

"We'll leave the hurting to the folks still living and breathing," Agatha added. "Which reminds me, we've done some hurting ourselves."

"'Fraid that we have," Beatrice agreed.

Just then, the two formless shapes began to materialize into something tangible. Human. A pair of glowing corpses appeared before me with flesh sloughing off their frames and boiling wounds upon their faces.

One smiling, the other scowling.

"We know you didn't get a chance to say goodbye. Which is partly our fault."

"*It's all* our fault, Agatha. And it's true that we can't bring George back, or take back what we took from you."

"So," Agatha said, rubbing her mangled hands together. "We've decided to do one last bit of magic, you know, before we leave for good. Consider it a parting gift."

Beatrice pulled me into a tight hug. "It isn't much, child, but it's the best we can do."

***

That was my last memory of the witches of Cold Rock Keep.

I woke up in my bed, with salt in my hair and seaweed down my shirt. My mother shrieked for joy when I did, and another man—a man I didn't recognize, but would later learn was a doctor, told me I had been asleep for some fourteen hours. The police, he explained, found me washed up on the shore. They thought I'd suffered a serious concussion. Perhaps fallen into a coma.

"You slept like the dead," he told me.

I told him that I felt fine, and that I was sorry for causing such a stir, but that right now, more than anything, I needed a little space to get my head in order. Just five minutes, I said. My mother and the doctor voiced their concerns, but ultimately respected my wishes. They left the room.

Alone, I went to my window. My house sat at the top of a hill and had a nice view of the town. From my perch, I looked out over a hundred sleepy homes. I looked out over a silent schoolyard, a run-down movie theater, and twenty or so boats bobbing at the dock.

Then I looked past that.

I looked out to the sea, to a little island with a stone spire. I looked out to Cold Rock Keep, and quiet as a breath, I said thank you. *Thank you for everything.*

You see, dreams are strange things. Sometimes a dream is merely a vignette, a slice of time so infinitesimally small that you wonder if it was ever there at all. Other times dreams are sweeping, so long and so vast that you live a second life inside of them.

That night, my dream had been longer and more real than any dream I've ever had. It spanned years. Decades. In that dream I played catch, traveled the world, shared pints of beer, and did lots and lots of fishing.

In that dream, I said goodbye to my brother.

JAGGED JANICE

I'm a government employee.

My name isn't important. All you need to worry about is what I have to say.

I work at a compound known as the Facility. Within it, we perform research on things the public would find unappetizing. Officially, we're listed under Experimental Weapons Development, but lately our umbrella has spread much wider.

Suffice it to say that there are things out there that go bump in the night. Things, both legendary and mundane, that exert their influence upon us and defy explanation. My job is to interview individuals who believe they've encountered such entities and determine if their accounts are fact or fiction. What my job is not to do, however, is share those interviews.

In this case, though, I don't think I have a choice.

**

The room is cramped, dimly lit, and smells vaguely of stale piss and black mold. A light hangs above the table between us, rocking back and forth and doing a poor job illuminating much of anything. Still, I can see the man's gaunt face and the fields on my clipboard.

It's enough.

It will do.

I ask the man to tell me his story, and we begin.

"It happened at the cabin," he says. He's twenty-something, with a long nose and five o'clock shadow. When he reaches for his cigarette, his hand shakes like a 1950s pickup truck. "Not my cabin," he adds. "It belonged to Emily, but she invited us up. The three of us."

My pen scratches across my clipboard. FOUR INDIVIDU-ALS. "For leisure, I'll assume?"

He cocks an eyebrow at me. "Yeah, I guess." A laugh escapes his lips. It's short. Awkward. "Why else do people go to cabins? We just wanted to get drunk, stoned, forget our problems for the weekend. You know, like normal people."

"Of course," I say, marking down his response. His eyes dart toward the cameras in the corner of the room, and his tongue slips across his lips. They're chapped, cracked and bleeding. He looks worse than a mess. What he looks like is a disaster.

"The cameras," he says. "What's the deal with them? You said you weren't a cop."

"I'm not," I reassure him. "The cameras are for my own records. Events—encounters with the paranormal, are tricky things. Sometimes we catch items in recordings we'd otherwise miss in person."

He stares at me a while. His lip curls in, his teeth gnawing at it. It's a look I've seen before, the sort of look where he's wondering if maybe he's being played. He's wondering if this is a sting operation, and he's taking the bait and I'm going to have him thrown into a psych ward, or worse.

"It's better if you tell me everything," I say, placing my clipboard on the desk between us. "I'm not here to have you put away, only to get some answers."

A moment of dead air hangs between us, and it's the sort of moment I recognize. He's weighing the situation. Sizing me up. He's wondering if he's comfortable talking about something this batshit insane to a total stranger.

But then he takes a deep breath, followed by a deep drag, and ashes his cigarette.

"Sure," he says. He taps on a finger on the desk. Gathers his thoughts. "It happened late at night. The four of us had been drinking in the cabin, doing mushrooms, but we all slept outside in tents since the place was full of spiders. Hardly ever got used."

"Why's that?" I check a box labeled INTOXICATED.

He shrugs. "Bad memories, I think?"

I tilt my head to the side, inviting him to continue.

"The cabin belonged to Emily's mom," he explains. "She passed away when Em was a little girl, and the place has been a mausoleum ever since. Em thinks it has bad mojo."

"What do you think?"

"What do I think?" He tastes the question. "I think that..." "He trails off, his eyes losing focus, gazing at the splintered wooden table between us. Suddenly, he seems far away. There's an emptiness in his expression. A disconnect. I wonder if he's thinking of legends and nightmares.

I wonder if he's thinking of Jagged Janice.

"Is everything alright?"

He blinks, then nods.

My pen scratches across my clipboard. SUBJECT APPEARS TRAUMATIZED. AVOIDANT.

"What's that?" he asks. "What are you writing?" He leans forward, narrowing his eyes on my form. I pull it away.

"It's private."

"How come?"

"Your knowledge of my notes could influence your account. I'd prefer it if such biases were avoided."

He looks angry as he sits back in his chair. Pissed. He's gnawing at his lips again, and his fingers tapping the table like a Gatling gun. There's no doubt in my mind that this guy's been through a lot, but I need to make sure he's telling the truth, and in order to do that, he can't know anything. Nothing at all.

"Fine," he says at length. "We'll do it your way."

Yes, we always do.

"Like I said, we were drinking in the cabin. Swapping old war stories from high-school. Talking about stupid pranks we'd pull, or places we'd tag, or teachers we hated. We reflected. Pretty soon, though, we got drunk enough that stuff went deeper. We stopped talking about all the silly surface bullshit, and we started talking about the stuff that really meant something to us—the things that set our souls on fire."

"That's a poetic turn of phrase. Are you a writer?"

He shrugs.

"Let me rephrase," I say. "Would you describe yourself as having an active imagination?"

The man studies me, gears turning in his head. Again, he's wondering if I'm goading him into an admission of insanity. He's wondering if I'm calculating what amount of antipsychotics it would take to counterbalance his paranoia, and what size straight-jacket would best fit his scarecrow frame.

But I'm not doing any of that.

The truth is, I don't care if he's insane or perfectly lucid. I don't give a damn about him at all. All I care about is whether or not he's seen Jagged Janice, and that he isn't another liar.

"My imagination isn't anything special," he says at length. "Now, can I tell my fucking story, or are you going to keep interrupting?"

I smile. "Tell your story."

He takes a breath, spares a half-second to glare at me. "The four of us are drinking in Em's cabin and she starts to get... low. Like, depressed. She's usually a pretty upbeat person, so I ask her what's up, and she says she's just been feeling a bit haunted since coming back to the cabin."

I lift an eyebrow.

"Her brother..." The man sighs, shakes his head as though de-termining how best to phrase his next words. "Her brother died at the cabin. Drowned to death a hundred feet from the door. Emily watched it happen."

"She watched her brother drown?"

He nods. "She was three years old. She didn't understand what was happening, not really. There wasn't anything she could do."

"I see." It's a sad story, but not really what I came here for. Worse still, nothing yet matches the Jagged Janice legend. "Any-thing else?"

The man looks up at me, and disbelief swims in his eyes. "Anything else? No, asshole. That's it. She watched her brother die and it made her feel like shit."

"I'm not here for Emily's story, I'm here for yours. You'll excuse me if I forget to feign empathy for a woman I've never met." I check a box labeled CONFRONTATIONAL and rest my pen on my clipboard. "Now then, you said you were drinking. Talking. What happened after that?"

His jaw is set. Clenched. He looks like he wants to slug me in the face and honestly, I wouldn't blame him, but instead he takes a drag on his cigarette and leans back in his chair.

"Fuck it. We drink and talk until our eyes get droopy, and then we go to bed. It's like any other night, I guess."

"That so?

"Yeah. Up until a point."

There's an implication in his words, but I'll deal with it later. For now, I need more details. I need to understand the setting of the Event as clearly as I can. "The police report," I say, glancing down at my copy of the document, "mentions the incident occurred inside of the cabin. Is that correct?"

"That's right."

"Can you describe it for me? The layout?"

He scratches the back of his head, brows furrowed. There's a picture being painted in his mind, colored by memories. "It's a tee-shaped cabin. Capital T. There's two bedrooms on either side of the T, and at the very top center is a bathroom. The bottom of the T is the living area and kitchen, then the front door."

"Simple enough." I make a quick sketch of it on my form. "According to the report, the Event occurred in the washroom. I'd like you to talk about that."

His mouth twitches. He sucks in on his cigarette like it's the last drag he'll ever have. Slow. Long. He burns it down to the filter, eyes bloodshot, and then he drops it into the ashtray. "You got any more of these?"

"Sure." I reach inside my jacket and pull out a pack, tossing it to him. The man catches it and flips it open. His hands are shaking. They're shaking so hard that he can hardly light the smoke after he slips it into his mouth.

"Let me," I offer.

"No," he says. "I've got it." The lighter strikes, and a flame dances to life. "You're the real deal, huh?"

"I'm sorry?"

He lights the smoke, breathes in, then exhales a storm cloud. "The real deal. You actually believe me, don't you?"

"Maybe," I say. Truthfully, I'm still making up my mind. "You said the four of you quit drinking to go to sleep. Back in your tents, I presume? What happened after that?"

He ashes the cigarette. "Nature calls. I gotta take a shit, so I get up and head to the cabin. When I unzip the tent, though, I can't see the dirt in front of me. It's dark outside. Pitch black."

"No moon?"

He shrugs. "Not much of one. All I know is I've got to do my business, and I'm not about to use the outhouse—it smells worse than death. So I make my way to the cabin. Once I get inside though, this weird feeling comes over me."

"Weird feeling?"

"Like I'm being watched."

Promising.

"The place feels empty. Lonely. It's just me, the bugs, and the light from my phone. The light's making shadows out of every-thing—the dusty fridge, the cluttered shelves, and the messy counters. There's a thousand shapes all around me, shifting with every step I take and this feeling of, I don't know.... Dread? comes over me. Like I'm not safe."

The man pauses. Sweat beads down his forehead. "Sorry," he says. "I just haven't thought about it in this much detail since the night it happened."

"Don't worry," I tell him. "Events are messy things, and more often than not, they leave scars."

"Okay."

"Take your time."

He gives himself a minute. Catches his breath. "Like I said, I don't feel safe in there, but I'm drunk enough that it doesn't faze me. I've still got a buzz going from earlier in the night, you know? I think to myself, I came to take a shit and some spooky shadows aren't gonna stop me." He chuckles to himself, shakes his head. "But a few seconds later, I'm in the bathroom and locking the door behind me. I figure, why take the chance?"

"So," he says, wiping his lips. "I'm about to unbuckle and do my business when I see movement. It's in the top corner of the bathroom—in one of those little toilet windows, like the type that's clouded on the bottom for privacy, or whatever, but clear on the top to let in light."

"I've seen those. Is that where you witnessed the Event?"

"That's where I saw the smile."

Jagged Janice. "Describe it."

"Honestly, I…" He sounds hesitant. Worried. "Wouldn't it be better to just talk about the Event instead?"

"The smile is part of the Event," I remind him. "It's important that we get as many details as possible, no matter how uncomfort-able your memories may be."

He looks down, and his eyes drift out of focus. "The smile is just a row of teeth. But the teeth are too big and too sharp to belong to a human, and there are just… so many of them."

I check my notes, consulting descriptions of Jagged Janice listed in old email chains from the early 2000s. "I'd like to hear more about those teeth."

"Why?"

"The teeth are important. Describe them, please."

The man is uncomfortable. He's shifting in his seat like quicksand, and when he talks his voice cracks, but he gives me what I want. "The teeth are jagged," he says. "Serrated, almost. Their length is all over the place. Some barely break her gums, others stretch down, cutting through her lips." His fingers move again. They're tapping on the metal table. *Tap. Tap. Tap.*

"When I see the smile, my heart starts pounding. I'm frozen there, standing in the dark bathroom with just the light from my phone. My mind's reeling, but I know that whoever that smile belongs to, I don't want them seeing me, so I hold my phone up against my chest. Tight as I can. I smother the light."

"The light," I say. "Did the woman showcase an adverse reaction to it?" Janice, according to her legend, loathes light.

"No," he says, shaking his head. "Or, I don't know? I can't remember small details. At that point, my body's mostly adrenaline. There's a storm of it coursing through me and screaming at me to run or scream or fight this bitch or just do something. Anything. But I can't. I just stand there, staring at her inhuman teeth, at her horrible, twisted smile with my phone clutched to my chest like a crucifix.

"Then the smile begins to fall away, lowering itself until it's just a blur behind the foggy part of the window. In its place are two eyes." The man takes a breath, trembling. "They're wide, angled all wrong and they're leaking this… black fluid. They dart around the washroom like she's looking for something.

"I stay still. Still as I can, like I'm fucking paralyzed. There's no light in the room, none except the bits of moon framing the monster in the window, so I let myself meld into the darkness. I don't move an inch, and I pray to god the she can't see me there."

He shivers, reaches for his cigarette and takes a drag.

"Then I hear the tapping on the window. Tap. Tap. Tap. It's followed by this chattering sound, and it takes me a second, but I realize it's her teeth gnashing together, open and shut, open and shut, over and over again. I don't want to look at her. I don't. But part of me can't stop myself, and I glance up and see her eyes staring back at me. Two tiny black dots in a sea of white. My breathing stops. My pulse races. Dribbles of piss run down my leg. It's just the two of us now, watching one another."

I lean forward, my interest piqued. Much of his description could have been pulled from the Jagged Janice legend itself. The small black pupils. The rows of inhuman teeth. I check off the features on my clipboard as he goes. "What does she do?" I ask. "When you lock eyes with her?"

He swallows. "She speaks."

"What does she say?"

"I see you."

I write the words down and circle them three times. They're not familiar to the legend. "Describe her voice to me. Does she sound old? Young?"

"Her voice is quiet. Hard to hear. The words sound like they've been pulled out of a wood chipper. Their pronunciation is all broken and unnatural, like it's been cut up by those... teeth."

"Curious," I mutter.

"Her fingers reach up, and she taps the glass again. *Tap. Tap. Tap.* I chance another look, and all I can see is her terrible, serrated smile in the window. It's making me feel nauseous. I've never been that scared, you know? I close my eyes, wanting the feeling to go away for just a second, but when I open them again the smile's gone. It's just me, alone in the bathroom."

He puts his face in his hands and lets the armor fall away. His shoulders quake with silent sobs. I give him a minute, then another.

"Is that all?" I ask.

No response.

"Sir?"

He keeps sobbing. I've been doing this job long enough to know when an interview is over. "A harrowing experience," I say, giving my form a final swipe with my pen. I stand up from my chair, reaching out to shake his hand with a disappointed sigh. "On behalf of the Facility, I'd like to thank you for taking the time to share this with me."

The man's sobs taper off. He blinks up at me, with red, puffy eyes and when he speaks, his voice is barely there. "It's not over," he says. "There's more."

My heart thrums as I pull back my handshake. A smile slips across my face as I sit back down in my chair, centering my clipboard in front of me. "Something else occurred?"

"Yeah," he says, wiping his nose on his sleeve. "The next few hours turned into a nightmare."

I click my pen, skin prickling with goosebumps. "You don't say?" Now it's my turn to take a breath, to center myself and calm my nerves. "How very unfortunate. Please continue, then."

"It takes me ten minutes before I can muster the courage to crack the bathroom door. When I do, I do it gently. Quietly. You can hardly even hear the shitty hinges creak, that's how careful I am. I peek out of the crack, looking for the smiling woman, terrified that I'm going to see her standing in the living area waiting for me, but I don't.

"There's nobody else in the cabin. It's just me. So I step out, moving across the hardwood floor. It creaks and groans with every step I take and each time that it does, my heart skips a beat and I expect to see her jump out of the darkness. I'm seeing that smile everywhere now. In every shadow. In every window. I want to shout and scream—I want to call out to my friends in the tent and beg them to pull me out of this horror, but they're past the cabin door. Out there at the far end of the yard. They're a world away."

"And your phone," I ask. "You never thought to use that to call for help?"

"Yeah, sure," he says, rolling his eyes. "I'm on a backwater island off the coast of rural BC. I've got great cell service out there." He shakes his head. "I couldn't get a cell signal if I climbed to the top of the tallest tree. My phone was a glorified flashlight."

"So what do you do?"

"I psyche myself up. I've got my hand on the front door, and I'm ready to fling the thing open and scream bloody murder, run to my friends and tell them we need to start the truck now because there's a fucking monster on the island and…. And that's when I hear it."

His fingers thrum the metal desk. *Tap. Tap. Tap.*

"In the window next to the front door, I see a long arm in a frayed sleeve, with crooked fingers playing against the glass. They're drumming a rhythm. Something... awful. It's noise masquerading as song."

"Then I hear her again. *I see you,* she says in a gravelly voice. The tapping gets faster. Heavier. I pull away from the window, from the door, and fall back into the shadows of the cabin. She must be twelve feet tall because her head cranes *down* into the window frame, all the way from the top of it. Her eyes are gleaming in the moonlight, darting around and swiveling again in ways they shouldn't be able to. She's searching again. For something—me, maybe. I don't know."

The man finishes his cigarette and slips a fresh one out of the pack. He lights it, trembling, and sucks in on the nicotine. His expression softens. "Then she's gone," he says.

"Gone?" I ask, disappointed. "Again?" There's nothing in the Jagged Janice mythology that indicates her vanishing and reappearing at regular intervals.

"Gone," he confirms. "I'm alone. Time passes. Minutes, maybe hours. I don't know. I just sit there in the living room, my ears and eyes straining for any sound, any movement, anything at all. I'm shaking and breathing in short bursts, terrified if I breathe too heavily she'll hear me. I wonder to myself how long it's been. How long there's still to go until the sun rises, and somebody wakes up and comes to check on me or use the washroom. I think about using my phone to check the time, but the idea of its light giving me away terrifies me, so I don't. I just sit there and wait."

"How long do you wait? Until morning?"

He laughs. Takes another drag. "Fuck no," he says. "It takes a while, but eventually I get calmer, or maybe too scared to keep sitting there doing nothing. Maybe I just need to reassure myself that this nightmare has an ending? I don't know." He gnaws at his fingernail. "I'm fucking quivering as I pull my phone outta my pocket. Shaking like a leaf. I turn it on, and my home screen lights up my face like I'm about to tell a campfire story."

"What time is it?"

"3:34 a.m. Two hours from sunrise." The man sighs, running a hand along his jaw. "It's too long for me. I can't do it, you know? Can't wait. I decide I need to do something now before that woman comes back. Because I have this horrible feeling that the next time she shows up she's going to be inside the cabin. She's going to find me. So I tell myself to make a run for it. Wake up my friends. It's easy, I think. I'll open my mouth and fucking scream my lungs out, and that way even if she gets in my way then at least everybody on the island will wake up, and maybe I'll get out of there in one piece. So I do it, I open my mouth and I scream.

"But nothing happens," he says quietly. His expression darkens. Tears slip from the corners of his eyes, and his lip trembles all over again. "No sound comes out. Instead, a hand that's long and crooked wraps itself around my mouth. It pulls my head back, and I smell rot and decay and seaweed, and a voice whispers in my ear like a lawn mower. *I see you.*"

Janice. I lean forward, gazing at him expectantly. "How did you get away?"

He wipes at his eyes, choking back the last of his sobs. "No idea. I blacked out. When I woke up, I wasn't in the cabin anymore. I was in a hospital bed surrounded by my friends."

"Same ones from the cabin?"

"That's right."

I check a box on my form labeled SURVIVOR. Then I chew on the back of my pen for a second before checking a second box: POST-TRAUMATIC STRESS AFFECTED.

"And what do these friends say? Anything useful?"

"They tell me it's all their fault," he says. "Em mumbles about how we should never have come out to the cabin in the first place. Steve and Haily are blaming themselves for letting me get exceptionally drunk." He cracks a bittersweet smile. "Everybody wants a share of the guilt."

My eyes drift down to the man's file. "You said the island was remote. I'll assume the hospital wasn't local to it?"

"No," he says. "It was off the island. An hour or so inland. I must have been out for a day at least though, because I don't remember ever travelling there."

"Interesting." A recurring aspect of the Janice mythology is a sense of mild amnesia and the presence of minor to severe bite wounds. "What did the hospital treat you for?"

He clears his throat. "A mild concussion. And water in my lungs."

"Water in your lungs?" I say, incredulous. "You're certain? Water in your lungs?"

"That's right," he says. "The doctors didn't understand it either. I never even got a chance to take a dip in the ocean, let alone drown in it."

"Okay, let me get this straight. So your friends pop by, leave you some get-well cards and you get discharged a couple of days later." I lean back in my chair, folding my arms. "Does that about sum things up?"

The man looks away, rubbing his arm. "Not exactly. Before they leave, I tell them about the smiling woman. I ask them if they've seen her lurking around the island, and Steve and Hailey look at each other like I must have hit my head harder than anybody thought. The look in their eyes... It's like they're terrified I've given myself brain damage. Steve squeezes my arm and apologizes over and over for doing shots with me. Says he should've gone easy for the first night. Hailey agrees. "

"And your other friend?" I ask. "Emily?"

"She's standing back. Staring at me, and her eyes are filled with... I don't know. Regret? But it's different from Steve and Hailey. She doesn't look like she feels sorry for me. She looks like she blames herself for all of this. I ask her one more time if she's seen the woman because I get the sense that she *has*."

I slide my pen down my clipboard and circle a word that says WITNESS before annotating it with a small question mark. "How does she respond?"

"She leaves," he says with a sigh. "I don't think she wants to talk about it—at least, not in front of Hailey and Steve. Pretty soon everybody leaves. It's just me again, in some tiny hospital on the outskirts of nowhere. The only company I've got is the apple tree outside my window and the shitty TV. I sleep pretty uneasily that night. Tossing and turning. I wake up at one point to the sound of tapping, and I stare out my window horrified, expecting to see that woman again, but it's just the apple tree. Its branches are brushing against the glass.

"I wonder to myself if this is just my life from now on. If every time I hear the faintest sound at night, I'm going to wake up in cold sweats thinking that woman's come back for me. Then the door creaks open. My body goes into full-blown panic, my breath hitches in my chest, my muscles tighten, and it's like that night all over again, with the smiling woman where I can't move an inch for fear.

"But it's just Emily," he says, chuckling in disbelief. "She pauses in the doorway and asks me if she can come in. I tell her that of course she can, and she does, not bothering to turn on the lights. When she gets to my bedside, I see her face more clearly. She looks rough. Her eyes have these heavy bags, and her cheeks are all red and splotchy from crying. She's wiping snot on her sleeve and telling me sorry, over and over."

"Sorry for what? Inviting you out to the cabin?" I say, doing my best not to roll my eyes. I've never seen a group of friends with such a guilty conscience.

"No," the man says. "She says she's sorry for not warning me about the woman. She says she thought the woman was gone, otherwise she'd never have come back to that place."

"What?" I snap forward, eyes latching onto his. "She told you she knew about her?"

He nods. "She says the circumstances of her brother's death aren't what she always said they were. He didn't drown—not accidentally, at least. He was murdered. A woman attacked them on the beach, a woman with a terrible smile and this tangle of black, messy hair that covered her face. She dragged Em's brother backward through the sand, muffling his screams with her hand and muttering 'to the sea with you.' Then she held him under the surf. She kept him there until he stopped moving and let the tide take him away."

"Disturbing," I say. "And she never brought this up to her parents?"

"She did. Her father told her it was just her imagination. He said that her brother had fallen into the ocean and gotten swept away, and it was already hard enough to deal with without Emily adding to it. So Emily just buried the memory. Moved on."

The man looks up at me, his expression despondent. "That's about when we hear it," he says. "In the hospital room. A tapping. *Tap. Tap. Tap.* It comes from the window to my right, the one with the old apple tree."

"The woman?"

"I don't look. I tell Emily not to look either. I tell her to focus on me, to ignore the sound. I don't know what she saw as a little girl, down by the ocean, but I know I don't want her to see what I saw in the cabin." He shudders. "I don't want her to see that smile."

"Does she listen?"

He grips a fistful of his hair, closes his eyes. "No," he says quietly. "She looks, and when she does, she screams. She screams so loudly that the lights come on down the hall, and I hear the night nurse call out and start running. Emily rushes toward the window. I catch sight of it from the corner of my eye because I still refuse to look at that pane of glass, but I hear Emily beating against it with her fists. Clawing at it with her nails. Then the nurse bursts in and pulls Emily away, calls a patrol car to drive her home."

The man takes a breath. He puts his face in his hands and rubs his eyes. "I text her an hour later. Just to make sure that she's okay and—"

"—Yes," I say, cutting him off. I glance at the folder on my desk labeled CORRESPONDENCE, then down at the watch on my wrist. It's three in the morning, and I'm jet-lagged. The meat of the man's story appears to have run its course and my eyelids feel like lead bricks. "If the texts are everything that's left then I can read them on my own." I rise from the desk and offer my hand to shake. He gives it a weak, reluctant squeeze, avoiding my eyes. Then he leaves the room without another word.

I sigh, sitting back down in the steel chair. Another long day. Another dead end. I adjust my glasses and pull out the text logs. There's only a handful of message receipts. The chance is slim, but the possibility that there's something in there about Jagged Janice entices me too much to set them aside for tomorrow.

I begin to read.

As I do, I make note of the timestamps. Words do a good job of painting a picture, but time and location lend context to every-thing.

01:34 Dorian: are you okay?

02:12 Emily: Not really

02:12 Dorian: did you see her?

02:45 Dorian: em, im sorry. that was a stupid text

02:45 Emily: It's fine.

02:46 Dorian: im guessing you dont feel like talking

02:46 Emily: Actually, it might be good for me

02:47 Dorian: yeah? okay. me too

02:47 Dorian: i never got a chance to tell you earlier, but i cant imagine how horrible it must have felt to see what happened to your brother and have your dad not believe you?? thats fucked

02:55 Emily: It's fine. We were never close anyway.

02:55 Dorian: sorry to hear. did you ever tell your mom? I mean, before she passed?

02:56 Emily: No. Mom was already dying by then and dad would've killed me

02:56 Dorian: fuck. im an asshole. how could I forget something like that? sorry agajn

02:57 Emily: You're not an asshole. You're right that I would have told her about Jonas if I could have

02:59 Emily: By then she was so hopped up on painkillers though that I hardly even recognized her

03:00 Dorian: the meds must have been pretty heavy. thats a lot to deal with for a four year old kid.

03:01 Emily: Yeah, her esophageal cancer was bad. She was in a lot of pain near the end and rarely in a good mood. Pretty sure dad was having an affair at the time too. Fuckin prick

03:01 Dorian: im sorry. thats a shitty memory to bring up

03:03 Emily: Dont be. I think I repressed a lot of old memories of her which probably isnt healthy

03:05 Emily: Honesrly, if it wasn't for you, I'd probably think I was going crazy right now

03:05 Dorian: why?

03:06 Emily: I saw her too.

03:06 Dorian: the smiling woman?

03:07 Dorian: em?

03:34 Emily: My mother

03:34 Emily: I see my mother

I stare at the last word in stunned silence. Her mother? Could she actually have been the origin of the legend? I rub a hand along my jaw, considering what I've heard of Emily's history. She had only been four years old at the time of her brother's death when she witnessed a crazed woman drag him into the sea, a woman who she couldn't identify because black hair obscured her face.

Could that woman have been her own mother? It doesn't seem terribly likely. But it doesn't seem impossible either. Children often reframe moments of terror in a bid to understand the incomprehensible.

I reach for my briefcase, unclasping the latches on the front and pulling out my laptop. I take a breath and then open up the database software. Emily's easy enough to find. Her last name is plastered everywhere across her social media, so I plug that in. The search function isn't the fastest, but it does the trick. It takes thirty seconds for the tiny, rotating hourglass to stop spinning, and when it does, I see her.

```
SUBJECT: EMILY KALDWELL
FATHER: HARLOD KALDWELL
MOTHER: JANICE KALDWELL [DECEASED]
```

I swallow, my hands shaking on the keyboard.

Had I finally found Jagged Janice? I pour myself a glass of water, finishing it in two giant swigs. It does little to calm my nerves. Still, it's one piece of the puzzle solved, but really it just creates more questions. It doesn't explain several aspects of the man's story. The water in the lungs. The vanishing. Certain pieces of his encounter don't add up, at least not compared to the original legend.

There's a knock on the door.

Three sharp raps with a knuckle. I get up to answer it, thinking maybe the man's forgotten his phone or wants to give me back my pack of smokes. When I open the door though, there's nobody.

I raise an eyebrow and head back to my laptop. I need to discover the source for these changes, these departures from the Jagged Janice mythology. This time I bring up my web browser, navigating to one of my preferred resources on urban legends. The website's a bit corny, but it's proven accurate, and its community aspect has been invaluable in my research.

After some scrolling, I bring up the Jagged Janice article. People can leave anecdotal encounters beneath the main text, and sometimes they do. Usually, they're all bullshit.

One of them catches my eye, however. It mentions seeing the serrated smile, the tapping fingers, and… that they found their infant child dead with water in its lungs. I shake my head. A coincidence, that's all. I keep scrolling. More keywords jump out at me.

"… there and then gone."

"… voice like a meat grinder."

"… to the sea with you."

I pause. Those were the words Emily said, words she remembered when she witnessed her brother being pulled into the ocean. *To the sea with you.* My mind spins, but a picture is forming. The guttural, difficult to understand voice. The drowned brother. The words.

"I see you."

No. She was never saying those words, not really. She was saying *to the sea with you.* The man misheard, or perhaps he couldn't properly understand because of Janice's damaged voice. In his panic, he likely defaulted to the simplest sounding phrase.

My heart races. I reach for my phone to make a call, to tell my boss what I've found. It wasn't long ago the Facility had an incident with a Man with a Red Notepad, one in which we learned the core principle of all legends and one which cost many people their lives: that legends evolve.

If the Jagged Janice legend has evolved, we need to allocate additional resources to locating it and neutralizing it. I continue to scroll, noticing many of the anecdotes have been posted in the last week. Several in the last few days. If even half of them are true, it'd imply highly increased activity on Janice's part.

I hear another knock at the door—three soft raps. I curse, kicking off from my desk and storming to the door, phone still pressed to my face, waiting for my boss to pick up. Once more, I swing it open, and once more, I look down a cold, empty hallway.

I slam the door shut and stalk back to the table. My phone continues to ring, and my boss continues to ignore my call. It's really not like her, but I tell myself to relax. She's probably sleeping. According to my watch, it's late as hell—3:34 in the morning, to be precise. That makes me an asshole, maybe, but this discovery is too big, too dangerous to ignore. Janice is out there, and she's on the move.

Three more knocks ring out, but these are softer than before. More gentle.

Almost taps.

THE MAN IN THE MOON

Believe it or not, the second trip to the moon made more headlines than the first.

There was so much more riding on it. After the nuclear exchange of 2029, most of the world had resigned itself to death. Looting was widespread. Riots claimed the streets. New York, Beijing and Moscow, once the population centers of millions, all became smoldering wastelands in the blink of an eye. The world as we knew it was over, and all that anybody wondered was how long they had left until their city joined the rubble.

But then something strange happened.

Maybe an angel touched down, or maybe the madmen at the top finally realized just how close they were to losing it all—their power, their wealth, their subjects. Whatever the case was, they called off Armageddon. Enough, they said. *We've had enough.*

And that was it.

Ninety million dead in the span of an afternoon was all it took to put things into perspective. After that, the world lost its taste for nuclear weapons. We lost our taste for war. After seeing the reality of what was waiting for us on the other side of our violent delights, the petty squabbles of our neighbors, our rival states, suddenly didn't seem to matter much anymore.

But that wasn't enough. No, it wasn't enough to simply *proclaim* our distaste for conflict, to dismantle our nuclear stockpiles and address our nations and come together in peace. No, what we needed was a grand gesture. Something spectacular.

We needed the *stars*.

So it was that the Return to the Moon initiative began. It was a joint effort, a collective push by Russia, China and the USA that was helped along by everybody from North Korea to Canada. This time, we weren't just going to land on the moon, say a few inspiring words, and be on our way. No, this time we were going to stick around. Colonize it. Create the very first settlement on a solar body that people could live on. It wouldn't belong to any one nation—it would be independent. A true symbol of our commitment to never again bow to the seductive temptations of tribalism and war.

It proved to be the gesture we needed. People rallied behind it, and it was supported by landslide margins on both the left and right, across practically every nation on earth. We saw it as real proof that we were willing to set aside the shadow of mutually assured destruction, and in its place walk together toward the heavens.

And it was a good idea. It's hard to fault the sentiment behind it, and even now I feel warm just thinking of the unity we felt in those days, but it was also the catalyst that set our extinction into motion.

When we launched the rockets, we always knew it would be expensive. Risky, too. The trouble is, we measured the costs in dollars, and the risks in headlines and isolated tragedies. We figured we'd have one or two failed launches here, maybe a crash-landing there. Nothing catastrophic. Nothing world-ending.

A week after the first astronauts landed, their instruments began picking up strange seismic readings. According to them, it was as though the moon was tilting on its axis. Soon quakes riddled the surface, wreaking havoc on research equipment and drastically slowing surveys for the forward operating base.

Then, two and a half weeks into the mission, Earth received its final communication from the moon.

ALPHA-3: Houston, this is Alpha 3. Do you read?

HOUSTON: Alpha-3, this is Houston. We read you loud and clear.

ALPHA-3: Roger. Houston, we have a situation.

HOUSTON: Go ahead, Alpha-3.

ALPHA-3: We've had some issues with the crew. We've had to restrain two members, and I'm beginning to think we may need to restrain more.

HOUSTON: This is the first we're hearing about this. What's going on up there?

ALPHA-3: Some of the crew have become violent. They attacked Major Donahue during a spacewalk. They looked like they were trying to pull her out of her suit, but we got to her in time and she's okay.

HOUSTON: Good work, Alpha-3. We'll need the names of those members. [STATIC] You said you suspect more members may need restraints?

ALPHA-3: That's correct, Houston. Tensions have flared in the last two hours, and arguments are becoming heated. We've had to break up four fights already.

HOUSTON: There's more fighting? [CONFUSED VOICES]

ALPHA-3: The crew are at each other's throats.

HOUSTON: Alpha-3, are you in a secure location?

ALPHA-3: Affirmative. I'm in the rover, the hatch is sealed. I know how much we have riding on this, Houston, but at this point I'd recommend a full crew recall.

HOUSTON: Understood. We're currently discussing it with the Alliance.

ALPHA-3: I appreciate that, Houston. I'm hoping that—Jesus!

HOUSTON: Alpha-3?

ALPHA-3: They're… they're all out there. On the surface.

HOUSTON: Say again?

ALPHA-3: They're on the surface, Houston. They're attacking one another. Bashing in their helmets with rocks and... Oh god. They're coming this way.

HOUSTON: Alpha-3, do not engage. Ensure your rover is sealed.

ALPHA-3: No. No. I can feel it too, now. I can feel it too.

HOUSTON: Feel what? Alpha-3, what's going on up there?

ALPHA-3: It's eating me. My brain. It feels like liquid fire and it's making me so angry... Fucking hell, Houston. This is... I think there's something crawling around inside my head, and its feet are like barbed wire.

HOUSTON: We're preparing an emergency extraction shuttle right now. Remain in place. Do you copy?

ALPHA-3: [UNINTELLIGIBLE GRUNTING] Can you feel that, Houston?

HOUSTON: Feel what, Alpha-3? Your first was broken and unreadable, say again.

ALPHA-3: It's watching me.

That was it. The final transmission.

Three days later, on the night of October 3rd 2034, the world ended. Cities burned. Governments fell, each dying in the ashes of a chaos nobody could comprehend. Blood filled the gutters in flash floods of violence. Families, once happy and loving, butchered each other in their homes as mothers feasted on their daughters and fathers picked apart their sons.

It was the end of times. The end of everything.

Then, a light emerged in the dark. A light that shepherded us away from total annihilation, that saved what we now call the dregs of humanity. The leftovers. It began on social media, taking

33

shape as a video streamed by a young woman in the throes of insanity. The video was called THE MOON IS WATCHING.

In it, she frothed at the mouth. She slurred her words. She moaned in disoriented agony as she spoke a broken warning about what the moon had done to her. Looking back on it now, it didn't tell us anything especially profound, but it spread like wildfire, going viral in the span of an hour as nations across the Earth shared it in silent horror.

"It's hurting my insides," she said, her body jerking and writhing. "It's crawling inside of my head, behind my eyes, across my brain. It's cutting me up. I... I'm not whole anymore."

She shrieked and her back lurched, twisting and snapping, her tongue lolling from her mouth like a panting dog. Her eyes looked around, hungry and eager. In her hand, she still held her phone, but it had become an afterthought. She didn't look at it. Didn't so much as acknowledge it as she broke off into a run, her ragged voice snarling as she collided with another person in a blur of pixels.

There's no video of what happened next. Her phone was discarded in the ensuing melee, but from the audio, it's clear that the person she attacked was a young boy. It's unlikely he survived.

That video was enough, though. More than enough. Its message, as harrowing and twisted as it may have been, taught us an important lesson that night. *Do not look at the moon.* Avoid it at all costs. Draw your blinds, lock your doors, and under no circumstances venture out in the dark. There are madmen in the streets— or Moonwalkers, as they've come to be called.

Catch them during the day and they're lethargic, almost braindead. But at night something overcomes them. Something sinister. They need violence to live like we need food and water. Somehow, it sustains them.

But even they aren't the true nightmare. No, worse than them are the Lucid. The one's like you and me. The ones who still think with their minds, who still eat and drink and haven't looked at the moon since the end of the world. They're the ones who break into your homes. The ones who steal your food and rape and kill with the practiced efficiency only real humans can manage.

They're the ones building new cults. New religions.

I'm not sure what the astronauts found when they went back to the moon. I'm not sure what they woke up. All that I know is that these days, if you decide the nightmare of reality is too much to take, there's an alternative to death. Folks take it sometimes. They walk out into the night, and they stare up at the sky.

They look at the moon, and the moon looks back.

SNIPPITY SNAP

It's just the two of us here. Myself and Ryan Halflow, a seventeen-year-old kid from Elktorch High.

He's typical as far as teenagers go. Impulsive. Disinterested. He and I are sitting in his parent's garage, in a couple of fold-up camping chairs, with cheap cups of coffee on our laps and half-eaten donuts in our hands.

We're talking.

I'm here because I believe he's witnessed an *Event*. A supernatural encounter of grave significance, and one which I believe could explain a series of grisly murders—murders which have gone unsolved, and plagued this sleepy town for close to a decade.

***

"It's just a stupid nursery rhyme," Ryan says, bookending his words with a smirk. "Something to keep the kids inside after dark. Militant parental shit, y'know?"

I adjust my tie and clear my throat. It's my first interview and I don't want to come across as an amateur. "I'm well aware of its origins," I say. "We're here to discuss your Event."

"My Event?"

I nod.

He stares at me for a few seconds, a smirk hovering on his lips. Eventually he huffs and folds his arms. "You're serious, aren't you? I was seeing shit, man. There isn't a mystery to be solved here. I was just high as a kite."

"High as a kite," I say, leaning back in my chair. "What kind of drugs were you taking then? LSD? DMT?"

"What? No."

"Psilocybin?"

He shakes his head, incredulous. "No man, I'm not fucking… I wasn't taking any of that."

"Then, what? Weed?"

He gives me a measured look. "Yeah. Just weed. Nothing crazy."

"Weed," I say, and it's my turn to smile. "Doesn't typically come packaged with vivid hallucinations, does it?"

His face falters. The cool demeanor, the dismissive aloofness—it fades and for a moment I see a twinge of anxiety, and that's when I know that I have him. I know that he doesn't believe in his own excuse.

"Yeah, well, I was drunk too," he argues. "I wasn't exactly in my right mind."

It's my turn to fold my arms. I appraise him like my orientation taught me to do: by maintaining eye contact, adopting a neutral expression, and above all else, not speaking a word. *If you want to make people talk*, my mentor once said, *then be silent.*

So I am. I'm as quiet as death.

Moments pass. There's nothing but the low hum of the light above us and my pencil, tap-tap-tapping on my clipboard. Ryan shifts in his chair. He mumbles. There're words on his tongue. I can tell. There're a whole world of questions he wants to ask, and I don't blame him. When a mysterious figure knocks on your door in the middle of the night, says he works for the government and just needs to talk, maybe you let him in. Maybe you don't. Either way, you've got questions.

Lots of them.

Ryan heaves a breath. "You said you worked for the government?"

I smile. He's testing the waters. It's not a slam dunk, but it's good enough.

"I work for the Facility," I say. "It's a fresh enterprise, one that most of the government, let alone the country, isn't aware of. My job is to investigate Events that my superiors deem noteworthy." I do my best to keep my voice level. Professional. But the job is so new, so exciting, that I can hardly contain myself. "Your Event has been selected."

Ryan eyes me. "Facility, huh? No offense, but that sounds fucking ridiculous."

He's right to be skeptical of me. Smart, even. I reach my hand into my jacket and pull out my leather-clad identification badge. "I showed this to you earlier when you answered the door, but perhaps you'd like a better look at it?"

I toss it to him. He catches it, looking from the badge back to me, trying to match the facial features. He runs his hand along the plastic, over the ridges of the raised employee number and then squints at the holographic security imprint.

"Looks real," he concludes. He hands it back to me, and I pocket it. "How come I've never seen the Facility on the news?"

"Like I said, it's a recent enterprise. The Facility is much more Area 51 than it is FBI. The work that we do, the Events that we deal with, they aren't the sort of thing that the public needs to know about."

"Why?"

"Think social tension, widespread panic."

His eyes widen. There's a gentle change to his facial features, a sort of relaxed acceptance. He may not like this meeting we're having, may not feel comfortable here, but the idea of being a part of something so clandestine is intoxicating to a teenage boy. I know this because I've been there before.

"What makes my Event noteworthy?" he asks.

"You made a post to social media three days ago showcasing a figure that I believe I recognize. That same night, a classmate of yours goes missing. A young man by the name of Benjamin Keen, and I'm wondering if the circumstances are possibly connected."

Ryan nods, taking a nervous sip from his styrofoam cup. "Yeah. I heard about Ben. He was around that night—at the party, I mean, but I never saw him. I hope he's alright."

"As do I." I appraise Ryan for several moments, monitoring his expression, his body language. It appears sincere. "The figure in the photo. Can you describe it in your own words?"

"The shadow you mean? Yeah. It looked like a demon or something straight out of a nightmare." He pauses, lowering the cup and looking at me seriously. "Are you in league with de-mons?"

"No, demons aren't within my purview."

He laughs, awkwardly. Like he's waiting for the punchline to a joke that never comes.

"My field of work is urban legends. Monsters. Myths. That sort of thing." I click my pen and bring it to the form on my clipboard. "It's getting late. If it's alright with you, Ryan, I'd like to get started. The night you took the photo, what led to that moment?"

He stares at me for a couple seconds, and then he realizes I'm not joking. He runs a nervous hand through curly brown hair. "It's a long story."

"Lucky you, my schedule's clear."

He frowns, then glances behind me. I turn, following his gaze, and in the small window of the garage door, I see a girl's face. It's only there for a moment before she ducks away.

"Who was that?" I ask. "Your sister?"

He nods, somewhat shaken. "You sure this isn't a prank? This seems like something she would get a real kick out of, screwing with me like this."

More disbelief. More skepticism. I sigh, resting my pen on my clipboard and leaning back in my chair. "I've seen things too, Ryan." The words come out quietly, with a gravity befitting their meaning. This time, I'm not acting. "Plenty of things. I've seen monsters, and spirits, but worst of all, I've seen people die."

He swallows.

"I watched somebody close to me lose themselves when I was very young. They became a monster, both figuratively and literally. The things they did to me—to my family and my life, were unspeakable." There's an emotion brewing inside of me, a sort of sadness mingled with pity and self-hatred. Tears leak from the corners of my eyes. They're the sort of tears that are against regulation, the sort of tears that indicate a lowering of the guard, and a dangerous vulnerability.

But I let them.

"That's how the Facility found me," I explain, locking eyes with him. "They swept up the broken pieces of a scared little boy and glued them back together. Now I'm not claiming to know your situation. What you've been through. All that I want to do is talk to you—because I know how hard these Events can be on a person, and what they can do to a developing mind."

It's a stupid line, maybe. Overdramatic and obnoxious even, but it's the truth. And on some level, I think that Ryan senses that. He doesn't laugh. He doesn't blow me off. Instead he sighs, leans forward and nods. "How does this work?" he asks, eying my clipboard. "Do I just start talking, or should I go slower so you can write?"

"Feel free to speak as fast as you like. I've had some practice with this."

"Alright," he mutters. He closes his eyes, takes a deep breath. It's his turn to lower his guard, his turn to let go of the armor. "It was three days ago," he says. "At Shannon Gilmor's house party. Her dad was out of town for work and Shannon decided she wasn't popular enough already, so she invited half the school to this thing."

"How many people attended the party?"

Ryan squints, furrowing his brows. "I'd say… maybe a hundred?" He shakes his head. "I don't know the exact number, but there were enough people that you couldn't keep track of everyone. People would come and go all the time. The front door was swinging on its hinges."

I make a note of it beneath the heading that reads WITNESS-ES. "Thank you. Go on."

"We were drinking, partying, just having a good time. Some people were playing beer pong upstairs, some people were getting stoned in the pool. The place was a fuckin' sprawl. I was downstairs in the living room, hanging with this goth chick from my theater class named Becca." His cheeks go a deep red. "She's pretty hot. Her and I… we were getting kinda… you know. Heavy. Making out. Hands down my—"

"Try to focus on the details most relevant to the Event."

"Right. Yeah. So after we fooled around a bit, she startedessing with me."

"Messing with you?"

He nods. "Talking about things like spirits and ghosts. That kind of crap. She told me she's attuned to them, that she could feel them and talk to them. It's totally ridiculous. So I started teasing her, calling her the *ghost whisper*. Just to be playful, you know? I asked her if she could get me Elvis' autograph next time she took a trip to the great beyond." Ryan takes another sip of coffee, and his hands are trembling. It's the first time I notice one of his index fingers is wrapped in gauze. "Becca told me she couldn't do Elvis, but she could show me another ghost."

"Another ghost?" According to my research, the urban legend I'm chasing isn't listed as a ghost. It's a physical entity. "You're positive that she used that terminology?"

"Yeah... pretty sure."

"Hm." I check a box on my clipboard labeled DIVERGENT. Nine times out of ten, a divergent Event is a dead end and nothing but a waste of paperwork.

Disappointing.

Ryan continues. "I asked her what ghost she was gonna introduce me to, since she couldn't get a hold of Elvis, and Becca got this twisted smile on her face. It was terrifying, but sexy too. Mischievous. She said it was a ghost I'd be really familiar with. One I'd know even better than Elvis."

"A family member of yours?"

He smiles, laughing a little. "That's what I thought too. But no, I told her I wouldn't go down there until she gave me a hint, and then she just came right out and said it. She said she was going to show me a local legend. A creature called Snippity Snap."

There it is.

I write the name down on my clipboard, my eyes growing wider with every letter. My hands are shaking so much that the words Snippity Snap come out crooked and uneven, but I don't care. It's the legend I'm chasing. The legend I've been chasing since I joined the Facility.

Elktorch's big bad myth.

"Snippity's a local celebrity," Ryan says. "She's the nursery rhyme you were asking about earlier. That little song folks hum to and from work. She's the monster that lives under our beds and watches us from the window at night. The reason kids come home after dark." He leans back, eyes glazing over, falling into a memory. "And Becca? She told me that Snippity Snap was *real*. She asked me if I wanted to meet her."

I take a breath, remind myself that the name alone isn't proof of the creature. The fact of the matter is everybody in this town already knows about Snippity Snap, so for the legend to be mentioned in this context isn't out of the ordinary. It's expected. I circle a box on my clipboard labeled INFLUENCED. It's not uncommon for people who believe they've encountered an urban legend to have just been heavily influenced by external sources—in this case, an attractive girl.

"And Becca," I say. "Had she had previous encounters with Snippity Snap?"

Ryan shrugs. "I don't know. Maybe? She was fuckingweird. Total nutcase. She led me down into the basement and said we needed to perform a ritual."

"A ritual?"

"To make Snippity appear." He takes another sip of coffee, and I catch another glance at his gauzed index finger. "Only reason I ever followed her down there was because I thought she was just playing around, being flirty and trying to get us some privacy so we could—well, you know, but once we started going down the steps, I started getting a really uneasy feeling."

"Uneasy how?"

"Like she wasn't right in the head. She closed the door behind us and we walked down the steps in the dark. I tried turning on the lights cause it's not like I needed a broken leg, but she snapped at me. Called me a pussy and grabbed my wrist. Next thing you know, she started pulling me down the steps two at a time, asking me if I was scared yet. I told her I came to party, not fuck around with ouija boards in the basement."

Ryan sighs, puts his head in his hands. "I nearly turned around, shrugged her off and went back upstairs, but all of a sudden she got real sweet. She put her lips against my ear and whispered that the two of us could fuck around all we wanted once she proved to me that Snippity was real. I was drunk enough that I agreed. I mean, shit, there was an implication there, right?"

"Anyway, she dragged me over to this sink in the basement. I didn't even realize where we were until she turned on the faucet and pulled my hand under it. Then..." His face suddenly pales, and he pulls his sweater sleeve over his hand—the hand with the gauzed finger. He looks like he's about to be sick. "Then she unzipped her purse and pulled out a pair of scissors."

"Scissors?" A smile flickers on my lips.

"Yeah," Ryan says slowly, noticing my smile. "Scissors." He looks at me like I'm crazy, and I realize I'm probably looking the part. The truth is, I know the ritual full-well. I've even attempted it myself unsuccessfully on several occasions. It requires four things:

absolute darkness, a spoken incantation, a pair of scissors, and, most importantly, a human finger.

If Becca went to that party with scissors in her purse, then it speaks volumes about her intentions. It's likely she was specifically looking for a victim. "The scissors," I say, already knowing the answer. "What did she do with them?"

Ryan takes a deep breath. "She cut my finger,and she said a sort of chant."

"A chant?"

"The first line of that old nursery rhyme, the one you brought up earlier. *Snip, Snap. Needle and thread.*"

"May I see your finger?" I ask.

He stares at me, and for a moment I think he might refuse, but then he slides his hand out of his sleeve, and there it is. His index finger, covered in gauze. He slowly unravels it. As he does, I see stitching across maybe ten or fifteen different cuts. It's badly mutilated. His eyes only look at it for a moment, before quickly wrapping it up again. "She was nuts."

I record the details on my clipboard.

```
Subject suffered multiple lacerations
that likely resulted in significant blood
loss. Strong possibility that the subject
was light-headed, and perhaps delirious at
the time of the Event.
```

"If you thought she was nuts," I say. "Then why would you let her do that to you?"

He opens his mouth as though to speak, but exhales instead. He shakes his head. His expression is guilt-ridden, painted in shades of shame and regret.

"I just mean to say that you're fairly large for your age, Ryan, and appear to be in decent shape. If you wanted to break free of this girl and her ritual, it shouldn't have been much of an issue." I gesture to him with my hand. "And yet you sit here before me, with so many cuts on your finger that it's hard to tell where one stitching ends and another begins. Such a phenomenon leads me to believe that something else happened. Something kept you there, and in pain."

He glares at me. Once again his eyes dart to the little window in the garage door, as though to make sure his sister isn't eavesdropping again. Eventually he drops his head, defeated. "I... I'm seventeen years-old and I haven't actually..."

"Haven't what?"

"You know," he says, his face getting red. "Done it."

"You're a virgin, is what you're saying?"

His eyes glance back to the window, nodding his head. "I was drunk and horny and willing to do just about anything if it meant..."

I fight the urge to criticize the kid. It's been years since I've crossed the river of puberty, but the idea of enduring a mutilated finger for a night in the sack seems frankly insane. Still, I'm not about to derail him while he's on a roll. "I get it. So what happened next?"

"She did it three times," he says, and his voice is hoarse. Choked-up. "She cut me with the scissors, and then she said that line, '*Snip, Snap. Needle and thread.*' When nothing happened though, I pulled my hand away and told her I was finished. She told me I couldn't be. Not yet. She said it'd only take two more cuts, and then Snippity would appear. She promised, and she pulled me down into a kiss and I sort of forgot about the pain and... and how fucked all of it was."

My pencil moves across the page, recording his story. The kiss isn't a part of the ritual, but it's a part of the coercion. For that reason, it's important. Whoever this Becca girl is, she's familiar enough with the legend to know exactly what it requires to be summoned, and she's willing to do what it takes to see that through.

"It was just the two of us there. I know that for a fact because there weren't any lights on when we'd come down, and nobody just hangs out in a pitch-black basement."

He swallows. "But I got this sense that we weren't alone. Like something was watching us, waiting somewhere in the shadows. Becca just kept chanting, though. She kept chanting that stupid nursery rhyme, except at this point her voice had changed."

"Changed how?"

"It lost its flirtiness. There wasn't any teasing anymore. It was all raw, and serious, and when she cut me it was deeper than before, almost to the bone." Ryan takes a shuddering breath, and his hand curls inside of his sleeve. "So I pulled away. I don't know why, but I started to think with a clearer head again. Maybe the pain started to outweigh the hormones. I started shouting at her, telling her she was fucking nuts. We got into a big argument. She seemed totally deranged, so I decided to get the hell out of there. I turned to leave, head back upstairs and tell everybody to steer clear of that psycho, but she grabbed my hand and cut me again."

He takes a moment. His teeth gnaw at his bottom lip while his eyes look detached and remorseful. "I'm not proud of it," Ryan says, "But I swung at her. Hit her in the face—hard as I could. She fell down, but I didn't care. I mean, she was crazy, right? Nuts. Cutting me after I told her I was finished, what the fuck was that?"

"An understandable reaction." I place my pencil down on the page, centering my clipboard on my lap. "Before you continue, Ryan, I want to impress upon you the importance of absolute honesty. I need to know the process of events exactly as they played out. It could save lives. Now, what happened after you knocked her down?"

"She screamed."

"Screamed?"

"Yeah. Screamed that I was a pussy and a coward. She screamed I was such a scared little bitch and that she hoped Snippity Snap would cut my head off."

I pick up my pencil and get back to work. Becca's aggressive attempts to perform the ritual are alarming to say the least, but they aren't unheard of. Entities like Snippity Snap have been known to have profound effects on those who follow them. Usually to tragic ends.

"Your finger," I say. "Is incredibly mutilated. You described three cuts, but there were clearly more. Did she manage to get a hold of you again?"

"Sort of. She grabbed my wrist, but this time I was ready. I turned around and I was going to—I was going to fucking clock her, man. I wasn't putting up with it anymore, but then…" His voice dies on his lips.

"And then what?"

"And then I saw her," he says. "Just like Becca promised."

"You saw Snippity Snap?" He nods, face draining of color. Ryan Halflow is the size of a quarterback, but in that moment he looks no bigger than a boy of five. "It was big," he says slowly.

"Twisted looking, like the thing had crawled straight out of hell. It had these giant scissors for arms that started at its elbows, and its face was wrinkled flesh, with no eyes, just these dark, sunken sockets." He sucks in a breath. "Its mouth was sewn shut with its own skin. And in between the threads of flesh…"

"Eyes," I mutter. "There were eyes in its mouth, weren't there?"

He gazes up at me, shaken. "That's right. A hundred of them. Milky white and swimming around. It was the sound of the scissors, though, that really got to me. Those two gigantic blades opening and closing. Snip. Snap. Snip. Snap."

He shivers, taking a sip of coffee. "It was the scariest thing I've ever seen. I knew if I got out of there and told somebody, they'd call me insane. Crazy. So I did the stupid thing everybody hates about my generation."

"You took a photo."

"Yeah. It was impulsive and stupid, but I needed to know that I wasn't just imagining it. That it was real. So I snapped the picture and made a run for it, but Becca grabbed me by the ankle. I hit the ground hard." Ryan's eyes glisten as his voice begins to tremble. His uninjured hand finds the back of his neck, rubbing it anxiously. "The next thing I knew, the scissor sounds stopped. No snipping. No snapping. Just silence. And then Becca started laughing."

"Laughing?" I frown, hoping I didn't come all this way for some twisted practical joke.

"Yeah. She's laughing. Howling. I didn't get it, but when I kicked my leg free, I felt it. The scissor blades were against my neck. That fucking creature was standing over me, getting ready to cut my head off."

My heart skips a beat. This is it. The real deal. To have a legitimate case this quickly is almost unheard of within the Facility. Most new agents take months to come across something real, with some having worked there for years without success.

Yet here I am, achieving it in my first week.

"Did you give it an offering?" I ask, eagerly.

Ryan gives me a look. It's an uncomfortable look, the sort of look that makes me realize that I'm losing my cool, that I'm letting pieces of me peek through that shouldn't be seen. So I straighten up. Flatten my expression. When I speak, my voice is level, professional. "What I mean to say is, did you allow yourself to be cut again?"

"I mean, I couldn't stop her. Becca just grabbed my finger and started cutting. Snip. Snip. I felt paralyzed, like I couldn't do anything. I just stayed there on my hands and knees with that fucking monster standing above me, ready to decapitate me."

Ryan chokes back a sob. "I remember feeling light-headed from the blood loss, and right when my finger started feeling numb to the pain, Becca stopped. I don't know if it was because she'd had enough, or because I was crying, or…" He swallows. "… because I pissed myself."

"But after that," I say. "It was over? Becca stopped and the creature let you leave?"

"I guess." Ryan exhales. "Once Becca stopped cutting, I realized the creature was gone. Before she could do anything else, I booked it up the stairs and didn't bother waiting for a ride. I ran all the way home."

"You didn't report it to the authorities?"

"Report what? That some girl half my size held me down with a monster in a basement and cut up my finger?" He snorts, wiping his eyes. "No, I didn't report shit to the authorities. I just wanted to forget about it, pretend it never happened."

"Why did you post that photo then?" I look down at my notes. "Particularly with the hashtag #SnippitySnap?"

He shrugs, looking out the window. "I don't know. I guess I just hoped that maybe somebody would tell me I wasn't insane. Maybe that they'd seen it too."

"You're not insane," I say. "For what it's worth, I believe you, Ryan. I also believe that you did the right thing taking that photograph, because without that there's a good chance I would have never come knocking at your door tonight." I reach across and give his arm a gentle, consoling squeeze. "Thank you for talking to me."

"No problem," Ryan says, wiping his runny nose with a coffee napkin.

"Before I go though, would you mind if I took another look at that photo? The uncompressed version on your phone, preferably."

He blinks. Once again, his eyes dart over to the little window in the garage door, and I wonder if he's back to thinking his sister is playing a joke on him. It doesn't matter now, though. I have more than enough information to work with—but I'd like just a *little* more.

"Ryan?"

He nods. "Yeah, sure. Just a second."

He pulls out his phone and navigates to the image of Snippity Snap, then hands it to me.

I study the picture. It's similar to what I viewed on his social media, but given the poor lighting, the compression algorithm wreaked havoc on it. This version is much cleaner. For instance, whereas his Instagram showed only a shadow with a faint outline, this one provides additional details.

The shadow is there still, but now it's cleaner. The creature's scissor arms glint faintly with the light from the camera flash. There's a reflection in the steel. A face maybe, but it doesn't look like Ryan's—probably a consequence of the dim lighting.

I move my eyes over the photo, analyzing the creature in more detail. It's humanoid, mostly, but distinct in important ways. For one, it's taller. Its bow-legged and slouched, with a sort of zigzag to its posture, like a person suffering from severe scoliosis, but it still stands over six feet. A hundred eyes gleam in its flesh-sewn mouth. In the bottom corner of the picture, I spot something I didn't notice in the compressed version. It appears to be another human face. A girl's. It's Becca, no doubt, on the ground after Ryan had knocked her down, looking wild-eyed with a gleeful smile across her face.

Her expression unnerves me.

"Thank you," I say, passing the phone back. I make a final notation on my clipboard labeled SURVIVOR. "If it's alright with you, Ryan, I'd like to know Becca's last name."

"Her last name?" He blinks.

"Yes." I say, clicking my pen and placing it into my shirt pocket. "I think she and I need to have a discussion."

***

The front door swings open and a young girl is standing there. Her eyes are framed with dark mascara and darker bags. "Who the fuck are you?" she says.

I stand up straight, reach into my jacket pocket, and pull out my badge. "My name is [REDACTED]. I'm here to speak with you about an Event."

She narrows her eyes. Her name is Becca Galdun, and I believe she's been in contact with an urban legend known as Snippity Snap. She too is a seventeen-year-old attending Elktorch High. A classmate of one Ryan Halflow. Presently, she's wearing a green turtleneck with blue jeans, and a scowl the length of her face.

"An Event?" she says. Her eyes look me over, and then she glances back inside her single-story house, as though making sure the coast is clear. "Are you with the Facility?"

"I—wait, what?" The question catches me off-guard.

"The Facility," she hisses. "Are you one of their Men in Black?"

"Men in Black?"

"Don't be stupid. You know what I mean. I'm asking you if you're a Ghostbuster, or Hunter or whatever. You work there, don't you?"

I was cautioned that due to recent Events, knowledge of the Facility's existence may have grown more widespread. "I do," I say hesitantly. "You'll forgive me for asking, but how did you hear about us?"

Her face turns shades of anxious as she ushers me inside. Before she closes the door, she scans the front yard and the rest of the street. Then she bolts the door shut. "I spend a lot of time on [REDACTED DARKWEB ADDRESS]. You guys are pretty infamous there."

"Oh," I say, making a mental note to mention it to my superiors. "I'm actually here to speak with you about—"

"Snippity Snap?"

"Yes, actually."

"Good." She leads me into her kitchen. The house isn't particularly modern or renovated, but it's clean. There's barely a hair out of place. She rummages through a wooden cupboard and, a moment later, pulls out a kettle and a couple of tea bags. "Hope you like English Breakfast," she says, filling the kettle with water. "That's all I've got left."

"I'm not that picky." I pull out a chair at the kitchen table, then open my briefcase and retrieve my clipboard and forms. The kitchen is small. Cramped, really. The round table seats four, but there's only two chairs. "Are your parents available? Strictly speaking, I should be requesting their permission before interviewing a minor."

"My mom doesn't live here, and my dad's at work—don't worry though," she adds, "Neither of them care. They don't really give a fuck about anything."

"I see." I attach the forms to the clipboard and pull my pen from my pocket. I note that Becca Galdun is a child of separated parents. It's a minor detail, but one potentially important in determining her motivations and impulses.

My eyes scan down the form, and read the heading labeled INTERVIEW ENVIRONMENT. I glance around, taking in the kitchen and make notes as I go. The fridge is old, its white surface stained an off-yellow color and peppered with magnets. A short distance away is the stove, and between the two is a dull metal sink. Above the sink is a small window. Its blinds are closed, blocking the glare of the setting sun.

"It's quiet," I remark, checking my watch. The display reads five p.m. "I figured by this time the entire household would be home."

"Well, this entire household is just my dad and I. He works late. Doesn't make much money and needs to pick up shifts where he can." She pulls a couple of teaspoons from a drawer and a carton of creamer from the fridge.

"In that case, are you comfortable if we proceed without him?"

"I'm making us tea," she says sarcastically. "What do you think?"

"Right." I flip a page on my clipboard, returning to the first form. "Just so I have the proper details, your name is Becca Galdun, correct?"

"Gal-*dune*, not Gal-done."

"Ah." I make a note of the proper pronunciation. "Thank you. Am I correct in saying that you attended a house party on 321 Hendra Ave with one Ryan Halflow?"

She shuts off the tap, closes the kettle and plugs it in. "I didn't go there with him, no. But I did meet him there."

I check a box on my clipboard labeled IN ALIGNMENT. The second question I asked was a small lie, one used to determine the validity of a potential informant. It ensures multiple stories can be corroborated. So far, her story matches Ryan's. "When you met Ryan there, what did the two of you do?"

She turns around, placing both of her hands on the edge of the counter. I notice one of her fingers is badly scarred. "Why don't we skip the bullshit? I took Ryan into the basement to kill him."

My mouth goes dry. It was a suspicion I'd had, but to hear it announced so brazenly throws me off. "Excuse me?"

"You and I both know it." She gestures to me incredulously. "You assholes are the whole fucking reason the world's been going to shit. Don't think I haven't heard about the experiments you did to make the Man with the Red Notepad a reality."

"That…" I begin, unsure how to phrase it without giving away pertinent intelligence. "… was not my department."

She smiles, but it's scornful. There's pain inside of it. "No, of course not. You're one of the Inquisitors. The field agents. You talk to people like me who have met the monsters you want to subdue. To weaponize."

I pause, considering my words. "You're awfully knowledgeable about my line of work."

"More than you know."

"What else do you know?"

She looks me over, her eyes flicking from my clipboard to my face. "I know that you're new. Your badge number begins with the letter A. That means you're as fresh as fresh can be, just barely out of orientation. I also know that you were hired after an agent investigated an encounter with an entity known as Jagged Janice. That agent hasn't been heard from since. He's probably dead, and now you're his replacement." The kettle starts to scream. "Follow his lead, and you'll be dead too."

"Is that a threat?"

"No," she says, turning back to the counter and dropping a couple of tea bags into two mugs. "I'm just a little girl, who am I to threaten a massive proto-military shadow organization?" She smiles, unplugging the kettle and pouring the boiling water into the cups. "Honey in your tea?"

I frown. "Please."

"I'm just telling you what I've read, you know. Fresh operatives at the Facility don't appear to have great track records." She sets my mug down in front of me, then sits down at the table. "I want to be rid of this curse. I really do. But look at you—the perfectly pressed shirt, pants and probably socks. The meticulously organized briefcase. The cookie-cutter hairstyle. You look more interested in landing a promotion than putting a stop to my nightmare."

The words sting, but they're not far from the truth. On some level—on many levels, I felt excited about discovering a real case this soon. Ecstatic at what it implied for my career. A successful capture of an entity like Snippity Snap would bring serious accolades within the Facility. "Understandable," I say. "I'm here to help, if I can."

She appraises me, leaning forward and resting her chin on steepled fingers. "Fine. It's not like I have any other options."

I bring my pen back to the clipboard. "Why did you intend to kill Ryan in that basement?"

"Honestly? It was him or me."

"Him or you?" I'm well versed in the lore of Snippity Snap, and there's nothing in there about ultimatums. "Can you expand on that?"

"The first time I saw Snippity Snap," she says. "I was just a girl. Seven going on eight. It was the nursery rhyme that did it—that old urban legend, except back then it was more recent. My mom used to sing it in the car, and I think it was because of that woman's funeral."

"Hope Delvine," I mutter. It's a name I've seen come up again and again in my study of the legend. A potential identity for Snippity.

Becca nods. "Yeah, I think that was it. She was murdered by her husband. The asshole stabbed her six times with a sewing needle, then cut her throat with a pair of scissors."

"That's right. Gruesome stuff."

"That's putting it lightly." Becca picks up her tea, gives it a gentle blow, and then takes a sip. "Anyway, I guess she used to write poetry in her free time and one of those poems was read at her funeral. The local paper published it."

"So that's the origin of the rhyme?"

"I think so. Since the events surrounding her death were so horrible, local kids picked the rhyme up and started trying to scare each other with it. Pretty soon, the poem became a sort of song, or a chant. Next thing you know, it's a full-blown urban legend. People are sharing it at sleepovers, campfires. All over the place."

A fascinating discovery. I remember getting chain mail when I was in highschool about an entity known as Snippity Snap. The text contained an old nursery rhyme, but I had always assumed the origin of it would be much older than ten years.

I hum to myself, and the tune comes back.

> *Snip Snap,*
> *Needle and thread, run through my head!*
> *Snip, Snap*
> *All that you've said, rather be dead!*
> *Snip Snap,*
> *Just leave me be, all that I need!*
> *Snip Snap,*
> *Please!*
> *Snip Snap,*
> *Please!*

"Some friends and I were chanting it one night," Becca says, squeezing her scarred finger. "And I got this stupid idea in my head. I thought that maybe since Hope was killed by a pair of scissors, and the refrain was Snip Snap, then maybe the scissors had something to do with the urban legend. Maybe scissors could make the fabled monster appear."

Her voice fades to silence, and her mouth hangs there for a moment. When she speaks again, it's slow, and full of regret. "So we tried saying the rhyme again, this time cutting at the air with scissors."

"You were actually trying to summon Snippity Snap?"

"We were eight," she says defensively. "It sounded scary, but deep down even we knew it was ridiculous. I don't think a single one of us thought anything would actually happen. Back then we didn't have all the wonders of the iPhone to entertain us, so we had to get creative."

"Did it work?"

She shakes her head. "Not that time."

I flip through my clipboard to the form entitled ORIGIN. I check a box labeled ATTEMPTS and then place a single tally beside it. Knowing the rough number of failures before a summoning succeeds is important, particularly if the intention is to capture the entity in question.

"After that," Becca continues. "We tried cutting something with the scissors. Not air, but something tangible. Paper, at first, and then cloth—since the whole rhyme was about sewing. Still, we got nothing. Then I had a thought. I figured since Hope was murdered, maybe there needed to be some kind of mutilation involved. A sort of blood for blood kinda deal. So I cut my finger, and then I said the rhyme. My friends were obviously grossed out but... it didn't take them long to become believers."

In spite of myself, I lean forward. I feel for this girl, for Ryan, for this whole town that's suffered under the shadow of this nightmare, but I can't pretend I'm not excited. It's only day two of my investigation and the discoveries are already proving massive. "Did she appear?" I ask. "Snippity?"

Becca glares at me. "Are you recording this? Word for word?"

"I'm only taking notes."

She raises an eyebrow, and I recognize the hesitancy in her features, her body language. "Becca," I say. "Before we continue, I think it's important that I impress upon you that I'm not law enforcement. The legality of your actions doesn't concern me. Not particularly. I'm strictly here for the details on the Event."

She snorts. "Yeah, sure. Then you can turn right around and hand those details to the FBI as soon as I'm finished talking." Her fingers grip her coffee mug, and they dance along its circumference. "I know how this goes."

"That's not the case at all. Your details, and those of the Event will be kept in secured, encrypted storage. These paper copies will be incinerated. It's bad for business if we run around getting our informants arrested."

She studies me for a few moments, and then her expression softens. "Makes sense, I guess. Of all the criticism I see for the Facility on [REDACTED DARKWEB ADDRESS] there's nothing about you guys being rats."

"At least they're right about that."

Becca leans back in her seat with a sigh. "After I mutilated my finger, Snippity Snap appeared."

A lump forms in my throat. I hastily flip through several sheets on my clipboard before I find one labeled INITIAL

ENCOUNTER. "Can you tell me where exactly it appeared? Was it in this house?"

"Yes." Becca points down a hallway to the right of me. "We did the ritual down there, in the bathroom. It's the only room in the house that doesn't have any windows, so it was ideal for the summoning."

My pen scratches across my form. "When Snippity Snap appeared, where was it standing relative to you and your friends?"

"In front of the bathroom door, about, I don't know, six feet away from us? It was dark, though. So dark. None of us noticed it was there until we heard that awful sound. The shears opening and closing. Snip. Snap."

Becca grimaces. "When I saw it, I froze. To see that monster, with its two giant scissors for arms and that horrible, sewed face with its loose flesh and all of those eyes...." She shudders. "I lost whatever nerve I had. I shouted at it to leave us alone. To go away."

"It sounds like you were quite brave."

Becca glances toward the hallway. It's a brief look. Just a half-second at most, but there's a nervousness in her expression, a deep panic. Then it's gone.

"Is somebody here?" I ask, shifting in my seat to look down the hallway.

It's empty.

She shakes her head. "No. Sorry, I just thought I heard my dad come home, but it's only six. He won't be back until seven or eight."

"Is that right..." Part of me feels off, like something isn't quite right, but I do my best to ignore it. I'm a professional now. A field agent. Snippity Snap is a creature that requires a summoning to appear, and such parameters haven't been met. Becca on her own isn't any threat.

"What did you do?" I ask, returning my pen to the clipboard.

"I—" Becca looks suddenly flustered. Distracted. Her previous calmness is lost, and something has replaced it. Fear, maybe? It's difficult to say. Traumatic memories can have severe effects on a person's mental state, particularly if they've been largely repressed.

"Miss Galdun?"

"I didn't do anything," she says quietly. "None of us did, except for Heather. Snippity got her first. It caught her arm when she tried to make a break for it—when she tried to run past the thing." Becca shivers. "Snippity cut her arm off. I remember it hanging there, dangling from her elbow. The only thing keeping it attached was a few strings of flesh, and they tore one by one, until her arm fell on the tile floor."

Becca's face screws up with the onset of tears. "I'll never forget the smell of Heather's blood, or the sound of her screaming. Her arm was spurting like a fountain, warm and wet. It was everywhere. All over us." She chokes back a sob. "It was the most horrible thing I've ever seen. I was so fucking afraid."

I open my mouth to speak, but there are no words to express how sorry I am for her. For her friend. To have suffered through an experience like that at such a young age is almost unimaginable. But unfortunately, it's something I can relate to.

"I'm sorry, Becca," I say. "But I have to ask you some questions about that."

She nods, reaching for a napkin on the table. She brings it to her nose and blows into it, dabbing at her eyes with a sweater sleeve. "Go ahead."

"At the time all this occurred, there were no adults in the home to hear it?"

"No," she says, taking a deep, shaking breath. "My mom was at work, and my dad was outside on the street tuning up his Camaro, which just happens to have an engine loud enough to pass for a jumbo jet." She sniffles. "It was just me and my two friends trapped in that bathroom. Nobody heard us."

I circle the word WITNESSES on the form, and as I do, I hear a faint sound in the distance—like metal scraping on metal. My pencil stops on the page. "Do you hear that?" I ask.

"Hear what?"

"That metallic sound." It's barely there, almost imperceptible. It doesn't stop a sensation from growing in my chest, though. Something's triggering my fight-or-flight response.

"I'm sorry," she says. "I don't hear anything."

For a moment, I feel foolish. The sound is so faint, so quiet, that I'm wondering if maybe I've allowed myself to become too invested in Becca's story. I wonder if I'm frightening myself. My hand brushes over the side of my jacket, where I can feel my service weapon holstered.

"Are you okay?" Becca asks.

"It's nothing," I say, returning my hand to my pencil. "I'm just hearing things. I didn't get much sleep these past couple of nights, and I think the consequences are coming home to roost. Jet lag, and all that." I plaster a smile on my face. "Please, continue."

"... Right." She eyes me for a moment, and then nods. "Okay. Where was I? There was blood everywhere. I couldn't see much, but I could feel it all over me, in my hair, my eyes, my mouth. Heather bawled her eyes out, and I could just barely see the creature standing over her, its shears reflecting what little light was in the room. I watched its mouth open and close, with all of its glowing, swimming eyes, and this... sound escaped it."

"Sound?"

"Yeah, like it was speaking."

"What did its voice sound like? Was it masculine, or feminine?"

"Neither," Becca says. "It sounded mechanical. It was sharp and grating, almost like a sewing machine."

"Curious." I make a notation on my clipboard. *Deviation*. In the legend, the voice is typically non-existent. The creature is silent, save for the sound of its shears. "So it wasn't speaking words?"

"No, but somehow I understood it anyway. I don't know if I just saw the writing on the wall because of what it did to Heather, or if I was attuned to it or something, but... somehow I knew what it wanted. I knew it wanted an offering. Someone to suffer like it had."

"Suffer like it had? You believe this creature is Hope Delvine?"

Becca shrugs, reaching for her mug, but her hands are trembling. They're shaking like a pair of maracas and the tea splashes over the rim, scalding her. "Fuck!" she shrieks.

I jump to my feet. "Are you alright?"

"I'm fine!" she roars, and her eyes are wild. There's venom in her voice.

I freeze. The sudden intensity of the moment feels wrong and out of place. "I'm trained in first aid," I explain. "It's probably best if you let me have a look at that burn."

"It's fine," she says, this time more calmly. "I'll deal with it." She walks to the sink, running her hand under cold water for a minute before returning wordlessly to the table, picking up a rag and dabbing up the spilled tea.

"Yes," she mutters. "I do believe that Snippity Snap is Hope Delvine. It's the only thing that makes any sense. Hope's rhyme summoned the creature, didn't it?"

"Fair point." I record the theory on my clipboard. It's certainly possible that Snippity Snap is a vengeful spirit. The pieces do add up. Still, it leaves another lingering and uncomfortable question. "What did you offer?"

Becca looks up at me. "Sorry?"

"You said it knew it wanted an offering. Someone to suffer like it had."

"Oh." She looks away.

"So what did you offer?"

"I offered it the only thing that I could." Becca takes a breath, puts her face in her hands. "I offered it Heather."

"You offered your friend to that monster?"

"Give me a break!" Becca snaps. "She was dead anyway! I mean, half her fucking arm was amputated. Besides, it wasn't like any of us were escaping while that thing was standing in front of the door."

I write the details down, but each word digs a pit in my stomach. A sickening sadness grows inside of me for that poor girl. It's difficult to imagine the horror she must have felt. "How did you offer her?" I ask, quietly. "Was there a ritual involved in that too?"

Becca blinks and tears slip down her cheeks. "No... God. There wasn't any ritual. I just told it to take her, to take Heather and leave me alone, and then it did."

"Leave you alone..." I stare at her, wondering if her terminology was an accident, intentional, or a psychological slip. She asked it to leave *her* alone. Becca. Not both of them. Not her and Fran. I reach for my mug and take a sip, reminding myself not to judge too harshly. Becca was just a young girl herself, after all. To be confronted by a nightmare at that age would drive anybody to act in strange ways.

"After you offered it Heather," I say, placing my mug back on the table. "What did Snippity Snap do to her?" I'm not sure I want to hear the answer, but I know that it's important.

Becca shrugs. Her eyes are red and puffy, and a trail of snot winds its way from her nose to her lip. She lifts a hand into the air and raises two fingers. She makes a cutting motion. "Snip," she says.

"Snip?"

"The monster took her head off. It was over quick, thankfully, but there was so much blood. Both of us—Fran and I, were drenched in it." She smiles, but it's a broken and twisted sort of smile. "On the bright side, we didn't have to listen to Heather screamanymore. Just each other."

"After Heather was killed, did Snippity leave?"

"Vanished. Like it was never even there."

I lean back in my chair, frowning as I look over my notes. From this interview alone I've accumulated a small textbook on Snippity Snap, much more than the Facility's managed since its inception.

Still, I suspect I'm only scratching the surface.

"I heard about that, you know. Heather's death."

Becca squirms in her seat. "Not surprised. It was pretty big news around here."

"They attributed the murder to a local man, didn't they?" I fold my arms, studying Becca's expression. "The newspapers called him the Elktorch Slasher. He was arrested not far from here."

"Yeah," Becca says, bitterness in her voice. "They threw my dad in prison for three months. The cops were convinced it had to have been him. I mean, who else was at the house, right? It's not like we have serial killers in sleepy Elktorch."

"He was exonerated, though," I say. "After two more murders occurred."

Becca's quiet. She glances back down the hallway and swallows. "Yeah. After two other people were killed, the police finally realized my dad was innocent. Dumb fucks. They decided there was a serial killer on the loose, after all."

Pieces begin to connect in my mind, and I'm not certain I like the look of the puzzle. "The people who were killed," I say darkly. "Did that have something to do with you?"

She stares at me. There's a look on her face somewhere between annoyance and impatience. Her hands ball into small fists. "No shit. Of course it did. My dad was in prison for murdering a little girl, and I knew the only way he was getting out of there was if—"

"—Snippity Snap killed again."

"Bingo," she says with false cheer.

"You committed identical murders to prove your father's innocence."

She rolls her eyes. "Are you here to present me with my Daughter of the Year Award?"

Outside, the sun's nearly set. Its last rays cast shadows across the room, filtering in through the narrow openings in the blinds. The way they play across Becca's face, it's difficult to discern her expression.

"You traded people's lives for your father's freedom," I say. "They didn't die peaceful deaths, you know."

She slams a hand on the table, shooting up out of her chair. "You really think I don't know just how horrible each and every one of their deaths were? You really think that shit doesn't keep me up at night, hating myself and wishing I had the courage to just let Snippity Snap take me instead?"

"Take you instead?" I say quietly. I speak my next words with a measured calmness, though my heart's beginning to race in my chest. "Miss Galdun, did you make some kind of deal with that creature?"

Becca glares at me, one side of her face draped in shadow, the other in shrinking sunlight. We sit in a tense silence. The corners of her mouth twitch with unsaid words.

"Becca," I say, this time more forcefully. "Did you make a deal with Snippity Snap?"

"I did what I had to do."

"What does that mean?"

She closes her eyes, runs both hands through her dark hair, and groans. She doesn't want to speak. She doesn't want to tell me this next part, but then her mouth opens, her voice cracks, and it all spills out. "I summoned it," she mutters. "When I mutilated my finger. When I said the rhyme and brought it through the veil and into our world. I created it, and it wanted me. Never Heather. Always me."

I study her, my eyes straining in the waning light. I never took Becca for an especially empathetic girl, but perhaps one who had been thrust into a situation she didn't understand, or one she existed in against her will. I'm beginning to believe, however, that I was mistaken. There's a cunning to her I didn't account for.

I assumed she was like so many other children who'd encountered entities or spirits. Enamoured. Perhaps believing themselves special for having had the experience, pulled into their orbit like a macabre cultist. But Becca wasn't manipulated. She wasn't. She chose to commit the murders. She chose to massacre innocent people, multiple times, all to save herself.

"Would you mind if we turn on a light?" I ask. "It's getting difficult to write."

"Sure." Becca reaches up and tugs at the chain of the ceiling fan. A light flickers to life. "That better?"

"Much."

She settles herself back into her chair. There's a look on her face that doesn't sit right with me. It's too eager, too enthusiastic. It's making me think that I should probably finish this up and get on my way, but there's still one more question I need to ask. One of incredible importance.

"How does it work, then? Your deal?"

Becca's lips split into a joyless smirk. "I give Snippity Snap life, in the form of blood and pain. I help it satiate its hunger. In exchange, it lets me live a little longer."

"Why does it want you? I understand that you summoned it, but that doesn't explain—"

"Are you deaf? Or were you just not listening? I didn't just summon the thing, I fucking *created* it. I pulled Hope Delvine's twisted soul out of the ether, and ripped it six ways to Sunday." Becca reaches a hand up and grips a clump of her air, pulling at it with a pained, manic glint in her eyes. "I didn't mean to. I didn't realize it would create that monster. But it did. It gave birth to that thing, and now Snippity Snap wants me to pay. Blood for blood, she says. Agony for agony."

My skin prickles with goosebumps. There's a new sound in the house, and it's coming from the hallway. It's sharp. Discordant.

Scissors. Opening and closing.

Snip. Snap.

Snip. Snap.

My heart thunders in my chest. A primal part of me screams that it's time to bolt—that it was time to bolt ten minutes ago, but now my palms feel clammy, and my head feels clouded with adrenaline. I clear my throat, rising from the table. "That should do for now. I'll take this information and do some research at my hotel." I speak more quickly than I should. More anxiously. I've broken a cardinal rule and allowed unease and fear to slip into my voice. "Hopefully tomorrow I'll have outlined a solution for your predicament."

"I'm not finished telling you my story though," Becca says, and this time the tears are gone. Her expression is cold. Calculated. She stands up from the table and there's a hunger in her eyes. "Stay awhile longer. We're just getting to the good part."

I bring a hand to my jacket, hovering over my service weapon. "I think the good part can wait until tomorrow." I give her a curt nod and a false smile. I turn around to leave.

Something presses against my throat.

Ryan Halflow towers in front of me, a pair of scissors in his hand. He presses the cold steel blades against my neck. "Don't move," he says. "And I won't kill you."

There's the squeal of a chair sliding on linoleum, and a moment later Becca strides in front of me. "I honestly didn't expect it to be this simple," she laughs. "But it was. You actually walked right in here after hearing Ryan's sob story. Now I've got a perfect offering that nobody's gonna bother looking for." She claps her hands gleefully.

"My employer knows where I am," I say, and it's the truth. "Down to the square foot. We're GPS tracked at all times."

"Sure you are," she says in a singsong voice. "But the Facility isn't going to risk revealing itself to the public. Not in the name of avenging some stupid intern. In the meantime though, you'll keep Snippity Snap satisfied for a few months."

She smirks, her tongue sliding across her teeth. "Think of it this way, your death will save another life. Isn't that what you wanted? To help people suffering from these mean old legends?"

"Listen," I say. "I can help you. I wasn't kidding about that. I have enormous resources, more than you can possibly know and—"

"I know all about your resources," Becca snaps, grabbing me by my hair and pulling my throat against the edge of the shears. I feel a thin trail of warmth trickle down my neck. "All you've managed to do at the Facility is fuck things up. You think I'm going to risk you pissing Snippity Snap off, all on the off chance some fresh out of orientation dimwit can solve a nightmare I've suffered with for a decade?"

She lets go with a violent jerk. I wince as the blade slides across my flesh, drawing more blood. Her face contorts in a mixture of revulsion and glee at the sight of it, and I realize this is the real Becca. Everything before this had been an act.

"I'm better off doing what I've been doing all along," she says. "Keeping Snippity Snap satisfied one life at a time. Offering it people that nobody's going to look for. People nobody gives a fuck about." She steps away, and a moment later the dim, flickering kitchen light goes out.

Then, from somewhere in the darkness, I hear her voice. "Do it, Ryan."

Ryan grabs my hand in a flash, pulling the scissors down from my throat and closing them on my index finger.

"Snip Snap," Becca chants beside me. "Needle and thread, run through my head!"

The pain of the shears slashing my fingers is dull, faded against the backdrop of my boiling adrenaline. Ryan has one of my hands, and I'm quite certain he could overpower me even without Becca's help, but I still have my service weapon. It's on the side of my torso, inside my jacket. With my free hand, it'd be an awkward reach, but if I could get to it before they realized what I was doing...

"It's not working," Ryan says, and I faintly see blood running down my finger. My eyes are beginning to adjust to the darkness. "I did what you said, Becca. I cut up my finger in the bathroom earlier to get her to cross over and—"

"Did she?" Becca barks.

"I don't know," he says, panicking. "Maybe. I mean, I thought so, but—"

"But what?"

"I didn't want her to get me."

"For fuck's sake!" Becca shrieks. "If you want to be a part of this, then you need to grow a pair, Ryan! Snippity Snap listens to me. She'll take whoever I offer!"

"I'm sorry, Bec."

I faintly see Becca grab Ryan's wrist, and the next second I feel her smaller hand grab my own. "Hold him still!" she commands. "Can you at least do that right?"

Ryan shuffles around me, and I realize that my window to draw my weapon and get out of this situation is quickly deteriorating.

Time to act.

I take a sharp breath and lunge sideways, reaching for my sidearm, but Ryan's quicker. He tackles me to the ground and grabs both of my arms, wrestling them behind my back and holding them there.

"Fucking christ..." I mutter, my face pressed against the cold linoleum. I'm beginning to wonder if Becca's father even lives here. If he's even still alive.

A shoe rests on my face, and I hear Becca's shrill laughter. "You strutted in here thinking you were hot shit, didn't you? You thought that just because big daddy gubbermint handed you a job working at their spooky old monster factory, that you were beyond the reach of real monsters." Her sneaker kicks me in the cheek, and I feel pain blossom across my face.

"Let me tell you a secret," she says, and I realize her voice is closer now, nearly against my ear. "You're not beyond the reach of real monsters. In fact, you're going to meet one very shortly."

I hear her reposition herself. She grabs my finger while Ryan holds my arms behind my back. "Let's try this again," she says, closing the scissors on my finger in a river of blood. "Snip, Snap! Needle and thread!"

I grimace, my mind reeling. I curse myself for getting pulled in by a couple of teenagers, and if I ever manage to get myself out of this mess, I swear to never underestimate an informant again. "Becca," I mumble, my mouth pressed against the floor. "There's another way to deal with Snippity Snap. Let me help you."

Another cut. This one deeper. Much deeper.

I slam my eyes shut, roaring in agony. Maybe a neighbor will hear me, I pray, or maybe somebody on the street will investigate. I holler again, shouting my lungs raw.

"Aw, he thinks somebody's going to hear him," Becca says in a doting voice. "Unlike you, I actually came here with a plan though, dipshit. You probably noticed the 'For Sale' sign on the house next door. That means nobody's home. And as for my other neighbor? They're on vacation upstate, not due back for another week."

She crouches down in front of me and jams the wet tea rag into my mouth. "I'm just putting this here to shut you up. I can't stand the sound of your whimpering."

I struggle, doing my best to keep shouting, but my voice is muffled. Barely audible.

"As for your earlier statement," Becca says, rising to her feet. "There's no other way to deal with Snippity Snap. Hear me? All you have are theories, but one botched theory means I'm *dead*." She steps around me and reaches down, grabbing my finger again. The scissors close. Another cut. Another muffled roar of pain. "Personally, I'd prefer it if *you* died instead."

Ryan howls with laughter. "This is going to be so amazing, Beccs. I can't wait to see Snippity!"

"You already have," she growls, cutting me again. "Snip, Snap! Needle and thread!"

"No!" he says, and his voice sounds panicked, insulted. "I've only seen the photo! I wish I could've been there with you guys when you killed Ben in the basement. You looked like you were having so much fun!"

"Well if you didn't bitch out earlier, Snippity Snap would already be here!" Three more cuts in rapid succession. Becca's chants are growing angrier, more frustrated. "Where the fuck is she? Get over here, Delvine, you stupid cunt! Take this offering!"

I spit out the rag, coughing. I'm beginning to feel lightheaded from the blood loss. "That whole story you fed me about the house party and not knowing what happened to Ben—"

"All bullshit," Ryan says gleefully. "I sold it pretty good though, didn't I? You can thank our theater teacher Miss Dill for that! I wasn't lying when I said it was a real picture of Snippity Snap, though. It really was. It just wasn't me who took it."

I feel the blood soaking through the back of my jacket. How much have I lost? Too much. Time's running out. I kick and thrash, but Ryan tightens his hold.

"So what," I grunt. "You grabbed Ben's phone, then played it off like you took the picture?"

"That's right," Ryan says, and Becca keeps cutting. "We figured we might attract some weirdos interested in the paranormal— some awkward kids with no friends. The sorta kid that nobody would bat an eye about dying in some fucked ritual, because they probably did it to themselves.

"Instead," Becca says, her voice thick with disbelief. "You contacted him. The fucking *Facility*. It was honestly dumbfounding. I really didn't think we'd sold it that well, but apparently it was good enough to fool you dimwits."

Damn it. I had it all backwards. Snippity Snap wasn't the monster. It was these two, and if I didn't get out of here somehow, they were going to cause the deaths of more innocent people. I wrack my mind, trying to formulate a plan. If I could just reach my pistol...

It's no use. Ryan's too strong. I need to think of a way around him, a way to remove his strength from the equation. I clench my eyes, trying to focus through the pain, trying to focus on a strategy that doesn't end up with me dead, cut up into neat little pieces.

I know Becca can't be reasoned with. If she didn't already prove that before, then she's certainly proven it now. Ryan, on the other hand, seems different. It's almost like he's being manipulated, like he's just along for the ride in Becca's master plan.

If I can get through to him, then I might have a chance.

"Ryan," I say in a measured voice. "I can get you the support you need. If you stop this now we can put it behind us, and that means no prison and no charges. You only need to let me go and—"

I scream.

I scream so hard that my throat becomes raw and my body writhes in anguish, my eyes stinging as they let loose a torrent of tears as my adrenaline spikes, causing my legs to kick out and my torso to twist violently.

"Snip," Becca says. She grabs my face, stuffing my amputated finger into my mouth. "That's enough talking from you." I choke on it for a moment before spitting it out, bawling in pain. All I taste is blood and flesh.

"Snip Snap," Becca calls. *"Needle and thread!"*

There's a sound in the hallway. Metallic. Sharp.

It arrives over the chorus of my whimpering agony. It's the sound of two giant shears opening and closing. Snip. Snap. Snip. Snap. My pain dulls, eclipsed by my racing heart and mounting panic.

"Becca," Ryan breathes. "Look—"

"I see it, dumbass." Becca steps in front of me, the blue of her jeans just barely visible in the inky blackness. "Snippity Snap," she loudly proclaims. "I offer you this life in exchange for my own!"

The scissors open and close. Then it speaks. It speaks in that terrible, sharp and jagged sewing machine voice Becca described. I have no idea what it says, but Becca steps back.

"Good girl, Snippity," she says, then "hold him still, Ryan."

I crane my neck, and I can see it. The shadow in the dark. The local nightmare, with its two gleaming, steel shears, and its many swimming eyes, all buzzing inside of a flesh-sewn mouth. It speaks again. That whirring, sewing machine ramble.

"Hope," I choke, desperate to try anything. "Hope Delvine, right? I know it's you in there. I know you think it's worth it, these blood offerings, but Becca Galdun's the one who's chained you here. She's the one who ripped you out of your afterlife, and brought you here to make people suffer. Just—"

Becca's foot connects with my face, and I hear a sharp crack. The pain tells me my cheekbone just fractured, badly enough that I can feel blood trailing down my jaw, but it's hardly a consideration. I keep talking. I have to, because it's all I have left. "Please, Hope! You are not an evil person. You were an innocent woman who was murdered by her husband!"

Snip. Snap. The shears open and close.

"Ryan," Becca shouts. "Shut him up for fuck sakes!"

I feel Ryan lift his hand from my wrist, clambering toward my face, and that's when I move. It's the only moment I'll ever have. I roll over, my hand darting inside my jacket and even as Ryan grabs me by my hair and smashes my skull against the linoleum floor, it's already too late.

Because I feel cold steel in my grip.

There's a loud bang and a blinding flash, and Ryan stumbles off of me with a look of confusion on his face.

I pull the trigger again, and he drops.

Becca rushes at me, but I swing my hand back and bash her across the face with the pistol grip. She crumples to the floor. I only look at her for a moment, my breath heaving in my chest, before my attention is pulled toward the real danger. The creature moving closer.

I study it, wrestling against my fight-or-flight response and trying to determine a game plan. I could run, I think to myself. The creature's not moving that quickly, with its crooked legs and twisted spine. I have little doubt that I could physically escape it, but to what end?

What happens once I leave? Does it follow me?

No. Too many variables. I raise my firearm, pointing it at the monster. My finger trembles on the trigger. I could dump a clip of bullets into Snippity Snap and blow the creature away. I'd fire them straight down its throat, into that flesh-sewn mouth, and its hundred white eyes.

No. That won't work either. The truth is Snippity Snap isn't the real monster here.

My eyes drift to Becca, and she's groaning on the ground, a hand cupped against her battered jaw. She lurches up to her hands and knees. Her expression is difficult to make out in the darkness, but I don't need to. Her growls paint a pretty picture all on their own.

She's angry. She hates me right now.

Good.

"Kill him!" Becca screams at Snippity Snap. "I summoned you to present my offering! Now accept it, you ungrateful bitch!"

Snip. Snap.

A thought occurs to me between the sound of shears and Becca's shrill demands for blood. It's true that Becca did summon Snippity here. In fact, she'd summoned it here the same way she'd summoned it the first time she tore Hope's soul from the ether and chained it to this world. She'd made this creature a reality by uttering the first lines of Hope's poem; the old nursery rhyme she'd written before being murdered by her husband. So what if...

It's a long shot, but it's all I've got left.

I step toward Becca, my pistol pointing at her while my other hand gestures to the scissors in her hand. "Give them to me," I order.

"Fuck you!"

I pull back on the cocking hammer. "Give them to me, or I blow your brains all over the kitchen floor." I glance at Ryan's corpse, jerking my head toward it. "You can join him. I've got plenty of bullets left, and you *did* seem like good friends."

There's a glint of defiance in her eyes, but I think she's realizing Snippity Snap isn't moving fast enough. She doesn't have me cornered, and she's lost her enforcer. Most importantly though, she knows that I've got nothing to lose.

If I die here, so does she.

She slides the scissors across the floor. I keep my pistol steadied on her as I reach down to pick them up. In my peripheral, I track the creature Hope Delvine's become. It shambles toward me slowly, its voice speaking in that mechanical whir. I wonder if it's begging me to put it out of its misery.

I strafe away from it, into the black hallway it emerged from. As I do, I sling my fingers through the scissor grips. I bring the blades to my hand, still holding the pistol, and extend my undamaged index finger.

Here goes nothing. I close the scissors on my flesh, cutting across my finger and announcing loudly, "Snip Snap. *Please!*"

The creature takes another step.

Snip. Snap. The shears speak promises of violence.

Damn it.

Becca rolls her head back, laughing. "You think I haven't tried that? You dipshit, this is exactly why I didn't want your help. You'd just end up getting me killed."

It was a hail mary, I confess. I thought maybe if the first lines had summoned the creature, then the last ones could send it back. Oh well. I'm still not out of ideas.

Not entirely.

I spit out a mouthful of blood. Shooting Hope feels wrong, given her tortured existence, and beyond that, it's probably pointless. She's not living, after all. My only real move is to run. To get away, return to the Facility and come back with some reinforcements to deal with this creature.

Yeah. That could work. I take another step back, fading into the darkness of the hallway.

"You don't get it, do you?" Becca sneers. "There's no escaping Snippity once you've been offered. You think you're the first person to run away? It always comes back. Always. It'll snap you the moment you rest those tired eyes."

I snarl, my finger twitching on the trigger and desperate to put six rounds into Becca's head. She deserves to die for everything she's done—for the willing horror she's inflicted on so many, and the gleeful torment she put me through. Still, there's a dilemma in that. If she was the one who created this monster, then perhaps she needs to be one to end it. She needs to offer herself to Snippity Snap. If she dies without Hope taking her toll, then who knows if there's even a way to put that genie back in the bottle.

The creature could roam the world forever, snapping people until the end of time.

Snip. Snap.

Its feet plod forward, slapping against the floor with each step while its scissors drag behind it, squealing as they carve up the linoleum. But as it passes the kitchen table, the creature suddenly jerks to a stop.

I blink, not sure what's going on. Evidently, neither is Becca. She stares at Snippity Snap, only six or seven feet away from her, with a slack-jawed look on her face.

Snippity's head tilts downward. Its hundred eyes begin vibrating in horrid excitement. Again, the mechanical whir of its voice starts up, except this time it gets louder and louder, like it's screaming in anticipation.

It's standing above Ryan Halflow's corpse.

No.

Not a corpse. Ryan's arm twitches, and he tries to raise himself onto his hands and knees, but he's lost too much blood. He doesn't have the strength. He collapses into a heap on the floor.

"Beccs," Ryan coughs weakly. A pool of blood lies beneath him. "Call an ambulance… and tell Snippity to get away—"

Snip.

There's a thud. Ryan's messy head of hair rolls across the kitchen floor. Becca shrieks, crawling away from the creature and toward me in the hallway.

I point the gun at her and fire.

Once.

Twice.

She drops, blood leaking from her arm. Tears escape her face, and this time I know they're genuine. "Please," she begs me. "Please help me!"

I gaze at her, and a piece of me wants to reach out, to help her up and get her out of there. It wants to save this young girl. But then I remember everything she's done. I remember the manipulation she put Ryan through, manipulation that resulted in two bullets in his chest and his head rolling on the kitchen floor. I remember her cutting off my finger. Laughing. Gleefully laughing.

Becca stumbles to her feet, and Snippity Snap plods toward her.

The kitchen becomes bright. There's a flash, and a bang, and then a gentle stream of smoke drifts from my handgun. Becca drops, her knees bleeding and voice screaming. She squirms on the ground, whimpering as each movement of her arms and legs proves too agonizing to complete. Crippled and broken, she starts crawling toward me like a worm.

"Please…" she groans.

But my sympathy has run out. The truth is, Becca's right. There's only ever been one surefire way of ending this horror, and now I intend to see it through.

Snip Snap.

Behind Becca, Snippity's shears open and close. Its feet slap the linoleum with each laboured step.

"You fucking asshole!" Becca shrieks. "Your job was to help me, not murder me!"

Her body slides toward me, inch by inch. But not fast enough. A few feet away from her, Snippity Snap takes the first steps into Becca's trail of blood. It speaks again in that strange, sewing-machine voice, and somehow I sense a level of joy in it.

It's been waiting for this moment for a long time.

"You murdered me!" Becca screams. "You hear me? You fucking child killer!"

Snippity's feet step over her, its scissor blades pressing Becca's neck to the floor.

"Don't you dare think you're safe!" Becca snarls. "It'll kill you too! It'll kill you unless you let me keep it away from you!" Her eyes are wild again, desperate. "I can help you! I can give it other offerings and keep it away from you!"

"All you have are theories," I say coldly. "And one botched theory means that I'm dead." I don't mean to, but a grin slips across my face. "Personally, I'd prefer it if you died instead."

Snippity's eyes vibrate, and its crooked body trembles as its voice spins louder and louder.

"Please!" Becca shrieks. "What the fuck are you waiting fo—"

Becca's head rolls toward my feet. It bumps against my leather shoe, coming to a rest. Her tongue lolls from her mouth, and her messy eyeshadow runs down her cheeks, still wet from the tears staining her face. For a moment, I see her eyes move. They're full of terror, and rage, and hatred.

And then they're still.

When I look up, Snippity Snap is gone.

I heave a sigh and stumble along the wall before flicking on the dim light. My hand throbs in agony. I step over the two corpses on the floor, each of them riddled with bullets from my service weapon.

For a job that started out so promising, it really went to shit.

I pass by the table. As I do, I reach out and take a sip of my tea. It's cold. Bitter. But I don't care, I just need something to quench my thirst. Something to get my head in order. I pull a rag from the oven handle and wrap it around my still-bleeding wound. My finger is still right where I left it, on the floor, lying next to Ryan's corpse. It's pale and pruned and a reminder of how arrogant I was to underestimate them both. To let my guard down.

I pick up the finger and pocket it.

It takes me a few minutes to track down a plastic bag, but once I do, I fill it with ice from Becca's freezer and drop my amputated finger inside. Hopefully that'll keep it fresh for a few hours.

Then I sit back down in my chair.

My eyes look around, taking in the carnage. Two school kids shot dead, both of their corpses riddled with bullets from my service weapon, and both of them beheaded. Oh, and I also happen to be covered in plenty of their blood.

I groan. I'm beginning to see why so few new agents manage to make any successful captures. The truth is, this shit is hard. I reach into my jacket pocket and pop a piece of spearmint gum. I'm not exactly certain what the protocol for this is. The Facility isn't going to be happy that I let an entity like Snippity Snap slip through my fingers, especially not after they've seen just how potent of a weapon it can be, but they're not going to burn me either. Keeping this hush-hush is far better than the alternative, which is admitting to the world at large that there really are monsters under their beds.

That things really do go bump in the night.

Worst of all, it would mean others like Ryan and Becca; people seeking to wield these entities, people seeking to follow them. In a word, it would mean competition. And the Facility does not want competition.

I take a deep breath, steel myself, and pull out my cell phone. I dial my handler.

Boy, have I got a story for them.

QUICK SAVE

The game does something strange. The screen flickers and the Tower of Wind becomes crooked, its pixels jagged and uneven. Jon frowns, wondering if he's encountered a glitch.

Weird.

He rounds the corner and goes down the Sunset Path, a little dirt trail that winds its way into a forest, winds its way toward his in-game home, a small cabin by the lake. He means to drop off his loot, grab a glass of water in real life, and then head out on a new quest.

But his cabin isn't there. Not where it should be, at least.

Instead, there is another cabin, this one built with rotten lumber, with broken windows and a door hanging from its hinges, groaning in the gentle breeze. Jon swallows. A scatter of blood decorates its front steps. He's never seen this aspect of the game before—that his cabin, his home base could somehow have been attacked. Raided.

Perhaps, he thinks, this was just an October patch. Something for Halloween.

Yeah, that must be it.

He guides his character up the steps, and in through the door. Darkness greets him. Jon squints at his computer screen, trying to make out anything in the ocean of black pixels, but all he can see is the faint outline of broken furniture and a shape on the floor.

A body?

Unease takes root in his stomach. The game music, usually soaring with notes of high-adventure, suddenly becomes a stuttering, sharp mechanical drone. The change is so jarring that he rips his headphones from his head. He throws them aside.

But the music persists.

Now it's coming from his computer speakers. Loud. Lurching, moaning with all the unnatural melody of a cannibal's teeth digging into still-living flesh. He reaches for the volume, but it doesn't give. He can't escape this music, this treacherous soundscape.

This way, a voice whispers. His computer screen flickers, and in the darkness of his cabin he spots a gentle light down the hall. It's coming from where his loot-room should be, if this had actually been his in-game cabin.

But somehow Jon realizes that it isn't. It's a different place. A more sinister place.

Jon's fingers twitch as he moves his mouse over his desk, as he guides his character down the corridor, toward the glimmer of light. His pulse races. Whatever the developers patched into the game for Halloween, it's compelling content.

This way, the voice says again, and now it's louder.

As Jon moves through the cabin, his character's eyes adjust. The darkness recedes. Now he can see broken pottery on the floor, moldy food on the table, and cobwebs dressing the rafters. The cabin is worn down. Dilapidated. It's only after Jon rounds the next corner, however, that he realizes the cabin looks horribly familiar.

It's not his in-game cabin. No, not by a long shot.

What it is, is his house. The one he lived in as a boy. Down to the little pencil etchings carved into the kitchen wall, showing his height over the small years of his life. The layout is identical.

But how?

He moves through the mausoleum of memories, awestruck and terrified. Graffiti lines the surfaces. Needles litter the carpet. There are bones in the fireplace, painted black by ashes and age.

There's a *thud* from downstairs, loud and sudden. Jon bolts up from his desk. The sound doesn't come from the game; it comes from downstairs. *His* downstairs. In real life.

"Hello?" Jon calls, and he steps away from his computer.

But then all the doors on his computer screen begin opening and closing, opening and closing. They're crashing, louder and louder. The voice is beckoning him again. It's calling out to him to *remember*.

Remember what?

Jon thinks about opening his bedroom door. About going downstairs to check on that thud, but then he figures he's probably overreacting anyway. He figures he's probably just a bit too spun up from how eerie this Halloween update is, and it's making his imagination see the sound of an acorn falling on his kitchen roof, or his old house settling, as something sinister. Malicious.

He takes a breath. He sits back down in his computer chair and resolves to explore this fascinating, horrifying update.

The slamming doors in the game stop. The old house is suddenly still. Silent. Then, at the top of the stairs, a single door creaks open to reveal a familiar sight. Jon's childhood bedroom.

"Up here," says the narrator. Jon trembles as his fingers tap the keyboard, moving his character up the steps and into the room. When he enters it, there's a crash. It's the sound of a door being kicked down.

Not in the game.

In real life.

Heart pounding, Jon bolts up to investigate.

But a voice calls out from his computer speakers, one that he recognizes. "Don't leave me alone," it says, whimpering. "Don't leave me alone again."

It's his mother, June.

How the hell?

No. There'll be time to question that later. For now, there's a very real chance somebody is breaking into Jon's house. Jon opens his bedroom door. He timidly looks down the stairs to check that there's nobody inside, that he's hearing things and it's all in his head. But he spots a shadow. Two of them. They lurch across his kitchen counter, voices muttering in alien tongues.

Panic seeps into Jon. He closes his door as quietly as he can, praying that the intruders don't notice. He reaches for his phone. Reaches to dial 911, to report a break-in at his residence.

"This is 911, what is your emergency?" asks the operator.

"There are burglars downstairs," Jon whispers. "I don't know if they have weapons."

A second passes. Then another.

"Hello?" Jon says.

"Don't leave me alone here, Jon," says the operator. "Please help."

What the fuck? Jon drops his phone, shaken.

His mother's voice calls from his computer again. From the game. Jon's gaze swivels to the monitor, and a cold sweat spreads across his body, his flesh prickling with goosebumps. The screen is fizzling. Crackling. The display is all purple and blue, and the bedroom Jon's character is standing inside of blinks from bright and whole, to broken and dark.

"JoN?" the voice repeats, but this time it's distorted. It's nothing but a grotesque approximation of his mother's, like hearing her voice through a dying phonograph. "ArE yOu tHeRe sWeEt-HeArT?"

Jon stumbles from the computer. No. This is too much. It can't be real—this is beyond insane. The game's music blares, reaching an awful crescendo. Its ear-splitting mechanical droning floods his bedroom, his house, and Jon lunges for the computer's power cord, terrified that the shadows downstairs will hear this and—

Shouting erupts from below.

HELLO?

ANYBODY HOME?

They're voices that Jon doesn't recognize. Strangers. Intruders.

COME ON DOWNSTAIRS.

DON'T MAKE US COME UP THERE.

Jon brings his hands to his ears. He clenches his eyes shut. He tries to wake up because he must be fast asleep, lost in a nightmare. But he can't. Footsteps sound on the stairs.

Creak.

Creak.

WE JUST WANT TO TALK.

Creak.

Creak.

The intruders are up the steps now. They're coming to his bedroom. "Get out of my house," Jon screams. "The police are on their way!"

WE KNOW.

There's a loud bang, and his door trembles. Jon rushes forward, pressing himself against it and bracing it as best he can.

Panicked tears stream down his face. "Just leave me alone! Take whatever you want, just leave me alone!"

YOU'RE THE ONLY THING WE CAME FOR.

GET AWAY FROM THE DOOR.

There's another loud bang, this one deafening. Its force is enough to knock Jon off of the door, onto his hands and knees. Before he can get back into position, the door hinge explodes outward, and the door swings forward, crashing into him painfully.

He groans, dazed. Disoriented.

The room—his room, is changing now. It's morphing, just like it did in the game. It's becoming dilapidated. Broken. His bed is a mess, its sheets dusty and moth-eaten, his computer monitor is broken, his desktop long gone.

He's no longer a young man.

He's old. Too old.

The gray of his beard tickles his face as he shifts on the ground. He feels as though he may be fifty years old now. Perhaps sixty. Long, greasy hair extends from his head, coarse and thinning.

There are two figures standing above him. Dark, imposing. A man and a woman, both armed with guns on their hips. Both wearing kevlar vests.

"Dispatch," the woman says, speaking into a black box on her shoulder. "We've located the suspect. It's Lewis. Again."

A voice crackles from the radio. "Copy that. Any idea how he keeps getting in there?"

The woman looks down at Jon, frowning. "Looks like he broke through boards on the kitchen window this time. You want us to bring him in?"

"Negative. Relocate him to the shelter on 4th and 9th."

"Roger."

***

Jon fidgets in his seat. The window beside him passes in a blur of lights and scenery. The police cruiser's sirens aren't on, but they might as well be for how disoriented he feels.

The man in the passenger seat looks up at the rear-view mirror. He looks at Jon in the back. "What's this guy's deal?" he asks the woman driving. "Seems like he's a known commodity around here."

The woman nods, her eyes scanning the road ahead. "Name's Jonathan Lewis. Used to be an addict." She flips her turn signal and takes a right onto a neon-lit street.

"Used to be?" The man looks back at Jon. "This guy's a mess. You sure he isn't still using?"

"Pretty sure."

"Must have been some hard shit then."

"Not as hard as you'd think." The woman clicks her tongue as the car slows to a stop at the intersection. "You're gonna laugh, but try not to. He's in a lot of pain."

"Try me."

"It was video games."

The man covers his mouth, chuckling. "Alright, I'm laughing."

"I wouldn't be. It's pretty tragic."

"How's that?"

The woman sighs, looking at Jon in the mirror. Her expression is full of sympathy. Pity. He still doesn't recognize her, doesn't recognize the man, doesn't understand what police officers are doing arresting him, or why he's a frail old man in the back seat of a cop car.

But he's listening. He's listening, and he's terrified because deep down, this all feels familiar. It feels like something he's spent his entire life avoiding.

"Jon's mother had several health issues," the woman says. "Serious ones. She had difficulty taking care of herself to the point that she couldn't live alone, so Jon stayed with her well into his thirties. It put a lot of strain on Jon. He never got out much, never got much of a life of his own because he always needed to be nearby, just in case something happened to her."

Outside, the traffic-light turns green. The cruiser hums as the woman presses the gas.

"So he gamed to pass the time?"

"Bingo. Got big into it. I guess it gave him the chance to talk to people, to have adventures while still being close at-hand for his mom. He ended up falling into a bit of a rabbit hole in one of the games, though. One of those big, multiplayer ones with the massive worlds."

"An MMO?"

"Yeah. Sure. One of those. Anyway, one night while he was playing, his mother took a fall. A bad one. Hit her head and bled out on the floor while Jon was upstairs finishing up a raid in his bedroom."

"Jesus Christ. He didn't hear her?"

She shrugs. "Guess not. He found her a few hours later, cold as a fish. The experience destroyed him. Never was himself after that."

The words fall around Jon like prison bars. He doesn't want to hear them. They're lies. All lies. He would never do that—how could he? No. No. *No.*

"Wanna know the sad thing?"

"What's that?" asks the man.

"As far as the coroner could tell, the mom died the moment her head struck the linoleum. Right away, you know? So Mister Lewis here couldn't have helped her even if he did hear her fall."

The man looks at Jon in the mirror. "So why does he keep going back to that house? Seems like that'd be the last place I'd wanna be."

"Don't know. The social workers seem to think it's a coping mechanism. A sort of derealization. He comes back every Halloween on the anniversary of his mother's death, probably to relive the last time his life made any sense to him."

"Rough go."

"Yep." The cruiser rolls to a stop, and the engine cuts off. "Here's us." The woman unbuckles her seat belt, opens the door, and the cab explodes with bright light. Jon grimaces. Confused. Blinded. A moment later, the door beside him opens, and the woman is standing there beneath a blue street sign that reads *4th and 9th.*

"Out you get now," she says.

Jon shimmies out of the car, nervous. Afraid. His eyes dart from the busy traffic honking in the street to the throngs of people on the sidewalks to the towering building in front of him. Rusty bars cover its windows. Broken needles litter its steps. Fluorescent letters hang above its doorway, buzzing quietly.

BRIGHTER HOPES SHELTER: A NEW START

"Go on," the woman says. She rounds the police car and stops by the driver-side door. "You don't want to be on the streets tonight. It's gonna be a cold one."

Jon shivers. It's cold already. He takes a hesitant step forward, and as he does the passenger window of the cruiser rolls down. The man leans out of it. He waves to Jon.

"Welcome home," he says, a smirk on his lips. "Guess I'll see you again next year."

The cruiser pulls off into the street, disappearing in the traffic.

LULLABIES AND NOVEMBER ASHES

Third grade, for me, was not a pleasant time. Sure, there are bright spots in the year. There always are. Overall though, I rate third grade a 1/10, and that's probably being generous.

My mother and father were not exactly great role models in my life. My dad was cold and, in retrospect, probably a socio-path—or at least a narcissist. He rarely spent time with me and when he did, I could tell he regretted it. Usually, he did his best to forget I existed.

My mother was kinder. Sometimes she helped me with my homework, and she always drove me to school. When she dropped me off, she'd wave goodbye with a smile and, as if reading from a script, tell me she loved me and hoped I had a good day.

I liked my mom.

Sometimes, I think I even loved her. At least, when she wasn't drinking. Her vice made sense in retrospect, given the man she decided to shore up with, but what didn't make sense, espe-cially to eight-year-old me, were the relentless insults she'd throw my way.

Lazy.

Waste of space.

Brat.

Dumbass.

These were all mainstays of her vocabulary, never far from her lips once they'd been soaked with wine.

My escape from the depression of my home life was school. Growing up, I loved everything about it. I loved hanging out with my friends, loved learning new subjects, and I especially loved the teachers who always had time for me, and never drank, and always remembered my name.

One of those teachers was Mr. Gilad. A boisterous, heavy-set man with bushy eyebrows and an uncanny ability to brighten the room. He wasn't my teacher, but he was my best friend Oscar's, and because of that I often crossed paths with him. The first time I ever told him my name, he remembered it. Like magic. Every day after, he'd greet me in the hallways with his beaming smile and booming voice. "Walter! How was class today?"

I would always tell him exactly how it was. Usually it was good, but sometimes it was frustrating. Or boring. No matter what, though, Mr. Gilad always listened intently, eyes focused on me and a grin on his face. It was like we were the only two people in the world. He was the first person I met that inspired me to be better than I was, and the first person that made me believe I actually could be.

One autumn day, I was feeling particularly low. In the middle of the previous night, my mother had woken me up. I smelled wine on her breath, and I asked her if she had been drinking again. She told me to shut up, that it was none of my business. Swaying on her feet, she stood over my bed, staring at me. I remember feeling horribly nervous, because there was this sense of hatred in her eyes, and the way she studied me almost seemed like she was making a decision.

"Mom?" I remember asking. "Can I go back to sleep now?"

She didn't reply.

Instead, she left the room. I curled back into my covers, nervous and afraid, although what I was nervous and afraid about I couldn't exactly say. It felt like an intuition. Something deep inside of me, something primal, was screaming that the way my mother was looking at me was not okay.

A few moments later, I heard the creak of my door opening and then there she was again, this time with a half-drunk glass of wine in her grip.

"I wish I never met your father," my mother said, staring at me with dead eyes. "That way you'd never have been born, and I'd have enough money to enjoy my life."

She watched me until she finished her glass of wine, and then she left. Door closed. Glass on my dresser. Unsure how to process what I'd just witnessed, I cried myself to sleep.

The next day, I spent recess alone at the far end of the field. I didn't feel like I deserved friends. I didn't feel like I deserved to have fun. I didn't feel like I deserved anything. When the bell rang, I took my time getting back to class. As I entered the door of the school, I was greeted by an empty hallway. The rest of the students had already returned to class.

My stomach twisted, knowing I was in for a talking-to, and probably a detention once I got back. "Walter!" a voice shouted.

Mr. Gilad.

Out of all the teachers I could have crossed paths with, somehow Mr. Gilad felt like the worst. He was the one adult that actually cared about me. For him to see me like this, out in the middle of the hall when I should have been in class? It probably destroyed whatever goodwill he had for me.

"Sorry, Mr. Gilad," I said, my eyes downcast.

He wasn't angry. Instead, he knelt down in front of me. "Is something wrong?"

I shook my head, but for one reason or another, the floodgates opened. My face scrunched up in a grimace, and then I started to sob. Before I knew it, I was bawling my eyes out in the empty hallway.

He took me by the shoulder and ushered me into a classroom undergoing renovations. He closed the door and sat me down at the teacher's desk. "What's happened?" he asked me, his voice calm and kind.

I told him everything. I told him about my father's cold indifference, my mom's drinking, and how last night she had woken me up to tell me she wished I'd never been born. I worked all of it out between sobs, my nose runny with snot and my cheeks soaking wet with tears.

Mr. Gilad pulled me into a tight hug. "I'm so sorry, Walter," he said. At length, he let me go, and then sighed. "You know, it's tough to talk about these things at times, but it's important that we do. My parents weren't especially kind to me either."

It seemed strange to me that somebody like Mr. Gilad, the kindest man I knew, could have had parents who were anything less than saints. I didn't know what to say, but thankfully I didn't need to say anything, because he kept talking.

"Something important that I think a lot of people learn far too late in life is that none of us are defined by our parents or our upbringings. Our future is our own. We get to choose who we become."

"We do?" I asked him, calming down. I sniffled and wiped my nose on my sleeve.

"That's right, we do," he said, his voice adopting a more serious tone. His eyes, usually so bright and full of cheer, now looked sullen and filled with sadness. He seemed somehow distant.

"It took me a long time to realize that, Walter. For a long time, I felt like I needed to do what society wanted, or be the sort of person my parents wanted me to be. It was only recently that I realized that in doing so, I wasn't actually living my life."

Mr. Gilad sighed, shaking his head and muttering something beneath his breath. "I never felt fulfilled, because each day I felt like I was a part of a play, or an act. I felt like I was fighting tooth and nail against my instincts, and it was only making me more desperate to see them through." He bit his lip. "I was never happy."

It was a heavy conversation to have with an eight-year-old, and while a lot of its nuance went over my head, I decided I got the gist of what he meant. "So no matter what anybody says, even my mom and dad, I should just keep being me?"

He smiled, and the sadness in his expression seemed to evaporate near-instantly. He was back to the beaming, joyous teacher I knew and loved. "Something like that," he said, ruffling my hair. "Hey, here's an idea. Why don't you join Oscar and the rest of my class tomorrow? We're going to be doing a trivia competition in the morning. Oscar tells me you're one of the smartest kids in the grade, and it'd be a shame if you missed out."

I grinned, sniffling. "I don't know if Mrs. Applefig would allow it. " My eyes drifted up to the clock above the closed door. Its minute hand ticked forward to 10:32am. "Actually, I think I'm already gonna be in a lot of trouble for being so late."

My mood plummeted all over again. Maybe my mother was right. I couldn't seem to do anything right—even get to class on time.

"Well, then how about this," Mr. Gilad said, standing up and opening up a drawer in the teacher's desk. He pulled out a stack of sticky notes and a pen. "I'll write you a note explaining your lateness, as well as giving you permission to attend tomorrow morning's trivia competition. Sounds good?"

I nodded enthusiastically. "Yes, I'd love that!"

"Perfect," he said. "So would I."

He handed me two sticky notes. One excusing my late return following recess, and another requesting permission for me to attend trivia tomorrow morning.

By some miracle, I spent the rest of the afternoon smiling. Oscar and I walked home together after school, and the entire time we brainstormed team names. We eventually decided on "Braini-acs."

"You better get us the win!" Oscar teased.

"Well duh," I laughed. "One of us has to!"

The two of us joked around and goofed off all the way home. For such a bad start to the day, I can scarcely remember a day ending with me feeling happier and more full of life. When Oscar and I finally split off, we swore that tomorrow we'd go home as the trivia champions.

As soon as I got home, I cheerily started on my homework. Mr. Gilad had given me a practice trivia question: what tempera-ture does nitrate burn at? If I got it right, we earned an extra point immediately in the trivia competition. I thought long and hard about it, and decided I really had no idea. To be honest, I'd never heard the word nitrate before in my life.

Which meant it was probably a trick question.

It sounded like something way beyond a third grader, so may-be Mr. Gilad wasn't expecting me to know the answer. He had forbidden us from using the internet, and I bet you that if I got the right answer for it, then he'd know I was cheating. Instead, I wrote 'very hot' with a confident flourish of my pencil.

A short while later, I heard the front door open and my mom came home. She paid me a hasty smile before pulling off her jacket and opening the cupboard to start on supper. "Hey mom," I said, beaming. "How was work?"

"Long, honey," she said, her eyes bloodshot and jaw set. "How was school?"

"Great! I'm doing a trivia competition tomorrow with Mr. Gi-lad's class!"

She eyed me for a moment and then smiled. "That's lovely. I'm sure you'll learn lots."

"Me too."

A half hour later, my father came home. He threw his jacket over the kitchen chair and immediately asked where supper was. "I've been stressed all day, Sarah, and I come and you still haven't started dinner?"

I shrank into my homework, doing my best to ignore my parents' arguing.

"I have started supper," my mother countered, "I just haven't started cooking it yet. The ingredients are all ready to go—"

"Jesus fuck, Sarah!" my dad bellowed. "Can't anybody in this house do anything right?"

***

That night I woke up to the smell of alcohol. I lay on my side, curled in blankets, and heard the sound of breathing near my face.

"Worthless," my mother's voice whispered from behind me. I felt her hand wrap itself around my neck, and I didn't move, I didn't speak, I didn't so much as breathe. My body was paralyzed with fear.

"You stole my life from me," she hissed. "If only you would just go away."

Her fingers squeezed, their nails biting into my flesh. My throat contracted. I gasped for air, whimpering in pain and terror, and then almost as soon as she started, she stopped.

Her hand slipped away from my neck.

My back was to her, but I could tell from the shadow she cast on the wall that she was still there. Standing in the dark. Watching me. Drinking wine straight from the bottle.

A half an hour later, she finished and put the bottle down on my dresser. I watched her silhouette wipe her lips, and heard her mutter the word, "Tonight."

She left my room.

I listened as her footsteps creaked their way down the stairs and into the kitchen. A moment later came the sound of wood squealing against wood, like a drawer being opened, followed by the clatter of cutlery.

I stared at my wall, blinking back tears. Again, that primal sense of fear returned. That indescribable intuition that something was very wrong, and I needed to be far away from my bedroom, and far away from this house.

My heart thundered in my chest as I heard the creak of foot-steps on the stairs. This time, coming up. The sounds grew louder, the higher and closer they got to my bedroom. Soon, the footsteps were in the hallway. I could hear my mom's voice muttering, although I couldn't make out any specific words.

Please, I thought to myself. Please walk by my door. Please don't come inside.

The footsteps groaned on the floorboards as they approached. My mother left my bedroom door ajar when she left, and from its crack I saw a shadow in the hallway. I heard her voice.

"… Threw away my career for this. Threw away my entire life, and all so that you could take my money, take my time and destroy my marriage."

The rusty hinges of my door whined, and the door swung open slowly. A shadow grew on my bedroom floor, and I recognized its shape as my mother in her nightgown. She held something in her right hand, but it wasn't a wine bottle.

It was a knife.

I curled into a ball, every part of me screaming to do something. To run. To call for help. To throw something at her. My instincts told me I was going to die.

Instead, I lay there as still as a board, too paralyzed by fear to move or speak.

Who would I call out to? My father? He didn't care about me. How was I supposed to run? My mother was blocking the door-way. What was I supposed to throw at her? The only thing I had nearby was my lamp, and I knew it wouldn't hurt her enough to stop her from hurting me.

She walked toward my bed, standing beside it, knife in hand. I stared at her, hyperventilating with panic. She looked back into my eyes. She kept moving her lips, muttering words, but not loud enough for me to hear. Her face was painted with revulsion and hatred, and every so often she would lift the knife up and threaten at stabbing it down toward me.

Then she turned on her heel and left my room, closing the door behind her.

I lay there, sat-up in bed, my body too awash with adrenaline to even dream of sleeping or thinking or doing anything. I just waited, wired and awake.

I waited for her to come back and kill me.

***

She never did.

The sun rose, and with it came the sound of cars in the street and dogs barking in their yards. I nervously stepped out of bed. My feet were cold against the hardwood, but I barely noticed. All I could think about was my mother, and how she would react this morning. Usually she was full of smiles and affection after she'd slept off the booze, but after last night I wasn't so sure.

Something seemed to have changed in her.

When I made my way downstairs for breakfast, she wasn't there. Normally, she was eating her porridge and ready to grab my cereal of choice from the cupboard. This time, it was just me. The house felt empty. Lonely.

I clambered onto the countertop and opened the cupboard, pulling out a box of Frosted Flakes. I did my best to remember what Mr. Gilad had told me the day before. *It doesn't matter what my parents think of me*, I thought to myself. *I need to forge my own path and listen to my heart. I have to do what I think is right, and not let anybody, my parents or otherwise, get in the way of that.*

I thought about his words over my bowl of cereal. Even if my dad didn't love me, and even if my mom wished I'd never been born, I could still find my own path in life.

As I ate, I monitored the digital clock sitting on our kitchen counter. It was a habit I picked up because my mom was always very strict about ushering me into the car by 7:15am, so she could drop me off in time to get to work.

Right now it read 7:45am. She was nowhere in sight.

A minute later, I heard the familiar creak of footsteps on the stairs, and my mood picked up. Even after everything that had happened last night, my mom hadn't hurt me, and I still had my trivia competition with Mr. Gilad and Oscar to look forward to. Maybe mom realized she loved me too much to hurt me.

The creaking stopped as the footsteps reached the landing, and my dad bustled around the corner, adjusting his tie. He paused, seeing me at the kitchen table. "What are you doing here?"

"Waiting for mom," I said quietly.

"Excuse me?" he said, his voice rising.

I swallowed. My father always had a way of making me feel smaller than I already was. "Waiting for mom, dad."

He stared at me with something between irritation and disbelief. "Your mom's not home."

"What?"

"I said she's not home. Do you need a fucking hearing aid now too?"

I looked down, eating another spoonful of Frosted Flakes. Where did she go? I wondered. She was here last night.

My eyes drifted to the digital display. The clock now read 7:50am. Class was starting in ten minutes, and so was my trivia competition. It took at least ten minutes to drive to school.

"Dad?" I asked.

"Have you seen my briefcase?" he said impatiently

"No, sorry."

"Fuck!" he snapped. "That stupid bitch probably took it!" He adjusted his collar and reached for the coffeepot before realizing it was empty and flinging it across the room. It shattered on the wall. "Everything I do!" he screamed. "Taken for granted!"

Mr. Gilad's words echoed in my head. To believe in myself. To trust in my instincts. To do what I felt I needed to. I cleared my throat. "Can you drive me to school? I have a trivia compet—"

"Do I look like your mother?" he said incredulously. I stared at him, feeling tears welling in my eyes. Eventually, I shook my head.

"I have a real job," he said, grabbing his jacket from the wall and opening the front door. "I don't have time to play at being a parent." He muttered something about ingrates, and then disappeared through the doorway, shutting the door behind him.

I sat at the table for a few more minutes, too stunned to do anything. My mom was gone. My dad was gone. It was just me in the house now. My family didn't care about me. Nobody gave a damn.

No, that wasn't true.

Oscar cared. Mr. Gilad cared.

I snatched my jacket from the coatrack beside the door and exited after my father. I used the key we hid under the rock in our garden to lock the house behind me, and I started jogging toward the school. Usually, when I walked home with Oscar, it'd take us just over an hour. Unfortunately for me, Hillcrest school lived up to its namesake.

My school sat perched atop a large hill, overlooking the rest of Plumberry township. At the top, it was really a spectacular view. To the north, you could see most of the local streets, all the way up to the city hall, downtown. To the south, you could see far down the country road, all the way out to Lake Tyler and Gefferson forest beyond.

Still, it was uphill. Which meant it would be a longer walk to than from. I was determined, though. Mr. Gilad's words recited themselves in my mind like a mantra, pushing me ever forward.

I kept my eye on the watch on my wrist, figuring if I could get there before 8:30, I'd be in the clear. In both third grade classes, we did a sharing period from 8 till 8:30, where we talked about our day or new things we found interesting.

My sneakers pounded along the sidewalk, my backpack bouncing up and down with my binder, pencils, and markers. I made good time getting to the bottom of the hill, and at the distant top I could see the gates that marked the entrance to Hillcrest elementary.

I started my ascent.

It was slow going. As I went, I kept track of the watch on my wrist. 8:20am. I had ten minutes to reach the top, and I was barely a quarter of the way there. My breath was coming in big heaves and my legs, tired from jogging for so long, burned with soreness. I felt lightheaded and wobbly—out of breath.

I continued to climb, more slowly now. I didn't have a water bottle, and I was beginning to feel incredibly thirsty, but I knew I needed to get to the top before the trivia competition started.

Somehow, even after everything that had happened with my mom and dad, I felt like if I could just win that competition, then everything would be alright. My mom would come home, and she'd realize how smart I was and decide that drinking wasn't worth it, and my dad would be so proud of me that he'd start taking an interest in my studies.

My eyes drifted back to the watch on my wrist, and my heart fell. 8:45am. How had I been walking up the hill for so long already? I stopped, catching my breath and realizing none of it mattered anymore.

I was way too late for trivia, and I was probably going to end up in detention besides that. There wasn't any point in rushing now.

My day was already ruined.

I took the rest of the hill at a slower walk, and my legs thanked me for it. I hated my mom for leaving last night, and I hated my dad for not driving me to school. I hated both of them for making me miss out on trivia, and disappoint the one adult who seemed to care about me: Mr. Gilad.

Tears tugged at the corners of my eyes as I considered how ashamed of me he probably was. He went through all the trouble of securing me permission to attend his class this morning, and I gave him my word I'd be there. Then I didn't show up at all, and my dad didn't so much as call the school and let them know I'd be late.

He probably thought I was just as much of a lost cause as my parents by now.

"There he is!" a shrill voice shrieked. "Oh my god, he's here!"

I looked up as Mrs. Applefig came stampeding toward me, her lined face filled with concern and her tone thick with relief. "Walter, are you okay?" she wrapped me into a tight hug. "Thank goodness. Thank goodness."

I'd been so absorbed in my own thoughts that I hadn't even noticed I'd crested the hill and come up in front of my school. Mrs. Applefig smothered me with her hug, and all I could see was the blue fabric of her blouse. "I'm fine, Mrs. Applefig," I lied. "I'm sorry for being late."

"It's okay, sweetheart. It's okay," she said, pressing her face to mine. I felt something wet on her cheek.

"Gloria, is that Walter Thimby?" a man bellowed, and I recognized it as Principal Patel.

She wheeled around, nodding fiercely. "It is, Uday! It is!"

Freed from Mrs. Applefig's all-encompassing blouse, I became acutely aware of something very strange: my entire school was staring at me.

"Bring him over here," Principal Patel called out. "Everybody triple check your students and make sure everybody's accounted for!"

Mrs. Applefig ushered me into a line with the rest of my classmates, and I plunked down on the grass beside Jessie Wilson, a blonde kid who held the record for most school suspensions in third grade. He leaned over and whispered into my ear.

"Whew," he said. "Gotta say man, for a while there you had us worried."

"Had you worried?" I said, feeling too depressed to chitchat.

"Yeah," he said. He thumbed over his shoulder, back at the school behind us. "We thought you were still inside."

Still inside? I turned around and gazed at the school with narrowed eyes. Beyond the belltower in the center, I saw a dark cloud billowing into the sky.

Smoke.

"The back of the school caught fire sometime this morning," Jessie explained. "We did the fire drill thing, everybody ditched the classroom's and came out here, but I guess we're still missing some students." He grinned. "One less now, though."

I swallowed. The smoke was pitch black and heavy. It looked like it was growing thicker.

"Firefighters are on the other side," Jessie continued. "Fire's been going for like twenty minutes now, and it keeps getting bigger. They're calling in fire trucks from the next town over. Pretty wild."

I stared, transfixed at the pillar of shadow rising from the school. Beneath it, faint in the brightness of the morning sun, I spotted the flicker of flames.

The school was burning.

Just then, a cacophony of sirens sounded in the distance. A handful of seconds later, and two fire trucks roared over the crest of the hill, through the school gates, and swung around the parking lot toward the south side. I gazed after them in awe. I'd never seen fire trucks in action before.

"Mister Thimbly," Principal Patel said firmly. I blinked, pulling my gaze from the school. Mr. Patel crouched down, meeting me at eye level. "I need to know if you were with Mr. Gilad's class this morning."

"Mr. Gilad's class?" I said, confused. "No, I was late. I was supposed to be but—"

"Jesus," he muttered, shaking his head and standing up. "He wasn't!" he shouted to somebody I didn't recognize. They were in a suit and on a cellphone, and their lips were moving fast.

"That's not good," Jessie said beside me.

"What's going on?" I asked, fear beginning to take seat in my chest.

"Pretty sure I heard 'em saying we're missing twenty-two kids still, and one teacher."

My heart sank, a piece of me already knowing the answer to the question I was about to ask. "Who's missing?"

"Mr. Gilad," Jessie said darkly. "Nobody knows where he is, or his class."

"They're two doors down from us," I argued. "How can they not know where he is?"

Mrs. Applefig appeared in front of us, her finger pursed to her lips. "Shh!" she hissed. "It's important that we're all quiet. This is a very serious situation and it's crucial that Principal Patel is able to hear what's going on."

Jessie and I closed our mouths, nodding in acknowledgement. As soon as Mrs. Applefig shuffled out of earshot, he leaned over and resumed his whispering.

"That's the thing, they cleared the entire school. The fire alarm went off as soon as the smoke detector caught whiff, and Patel himself made sure to double check every classroom to make sure they were clear. All of them were empty."

I shook my head. "That doesn't make any sense," I said, defiance leaking into my voice. Oscar was in that class, and there was no way Patel would miss Oscar. He was the loudest kid I'd ever met. "They had to have been there! We were doing a trivia competition today."

Jessie shrugged. "Don't know what to tell ya' man, that's just what I heard."

My mind raced. Where could they be? Mr. Gilad had promised me there would be a trivia competition today. He hadn't told me to meet the class anywhere special. They had to be here.

My eyes scanned the crowd of assembled students. Each class was separated into small ranks, with their teachers standing out front. I went over every one of them once, twice, then once again to be certain. No Oscar. No Mr. Gilad.

No. Just no.

Again, I felt my emotions getting the better of me. Tears welled in the corners of my eyes, but I took a deep breath. Maybe they had met up at the school and then gone for a walk? I looked up at the cloudless sky and the warm sun. It was an uncharacteristically nice day for November. Maybe Mr. Gilad took them outside for the trivia competition, so that they could enjoy the weather?

Yeah. That was it.

A crash sounded behind me, and everybody's heads turned in near unison. I watched, transfixed in horror as the bell tower, now almost entirely enshrouded in thick black smoke, sagged, and then with a loud groan fell backwards onto the blazing south wing. The resultant collision was deafening. The roof of the school caved in instantly, and in its wake exploded an inferno of smoke and flame.

Screams erupted from the students.

My jaw dropped. I was watching my school, the one place I truly felt at home, burn to ash in front of my eyes. It felt surreal. Like I was dreaming, and couldn't wake up.

It was Mrs. Applefig's crying that brought me back to earth. She had a hand covering her mouth, and she kept muttering the words "Oh no. Oh no. Oh no."

A minute later, a school bus arrived, and all of us whose parents hadn't picked us up yet were loaded into it. I remember resisting at first, telling Mrs. Applefig that I needed to wait for Oscar, but she kept crying and telling me I had to get onboard. "Please," she said. "Please, Walter. Please, just go."

I relented, and fifteen minutes later the bus dropped me off at home. I used the key in the garden to get back inside, and when I did, I called out for my mom. She didn't answer, so I went into the kitchen and picked up my phone, calling Oscar's house. Maybe he was homesick?

The ringer rang once, twice, three times and then a voice picked up. "Hello?" it said breathlessly. "Sarah? Matthew? Is Oscar at your house with Walter? Please, we need to—"

"No," I said. "This is Walter. Oscar's not here."

The line went quiet on the other end.

"Is he not at home?" I asked.

"No," said his mother's voice, though it was broken and filled with sadness. I heard her stifle a sob. "I'm sorry, Walter. I have to go."

"Okay, Miss Cortez."

The line went dead, and I hung up the phone. I looked over at the clock. It read 10:54am. My dad wouldn't be home for another six hours, so in the meantime, I made my way to the living room and turned on the TV, hoping maybe there was something on the news.

I flicked through the channels until I spotted a newscaster in front of my school.

"—here in front of Hillcrest elementary, where a vicious fire has caused the bell tower to collapse upon the south wing. Fire-fighters have managed to get the blaze out, and efforts to locate survivors, as well as fully assess the extent of the damage have begun."

The woman speaking, dressed in a nice three-piece suit, turned her attention to somebody off camera. They exchanged a few words with her microphone down. A moment later, she looked back at the camera and raised her microphone to her mouth.

"I've just received word from the fire department that several remains have been located within Hillcrest. These remains are suspected to belong to the missing third grade class, taught by Mr. Heinrich Gilad."

An emptiness stole through me. The news lady continued speaking, but her words washed over me like white noise. *Several remains have been located within Hillcrest.* The words haunted me, replaying over and over again in my head. It wasn't until my father came home that I realized just how long I'd been sitting there.

"Walter?" he said, before rushing over to me. He pulled me into a tight hug. "Oh, god, Walter. I was so worried for you. I was in a meeting and I didn't hear until twenty minutes ago. Once I did, I came right over—"

"It's okay, dad," I said, though my voice was void of emotion. It was such an odd sort of feeling. All of my life I had craved this sort of attention and affection from my father, and yet now that I was receiving it, it didn't mean anything to me.

I felt empty inside.

My dad took me upstairs, ordered me my favorite pizza and rented the newest Harry Potter movie. He sat with me all night. Every so often he would ask me if I was okay, and apologize for yelling at me earlier, but I hardly registered it. My thoughts were consumed with thoughts of Oscar, and Mr. Gilad.

They were gone.

The next morning, school was predictably canceled. My father stayed home with me and put on another rented movie in my room. This one was Monsters Inc. I only watched it for twenty minutes or so before I wandered downstairs. I found my dad on the couch in the living room, his back facing me, watching the news lady I'd seen yesterday.

She was in front of the scorched remains of the south wing of my school, and it looked like a windy day, because her blond hair was blowing all over the place.

"—I'm again in front of the wreckage of Hillcrest Elementary's south wing, where twenty-two children and one man lost their lives early yesterday morning, in what can only be described as the greatest tragedy in Plumdale history…"

My dad reached for his mug on the coffee table and took a sip. It occurred to me that he must have taken the day off of work to stay home with me.

"… Yesterday morning a fire blazed, quickly spreading through the south wing and eventually reaching the bell tower. An old school, built in the early 1900s, Hillcrest Elementary was built primarily of highly flammable lumber, and the bell tower was no exception. At 10:13am it fell backward, onto the south wing, collapsing that section of the school and dooming the individuals trapped inside."

She touched her ear, and her eyes looked sideways, as if somebody was speaking to her.

"I'm just receiving word that the investigation has determined some rather disturbing details. I… I should caution viewers at home that what I'm about to say is not for the faint of heart."

The news lady cleared her throat, and I drew closer behind my father.

"Investigators have located two thick wooden doors in the wreckage. The deadbolts belonging to these doors were discovered in the outward, locked position. According to blueprints, these doors lead into the basement of the school, where the Hillcrest archive was held."

"Jesus…" I heard my father mutter, leaning forward and setting his mug back down on the table.

"The twenty-two students and teacher, who we have now positively identified as one Mr. Heinnrich Gilad via dental records, appear to have been locked inside the school's basement at the time of the blaze. Details pertaining as to why are still unknown. The stunning ferocity of the blaze, according to investigators, was due to old film reels housed in the school's archive. These reels contained nitrate, a substance which burns hotter than gasoline…"

A lump formed in my throat.

"One aspect of the tragedy that school Principal Uday Patel is wrestling with is that he never physically cleared any of the school's basement areas."

The camera cuts out, and I see my principal giving an interview on the school grounds, but in a different location during a different time of day.

"I checked everywhere," he said, adjusting his glasses and keeping his voice level. "Every classroom was personally cleared by myself, as well as a team of three other faculty members. We ensured to check all of them. I double checked them personally and suffered severe smoke exposure in the process. Of course, in the interest of protecting my students—"

"What about the basement?" the interviewer asked from off-screen, and I recognized the voice as the news lady from earlier.

Principal Patel's voice cracked as he began his reply. "I saw no need to physically check the basements. It seemed a dangerous task, given the relative size of them, and the speed at which the blaze was spreading. As I walked by the basement areas in each wing, I called down and asked if anybody was down there and needed assistance. I heard no response, and so I continued on. There simply wasn't time."

The screen cut back to the news lady, and a small icon in the corner read LIVE.

"Strangely enough, despite Principal Patel's calls, nobody answered. Given the amount of remains located within the school's archive, it seems as though such screams would have been loud and plentiful. One theory as to why Patel didn't hear any of the victims was that they had already suffered from toxin inhalation due to the nitrate film off-gassing. It's highly likely they'd already passed out—- sorry?"

The news lady brought a hand to her earpiece again. Seconds ticked by in silence, and I realized somebody must be speaking to her on the other end, because her expression slowly became more and more disturbed. Finally, she cleared her throat and brought the mic to her lips.

"For those watching at home, particularly family members of the suspected deceased, your viewer discretion is advised." Her voice trembled. "I can hardly believe I'm about to say this in sleepy Plumdale, but investigators have just determined that, based on observed damage to a child's hyoid bone, their throat is presumed to have been slit."

The news lady closed her eyes and took a deep breath. "According to dental records, one Oscar Cortez appears to have died prior to the start of the blaze."

I gazed, transfixed in horror at the television screen. My father was too stunned to notice me creeping ever closer, drawn toward the scenes on the display. "It is now being posited that perhaps this young man was killed in an attempt to scare the remaining twenty-one children into silence."

"Oh my god," my dad muttered. He ran a hand through his mess of hair, and I could tell by his sleeves that he was wearing his housecoat. He didn't even bother getting properly dressed.

I took another step closer and the floorboard croaked. My father turned around. "Walter?" he exclaimed. "Jesus, Walter! You shouldn't be watching this!"

He rushed around the couch, and the news lady's words became muffled against his chest as he lifted me up and carried me back upstairs.

"You need to take it easy, buddy," he said, ferrying me through the hallway. "I know you're going through a lot right now, and I know your worthless joke of a mother abandoned us, but the two of us gotta stick together, okay? And that means you gotta trust that I know what's best for you. Now I don't want to see you out of your room again today, alright?"

He gently lowered me onto my bed and hit play on the *Monsters Inc* movie. "You need to take some time for yourself. Don't worry about the news. This is all just conjecture right now anyway."

He paid me a remorseful smile and closed my bedroom door behind him. I laid there, staring at my wall and oblivious to the sounds of Sully and Mike from Monsters Inc. All I could think about was Mr. Gilad's words, playing on repeat inside of my head.

"I never felt fulfilled, because each day I felt like I was a part of a play, or an act. I felt like I was fighting tooth and nail against my instincts, and it was only making me more desperate to see them through."

Tears slipped from the corners of my eyes. Thanks to the news lady, I finally knew the answer to my trivia question.

Nitrate burned hotter than gasoline.

KNOCK, KNOCK. WHO'S THERE?

Ever play Nicky Nicky Nine Doors as a kid?

Yeah, I was an asshole too. The game was simple fun, which was perfect for smooth-brained oafs like me. You'd knock on the door, then run and hide before somebody opened up.

Lately, I've been the victim of something similar. Oddly enough, the knock always happens at the same time of night: a minute and a half past 4 AM. Bizarre, right? Who has that kind of discipline?

After the third night in a row, I decided I'd had enough and was going to catch the fucker and give him a piece of my mind. I set up shop beside my front door and waited for the clock to tick over to 4:01. Soon after, the knock sounded.

Like a bat out of hell, I swung the door open and shouted into the dead of night, "Do it again and I'll fucking kill ya!"

Nobody was there.

Or, if there was somebody there, they had done a good job of slinking away. It was odd, though. How had they escaped so fast? I spent some time looking for them, but I came up empty handed. I couldn't see so much as tracks in the snow.

The knocking kept up. Every night. Over and over. I couldn't catch them, no matter how hard I tried. Once, I even waited outside my front door, and when the clock struck a minute and a half past four, I heard the knock plain as day, despite nobody being there to make it. What the hell?

Soon, the knocking was followed by unintelligible whispers, and then the whispers were followed by small gifts.

Wood carvings ended up on my doorstep. They resembled tiny people, and upon closer inspection, people that I knew. The latest was a rendition of my mother and father, an artful piece with their heads twisted backward and a rune carved into their chests.

It unnerved me. Terrified me, really. The thing that frightened me most, though, was that I had no idea who could be doing this.

See, I haven't had any neighbors for the past two years. I live alone in the mountains, three hours from the nearest town, and the last time I saw somebody out here I was burying their corpse.

THE ISLAND

Last month, my team responded to a SOS in the southern Pacific. When we arrived, we were unable to locate any of the stricken individuals. All we found were two curious items in a local cave system: a journal and an audio recorder, both of which owned by an archaeologist named Albert Vess.

The contents of the journal are disturbing, but perhaps worse still is the audio.

Since reading the journal and listening to the audio, I've been feeling strange. Unwell. My mind feels like mush and my moods have been erratic. No medication has helped. My doctor thinks I just need some rest, but I'm not sure. It's... hard to describe?

I don't know why, but I feel like the island has something to do with it. I feel like the journal does. I've transcribed it below, but be warned.

It's an uncomfortable read.

***

06/01/21

The valley is steep.

For an island in the middle of the Pacific, it feels almost unnatural. Certainly uncommon. I've done plenty of these expeditions and I've rarely encountered geography such as this. The shoreline is sparse, thin. It gives way to a scatter of trees and a sharp drop-off into a hollow of palms and brush. It's incredible. Claustrophobic.

It's where we're going. All four of us.

Bernard, the research lead. Darian, the cave spelunker. And Allison, one of the most accomplished archaeologists I've ever met.

And of course, myself.

My stomach is still upside down, recovering from the sail it took to get here, but the worst is over. Once we finish our survey of the ruin below, we can set up camp and get some shut-eye. It's not so bad, really. And we're so very close.

This, I think, could be the discovery of a lifetime.

***

The sun is setting in the sky.

When we looked down into the valley this afternoon, we never anticipated it'd be this slow-going, or that the canopy of leaves would be this blinding. Alison recommends we make camp and get some rest. She says the ruin will be there to excavate in the morning, and we'll be better off with more daylight to spare.

Bernard disagrees. He says we've got lanterns and rations, and that the scene survey won't take that long. Besides, he's not planning on doing any excavating until he knows the ruins are actually there.

His remark catches us off guard. I remind him that there are already aerial photos of the ruin. That there's no need to prove it's actually there because we can see that it is.

It takes Bernard a minute to answer, and when he does, he admits the aerial photos of the ruins were doctored. He admits that the research he submitted to secure this grant was false.

"All I have," he says, "is what's written in here."

He shows us a leather-bound book with yellowed pages. It belonged to his ancestor apparently, a merchant captain who was shipwrecked on this island over a century ago. According to the journal, there really are ruins—but the thing is, they're *underground*. You'd never know they were there if you weren't looking for them and it's why nobody discovered them before.

I can hardly believe it. I want to be furious at him, but Alison is angry enough for the both of us. She's fuming. Darian doesn't seem to mind terribly, maybe because it's her first expedition and she still has stars in her eyes.

"Trust me," Bernard says. "This will be the discovery of our lives."

I suppose we don't really have a choice. The boat that dropped us off won't be returning for another week. For better or worse, I and everybody else are stuck on this little spit of land.

***

Alison heads into the trees to pee and when she comes back, she's a nervous wreck. Her shoulders are quaking. Her voice is uneven. "I heard footsteps out there," she says. "Footsteps and laughter, out there in the jungle."

I remind her that there's nobody out there. That this island is as empty as it's ever been.

"Then who's laughing at me?" she snaps. "The trees?"

***

The jungle ends in moonlight.

It opens to a clearing, a dusty expanse of stone boulders and saplings. We made it to the bottom of the valley, to the site of the supposed underground ruins. Bernard tells us there should be an opening somewhere. A hole. It might be tiny, or it might be large enough to fall into if you aren't careful.

The four of us split off, flashlights in tow. Alison in one direction—scowling, and Darian in another—beaming. She's young enough that I hope we really do find something, otherwise this might just sour her opinion on archaeology for good.

Before I can step off, Bernard stops me. He asks me if I can hear that.

"Hear what?" I ask.

The laughter, he says.

***

It's not forty paces away that something catches my eye.

It's small. Difficult to make out in the dark—even with the light of my lantern and the moon above, but it's there. It's making my skin crawl. Between two squat boulders is a circle of small stones arranged in a spiral. They frame a recess into the earth that's filled with decaying wood, charred black by the heat of flames. A firepit.

I gaze at it, stunned. This island should be deserted. As my mind churns, I spot something sticking out of the dirt and the ash. It's broken. Crumbling. It looks like mother nature has had its way with it, but it's unnatural enough to stick out to me. It isn't wood. It isn't stone.

It's... strange.

I bend low, digging into the mess, hoping the debris above has managed to preserve what lay beneath. A moment later, and I know that it has. My hands pull something free, something that's decomposed into three pieces. Something familiar.

A fractured human skull.

***

It's odd, but I stare at the skull for a long while. There's something about it that I can't quite put my finger on, but it's fascinating to me. I feel almost entranced by it.

Before I can properly process my find, I hear screaming. Shouting. I hear Bernard, Alison, and Darian all calling my name. They're shrieking for me into the night, telling me the good news.

They've found the ruin.

***

When I reach them, they surround a hole in the earth the size of a basketball. Bernard's lantern is sitting next to it. He's explaining in an excited tone how he nearly fell into the damn thing. He's explaining how he knew it would be here, about how he never once had any doubt.

I'm trying to tell him—them—about the firepit. I'm trying to tell them about the human skull split into three pieces.

"What does it matter," Darian asks, "if somebody died here? That was probably a hundred years ago." She's already getting herself ready for her first big find. She's tying a length of rope to a nearby boulder to serve as an anchor point. Bernard's strapping a headlamp to her helmet.

What it matters, I say, is that human skulls don't generally burn themselves on deserted islands. What it matters is that whoever burned that skull was doing it very much on purpose, and there are very few reasons that would ever be okay.

Bernard sides with Darian but tells me that I'm probably right, that whoever burned that skull was up to no good, but what do I expect the four of us to do about it? It's ancient history.

Before I can argue my point, Alison calls us over. She's on her belly at the entrance of the hole, flashlight angled down, trying to get a look inside the ruin. She tells us she thinks she saw something move down there.

Darian reasons that it's probably just water bouncing the light around, making shadows. She says she sees it all the time while spelunking. Underground lakes. I figure she's probably right about that. In a valley like this, it'll be a small miracle if these ruins aren't already flooded.

Still, the skull looms in the back of my mind. It unnerves me.

***

Darian rigs the rope to her carabiner and slips her legs into the hole. A moment later, and she shimmies the rest of her body through the opening until the white of her helmet disappears beneath the earth.

As she lowers herself down into the ruins, Bernard asks her for details about what she's seeing. For the first while, she says it's just a long, tight drop. Nothing to see. Just stone pressing against her on all sides.

Then she says it's opening up into a cavern. She says she's inside of them now—the ruins. Or rather, a cave system. "I don't see any ruins," she tells us. "All I see are…"

Her voice trails off. It sounds… concerned.

"There's writing down here," she says. "Lots of writing, all over the cave walls. It looks like it was scratched into the stone."

Bernard looks ecstatic. He asks her what language it's in, and whether or not she can read it.

She responds by saying that yes, she can read it. It's…. English numerals, she says. There are numbers all over the cave.

A pause. Two breaths. Her voice echoes out of the dark hole. "Are these dates?"

Nobody gets a chance to ask her about the dates, or exactly how many there are, because our attention is stolen. In the distance, from deep within the jungle, we hear the low sound of footsteps. Heavy, desperate footsteps.

Footsteps that are coming our way.

***

I call into the hole, ordering Darian to get out. I tell her something—somebody is coming. My heart is beating through my chest, my mind replaying images of the scorched skull. It feels insane. Absurd. There's nobody on this island. We know that. We have the records, and yet…

I feel that something is very wrong.

Alison holds our only weapon—a brush-whacking machete, and she's shrieking at Bernard, demanding whether he forgot to mention the existence of cannibal tribes on the island. Bernard's too shell-shocked to speak. I holler at him to help me heave on the rope, to bring Darian up faster. Thankfully, he does.

It's exhausting, but we manage to pull her up to the top of the hole, just far enough to see the white of her helmet and her terrified features. She tells us that she's stuck. That she can't move any further.

I hear the footfalls nearing. So close. Whatever's coming is running now, and the sound is like thunder in my ears. I watch as Bernard works at freeing Darian from the opening, and I realize it's taking too long. Much too long. I drop the line and rush over to help, pressing my hands against Darian's shoulders.

Then, all at once, the footfalls stop.

They stop just outside the perimeter of the clearing. For a moment, the night is silent. None of us so much as steal a breath as we listen for whatever is out there. Whatever is coming for us.

Alison suggests that our shouting may have scared it off. It's a comforting thought. That it might have been a large species of boar charging through the jungle, or perhaps an earthquake. Bernard agrees. He adds that we're all running low on sleep and very on edge, and that Alison was right—we should have just made camp and gotten some rest.

Then Darian screams, and her body slips, ribs snapping as she disappears back into the darkness of the ruin. A split second later, there's a grotesque cracking sound and the screaming stops. It's the sound of Darian's body striking the cavern floor.

It is, I think, the sound of Darian dying.

***

Something goes through us then. Alison. Bernard. Myself. Something goes through us like a bullet, shutting us up as we wait, desperate to hear Darian call out and say she's okay. That she's just a little bruised up.

I call out to her. Desperate. Horrified.

Alison appears at my side and hushes me with a finger. She glares at me, narrowing her eyes at me like all of this—this entire disaster is somehow *my* fault. Then she lowers herself onto her hands and knees, machete by her side, ear toward the hole.

She asks us if we can hear that. She tells us to listen.

Bernard and I press ourselves closer to the opening. We strain our ears. There's a scraping sound coming from inside. A low, sustained sound like something being slid across stone.

"There's something down there," Alison says. "I knew there was something down there and I told you, Bernard! I fucking warned you!" She erupts, lunging at Bernard like a maelstrom, scratching, punching—hurting him as much as she can. He curls up, but he doesn't try to fight back. He doesn't try to flee.

He sits there trembling. He sits there trembling, I think, because he hears the same thing that Alison and I do, down there in the cavern.

He hears the sound of Darian's body being dragged away.

***

We put it to a vote.

Out of the three of us, only Bernard wants to go back down into the hole looking for Darian. Only Bernard wants to face the nightmare he dragged us into. Alison and I, we have no idea what we're dealing with. Bernard's convinced that it's an animal. A family of bears, perhaps, that are using the cavern as a sort of den. There's no other alternative, he says.

What I don't say is that there's always an alternative. In this case, the alternative is we're not alone on this island. In this case, the alternative is that whatever's out there doesn't want to be found.

***

The hike back up to our base camp is long, and by the time we arrive it's raining and half-past noon. A wall of dark-gray descends toward us from across the ocean. Storm clouds. Lightning flashes on the horizon, followed by rolling cracks of thunder.

The sea laps and churns.

All any of us want to do is go to sleep, to rest and process our grief over losing Darian, but we have work to do. Bernard fires up the HF amplifier and attempts to contact rescue services. Static greets him over the receiver. He tells us he doesn't think it's working. He tells us the radio is fucked.

Alison tries her hand at it, and thank god she does because she gets the thing running again. Over the other end, like the voice of an angel, we hear the operator crackle out of the speaker.

"Everything alright out there, folks?"

"No," we say, in near-perfect unison.

God no.

***

The conversation doesn't go as planned.

According to the operator, it could be hours or even days before we're picked up. The storm front in our area is a bad one, they explain, and it's likely to impede any rescue efforts. Local authorities aren't keen on risking their lives for tourists. At the moment, they're attempting to contact military vessels nearby for a potential extraction, but we shouldn't count on that.

Their advice? Hunker down. Batten the hatches. Stay safe. Avoid becoming separated.

What if there's somebody out there, Alison asks them, trying to fucking kill us?

Didn't you say you had a machete? they ask.

Feel free to use it.

***

The night passes for me as a string of nightmares. I toss and turn for much of it. It's not clear why, but my stomach is in knots. I feel ill. Nauseous and unwell.

I wonder if it's the rations I ate. Maybe Bernard didn't prepare them properly? Maybe they'd gone bad? It doesn't matter. My body and mind are exhausted enough that the pain in my stomach is an afterthought.

***

I awake to silhouettes arguing. Alison and Bernard. My head feels like I just drank a bottle of whisky and hit it with a hammer. My mouth is dry. I'm sweating and shivering at the same time. Do I have a fever? Pieces of their argument reach my ears. They're not far from me, but they sound so distant. So faint.

—- killed her.

Give me a break, Alison! Darian's a grown woman who made her own choices. You think we knew she'd slip?

She didn't slip. You know damn well.

I stumble from the tent, and warm, tropical rain is pouring overhead. Wind whistles painfully in my ears. Alison and Bernard are standing beneath the awning nearby, looking at me, but their faces are a blur. I can't make out their expressions.

"What are you doing up?" Alison asks. "Eavesdropping?" She's holding the machete—pointing it at me.

Hands grab me by my arm, roughly. "Go to sleep," Bernard orders. He guides me back into the tent. Back into my sleeping bag. "You're not well. Tomorrow the storm breaks, and the rescue team should arrive."

I mumble a response, but my words are slurred. Barely there.

It's okay, he says

Nothing about this is okay.

***

I spend the night in and out of sleep, my mind swimming. My body feels feverish, alternating between flashes of panting heat and frigid chills. My dreams are of Alison.

In them, she's calling out to me. Begging me for help. She's trapped inside a pit filled with snakes, covered head to toe in red and blue serpents. They're slithering about her and I'm holding her machete and chopping at them, trying to save her.

Please, she says. *Please.*

***

The next morning, my head is pounding. There's an awful pressure near my temples, like my brain is expanding outward and trying to split my skull in three. I need water. I need aspirin.

Why is it so quiet?

I open my eyes to an empty tent. Strangely, there's no sign of Allison or Bernard. It's just me and... the remains of our HF radio. Red and blue wires lay strewn about the floor like electrical snakes. Its faceplate is split in two, the circuit board with it.

What happened?

Wandering outside, I find the storm has cleared. A sprinkle of rain is all that's left.

Did the rescue team already arrive? Perhaps Alison and Bernard have taken them down to the ruins to search for Darian.

***

I abandon the tent and take to the shoreline, calling out their names. It's a short while later that I find Bernard. He emerges from the jungle looking disheveled, manic. His eyes are wild, framed with heavy bags, and in his hand is Alison's machete. It's flecked in crimson.

CantfindAllison

His voice is stuttering, moving too fast for his lips.

Shesgone

I tell him to slow down. My head is in rough shape, and it's difficult to follow what he's saying. Bernard, I ask, is there blood on that machete? He shakes his head. He tells me to go back to the tent—to lie down. He says he'll keep looking for her. He says she has to be around here somewhere. She has to.

As he stalks off, I think I hear him mumble a prayer, but I'm so very tired.

***

My dreams are once more of Alison. Of Darian. This time, they're beckoning me to return to the ruin. They're weeping that Bernard has done this to us—that he's lost his mind. They're saying that he's trying to kill us off so that the discovery can be his, and his alone.

He pushed me into the hole, Darian whimpers.

He drowned me on the beach, Allison cries.

He's drugging you, they say in unison. Don't trust him. Don't follow him. Go back to the ruins and you'll see the truth. Do it before he cuts you into little pieces and eats you, burns your skull and splits it in three.

I open my eyes, and Bernard is fast asleep. The machete is tucked securely in his arms. As quietly as I can, I leave the tent and make for the ruins.

***

It's part way through the jungle that the footsteps sound behind me.

They're pounding the dirt, moving through the brush like a hurricane. Is it Bernard? I can't tell. My head is aching and my body is exhausted, but despite it all I press forward at a sprint. I press forward toward the valley below. Toward the ruins.

I hear laughter in the jungle. Manic, maddening laughter. It's following me, closing in. Whatever is happening on this island, I realize, begins and ends with those ruins.

I must reach them.

***

It's a small relief to see the rope still anchored to the stone.

I quickly toss Darian's line into the entrance of the cavern and squeeze myself through the opening. My palms burn, splitting open in warm blood as they halt my descent. Before I can make it to the bottom, something snaps from above and my rope gives way.

I fall a short and painful distance, with the rest of my rope tumbling down around me. Looking up, I expect to see Bernard standing at the small moonlit entrance. Instead it's just empty sky.

Bernard? I shout.

There's no response.

Flicking on my headlamp, I take a look around the cavern. The light reveals a tight cave structure, one splitting off into three separate tunnels. And carved into the walls, just like Darian said, are numerals. Dates.

What's odd though—what's borderline impossible, is the date the numerals list.

10-20-1972.

My birthday. It's everywhere.

***

I'm alone down here.

There's no sign of Darian. There's no sign of Bernard. The cavern is empty, echoing, and feels endless. I've made small attempts to scout the three tunnels, but each presents its own share of impassable obstacles—whether growing too tight to traverse, dropping off into abyssal black water, or twisting steeply upward.

I've chosen instead to remain beneath the entrance to the ruins. It is my hope I can shout, and gain the attention of the rescue team when they arrive. Until then, I take this time to update my journal.

I've filled in the entries of my flight from the tent, of my return to the ruins. I've filled in other details as best I can while their memory is still fresh in my mind, because even now I feel my stomach roll with hunger and my mouth thirsty for water. I feel myself slipping. These details may prove important to me at a later date. I just need to hang on and hope that somebody will come.

But I'm so thirsty. So thirsty. Perhaps just a sip from the lake? Only a taste.

Just to wet my lips.

***

I am… unwell. I feel broken? Aching. All over. I'm aching in my mind, and it hurts. So so much. It hurts. There are sounds around me. Sounds in the cave. I've recorded them ti stdy later but it is so difficult to think. So difcult to write.

Ar they talkin to me??

***

The sounds are so close. CLOSE. They're surrounding me frm every crnr of the caVern now and memories are playin in my head like VIDEOS or movies. Ow. I don't feel good I feel really really bad. I see… I see my hands pushing Darian into the hole, down into the RUIns oh god I see her eyes as she falls LOOK-INGAT ME

ImsorryImsorryImsorry

HAD TO

The radio it was just so LOUD and the rescue team would come so fast that I had to call it off. I had to tell them we were JUST PEACHY and that there was no need to rush because DARIAN SHOWED UP RIGHT AS RAIN!!! Of corse I needed to destroy the radio. snapped the faceplate on my KNEE

I HAD TO. whatif Alison called them back and told them I was FIBBING?

Alison, Alison. Always with her MACHETE she never let the amn thing go. What the ffuck was it, her child? I needed to wait forever for her to step off into the jungle for a potty break but once she did I GUTTED HER cause she was gonna ruin it all i SWEAR scouts honor she knew something was uppppp with me

BERnard oh bernie bernie beRNIe you knew the journal was TROUBLE ya knw it was NO good and ya brought us anyway becbuase yu wanted ANSWERS for the dreams you were havin since ya read the thing but dont worrydontworrydontworry

people are soeasy to strngle when there sleeping

Oh LORD! The voices… The SKULL. It told me IT NEED-ED THEM. it needed us all down here and wewere so close to beingpart of this beautiful place but NOBODY wanted to come and DARIAN didnt land on her feet so now ITS JUST ME

Its just me
Soon though, it'll be me and you.

***

That's it... That's the final entry.

Note that for Albert's less... lucid entries, I attempted to transcribe them as accurately as I could from his writing. The bizarre capitalizations, the sudden misspellings. All of it is authentic to his journal, if that helps at all.

Without access to the remains of any of the individuals, it's difficult to say if Albert was simply losing his mind or really did end their lives. The part about him cancelling the SOS signal, however, is accurate. Somebody sent out a call indicating that Darian had reunited with the group and was not seriously injured—and that rescue at that time was no longer needed.

We arrived three days later, shortly after their transportation returned to recover them, and found their tent cut into pieces, equipment destroyed, and no sign of any members of the expedition. At that point, a search team scoured the island. I was the one who located the cave system, entered it, and recovered Albert Vess' journal and audio recorder—though there was no trace of him, body or otherwise.

In addition, I visually sighted the writing on the cavern walls. The weird thing is that it doesn't match up to what was recorded in Mr. Vess' journal. The numerals I saw were different. The date they listed wasn't 10-20-1972, but instead 04-04-1991.

Not his birthday.
Mine.

THE TOMBSTONE IN THE SEA

There is a tombstone in the sea, a great stone marker that rises above the frigid waves of the Arctic Ocean. It's a new thing, built not long ago. But if you ask around, nobody seems to know who built it, or to whom it belongs. Most don't even know that it exists.

But there is an old man, frail and white-bearded, who has sailed the Earth for many years and has come to know many things. One of the things he has come to know is the location of this tombstone.

And another of the things is to whom it belongs.

***

The man's bones ache against the cold. He looks out to the grave marker—a twisting, decrepit cross that sits above the waves and he takes a deep drag on his corn cob pipe. He breathes out, and his breath becomes fog.

"It's not at all as I remember," the sailor says, guiding his skiff toward the grave. He is alone on his boat. It's only him, all by himself at the end of this frozen world, and that's just fine because even though there's a storm brewing, and even though he's tired and weary, he's here. And that was all that he ever set out to be.

When the boat nears the twisting headstone, the sailor throws out a line, mooring himself to the grave. Satisfied that his boat won't wander, the old man goes below decks. He searches for something, unclasps a steel chest filled with a great many things. He tosses aside instruments for navigation and seafaring, and tosses aside tattered shoes and socks and old, crumpled papers filled with half-written journal entries that no one shall ever read. He tosses it all, and then at the bottom of the chest, he pauses.

Smoke billows from the corner of his mouth.

"There you are," he mutters, resting his pipe on the deck. He pulls forth a book. It's an old thing, weathered and beaten, its spine a mangled carcass that seems magical if only for the fact that it still holds its yellowed pages in place.

"It's been a long time," says the man of the sea, and he opens the book. Outside, in the small port-hole window, lightning streaks the sky like the threat of a god. The air rumbles. Thunder—thunder and something else. Something wondrous.

Sinister.

The man opens the book and a feeling runs through him. It's the sort that burrows deep beneath his jacket, shirt and skin and finds a home inside of his bones. It's a chill. One both familiar and haunting. One he thought he would never again feel, but perhaps that was just the dream of a young man, desperate to believe that there would be a life for him at the end of all his mistakes and failures.

His old fingers tremble as they flip through the ancient pages. There are words upon them, but the words are alien and rotten-looking, written in strange symbols that the man cannot interpret. Each page is a different language. A new blasphemy. Finally though, he finds the page he has been searching for. It is a page written in symbols the man can understand. There are consonants and vowels, and sentences and small stains where long ago, tears fell upon the parchment like scars to flesh.

Most importantly though, there are memories.

By the light of the dying sun, the man reads words that he promised to never again utter. He reads words that have ended lives, ended worlds. This time he recites them without tears in his eyes, but instead a hollow emptiness, a vast loneliness in his heart. The man feels apart from things. Perhaps, he thinks, he has been apart from things for too long.

The boat is rocking now, moving like a leaf in the wind. The storm is surging around it with such sudden intensity that the old man knows it cannot be a coincidence, cannot be the work of nature alone. Through the porthole, he sees the sky is red and scattered with black clouds. Some of these clouds are lit up, filled with shimmering veins of lightning.

There is something here.

Someone.

A voice rises on the wind, impossibly loud and indecipherable. It sounds like shrieking. Hollering. There's a voice upon the wind and it's speaking to the man, but for the life of him, he cannot understand it—not anymore.

But then, he was never meant to. That voice, that ageless power that seeps into all things living and dead, was always meant to be beyond the understanding of men. So far above, so far beyond, that the thoughts and ponderings of mortals are barren before it. Empty. Insignificant.

But the man has come here for this voice. He has come here for this storm. Book in hand, he stumbles out from his cabin on the little boat, stumbles out into a growing maelstrom as his vessel twists upon the wretched gravestone, driven by the malice of the tide.

"Who are you?" he bellows into the wind. "Who are you, and what is it you're doing with my voice?"

Laughter echoes around him, infinite and maddening. It speaks words the man has long since forgotten, words the man has sworn to never again speak or hear, and yet if he could, he would scream them to silence this beast.

"Who are you?" the old man shouts once more, and this time his voice is broken by fits of coughing. He keels over. His frail hands grip the guardrail of the deck, his feet slipping. The sea is sloshing over him now, drenching him in a coldness worse than he's ever known, a coldness that's as inescapable as it is painful. "Speak your name!"

"I am the thing that has always been," the Voice says, slithering about him like a snake. "I am the Beginning. And now, I am the End."

No, thinks the man. That's not true. "*I am* the Beginning," he insists, and his voice is weak. Hoarse. "I was there when this world was a mote of dust, when all the universe was painted in the black strokes of the abyss."

"The strokes of me," says the Voice. It sweeps about him, and now the sea is towering, raging, and his boat, still tethered to the awful gravestone, remains upright only by the will of this monster.

"I watched you from the nothing, from the void. I watched you weave worlds and sing things to life. I watched you dance light into this empty space I called my home, inviting stars to banish my darkness, all so that they could shine upon your broken creations."

The man breathes. It cannot be.

His memories, lost as they were, are coming back to him now and perhaps it is a trick of this beast, but the man remembers the beginning. The time before time. He remembers the empty palette upon which he painted the colors of this reality, and he remembers the infinite power flowing through him as he shaped the first worlds, the first laws.

He remembers that he wasn't alone.

"You," he says, and for the first time, he is afraid. "The Shape in the Shadows. I dealt with you. I burned you up in the heart of a star, and then scattered you across eons."

Silence.

If the thing is still there, the old man doesn't know. The maelstrom, the lightning, the voice of a god fades away and now there is only the gentle froth of waves gleaming in the setting sun.

"Come back!" the man roars. "Where are you?"

But the man is alone. Cocooned in silence, he sits upon the deck of his vessel and reads from his ancient book. He has long forgotten most of what he has written—his power now so vacant that even looking upon his old words makes his mind ache. But he tries. He sits there for hours as day turns to night, and he tries to read the pages of that ancient book, but he can't.

If there is an answer to his misery, to his folly in those pages, then he can longer find it. It has left him behind. The only words that make sense to the man are the words written on the final page. Human words. Words written the day he stepped down from the heavens.

They tell a story of a sort. A reminder.

They advise the man that he buried something here, deep beneath these waves ages ago. Pieces of himself. Small fragments of eternity. The words explain that the man locked these fragments away so that he could walk among his children, so that he could see his creation just once through their mortal eyes.

The words speak of regret. Of concern.

They speak of the power of what lay buried, about the terrifying wounds it unleashed upon this world—great fires, floods, and plagues. All of it His will. His reaping.

The old man rests his face in his hands, and he weeps. He weeps until the tears freeze upon his palms, and his lungs, now estranged from infinity, wheeze under the weight of his mortal age. He weeps for a great many things—for his children, his arrogance, and his wondrous creation.

Most of all though, he weeps for the glimmering stars high above, and their bright lights that are fading, fading.

Gone.

THE HOWLER OF DOGBONE SPIT

"Of course The Howler exists," Todd says, an air of defensiveness about him. He shoves a sausage-like finger against my chest and leans his jowly face close to mine. "You're just denying it to act tough in front of the younger kids. Trying to make me look *stupid.*"

I want to tell Todd I don't have to try and make him look stupid because he does a good enough job of that on his own. I want to, but I don't, because Todd is twice my size with a fuse half as short, and could probably snap me like a twig if he wanted to. So I play it safe.

"I'm just saying it's a silly urban legend. There isn't any such thing as werewolves, or howlers, or whatever you want to call it. It's made up."

Todd and I have known each other for years. We both grew up attending Dogbone Summer Camp. Since turning fourteen this year, the two of us assumed the role of Junior Camp Counselors, which is really just a fancy way of saying we get to herd kids to and from camp activities.

"Then how'd all those kids go missing?" one of the younger campers pipes up.

I feel myself tense.

Another kid jumps in. "Yeah! My brother says a kid's gone missing from Dogbone every year for the past three years. He says there's gotta be a monster scoopin' us up. He swears he saw it standing on the rocks at Dogbone beach."

"Plus," a girl chimes in, "I've heard the howling—we all have. We hear it plain as day, coming right from Dogbone Spit, out there in the lake. There's gotta be something out there, right?"

The kids erupt, arguing over the existence of the Howler. Some of the younger ones have scrunched up faces on the verge of tears—no doubt the idea of a murderous beast stalking the campgrounds isn't doing much to keep their spirits up.

"Enough!" Todd shouts, and the campers shut off like a light switch. He narrows his bushy eyebrows at me and then says in a quiet voice. "It's fine, Derrick. You can pretend you know what you're talking about, or that you're so brave. But we all know you're a giant *fucking* pussy."

"Come on, Todd…"

"Oh, do wittle swear words hurt your ears?" He pantomimes, unwrapping a Giant*Chew*—a chocolate bar so disgusting I've only ever known Todd to risk eating them. "Don't be such a bitch." With one fell swoop, he stuffs the chocolate bar into his mouth. Like a trash compactor, his teeth clamp down, smearing themselves with great globs of half-devoured caramel.

"How about this?" he says, mouth full. "Since you're so convinced the Howler is nothing but a legend, why don't you go on a little adventure tonight?"

"Oh, to Dogbone Spit?" The urge to roll my eyes is almost overpowering. "Yeah, no thanks. For one thing, I'd like to keep my job, and for another thing the weather is supposed to be garbage and our boats are made of driftwood."

"Figured you'd have an excuse."

Some of the kids start chuckling, and one of them asks why I'm being such a baby. Todd goads them on. "You should have seen him last year," he says, and there's a smirk playing at the corner of his lips. "He cried his eyes out every night because he was so afraid."

"Fuck off, Todd!" I say, and my voice is shaking. "My dad died that summer. I wasn't scared of some made-up werewolf then, and I'm not afraid of it now! But I bet you are."

Todd opens his mouth to reply, but I'm already barreling through him.

"So here's my counter offer. I'll go there, but only if you're along for the ride. See, I think you're just trying to act big and cool for all the little kids here—I think when push comes to shove, the big bad Howler scares you so much because you know you're too fat to run away."

The words fall out of my mouth without thinking, and it's not until I hear some of the kids break out into fits of laughter that I know I've fucked up. Todd's ham-like hands ball into fists. If there weren't so many voices chuckling, I'd bet dollars to donuts I could hear him growling.

Then, it's like the storm passes. Maybe Todd realizes he's overreacting. Maybe he realizes that losing his cool is going to lose him his status as the 'fun' counselor. Whatever the case, he unfurls his fists and sticks his hand out.

"Fine," he says. "Tonight we'll go to Dogbone Spit. And I'll even escort you, since you're too scared to go alone."

***

It's dark when we put the boat into the water.

It should be a full moon, but you'd never be able to tell with the storm clouds obscuring it on the horizon. The sensible thing to do at this point is call it off. Reschedule. There's no good that can come of a rowboat getting caught out in a storm in the middle of a lake.

Of course, that's not what happens.

The truth is, we're both in too deep for that. We're young, reckless, and stupid, and neither of us want to risk losing face. So we push the little thing into the water as quietly as we can, making sure we don't wake up any of the senior camp staff, and I grab the oars and get to work.

***

The level of effort we're putting in feels lopsided. I've been rowing for damn near forty minutes while Todd sits back flipping the pages of his novel: some fantasy pulp titled *War of Salgrum Book 3: The Age of Reaping*. He looks totally drawn into it. Entranced.

"What's that about?" I ask.

He looks up, and there's sweat on his brow. He looks nervous. Worried? Whatever it is, it's a new look for Todd. "Just some wizards and stuff," he says. Then, as if remembering he's still supposed to be putting on a tough front, he adds. "What do you care? Thanks a lot, by the way, for dragging us all the way out here."

"Me?" I say, incredulous. "You're the one who started this whole thing!"

"No I wasn't," Todd snaps back. "I was telling the kids a campfire story and you barged in and ruined it. What was I supposed to do? Tell them 'yeah, I was lying to you, there's no such thing as the Howler after all' and just ruin it for everybody?"

"I…" my words die on my tongue. Was I the asshole here?

Silence stretches between us, and Todd goes back to his book. I never pictured him as much more than a bully, but seeing him read that dorky stuff and go to this extent to maintain the equivalent of 'Santa's real!' has me rethinking my opinion of him.

Maybe he isn't such a bad guy. Awkward and insecure—definitely. But take away the crowd and the social pressure, and he's just a quiet teenager with a short temper. I wonder, as my paddles slosh in and out of the dark lake, if Todd isn't just another kid with a rough past, trying to put on a tough front so people won't pick on him.

"Do we really need to go all the way out to the island?" I ask. "Now that we've both admitted the Howler is just a made-up legend?"

He sighs. "Let's just go there and snap a picture by the Big Rock on the beach. Then the kids will know we went, and we can say the Howler chased us off." He shoots me a smile. "They'll get a kick outta it."

"Sure," I say, smiling and dipping the oars into the lake. "Why not?"

* * *

Thunder rumbles overhead as sheets of rain crash down in a torrent.

When I thought the weather would be rough tonight, I never imagined it would be *this* rough. There's a storm brewing, and it's brewing quickly. Quickly enough that we don't have the luxury of turning back around because, in this piece of crap, I'm not sure we could make it all the way to camp without capsizing.

The tiny rowboat is tossing and turning in the waves, the whitecaps now large enough to occasionally dip into the hull itself. We're most of the way to the island now—just a little further, but god are my arms tired.

It turns out rowing is hard, and it takes a very long time in these old boats. They're not built for speed. They're built to paddle around the dock, not actually *go* somewhere. If you told the guy who made this thing you were planning on taking it out in a storm, he'd probably laugh in your face and pronounce you dead on the spot.

All this to say, we have one option: Dogbone Spit. At this rate, we'll probably have to stay the night. My arms feel like twin bricks of lead. Still, somehow I don't feel like I'm the worst for wear between the two of us. Todd looks drop-dead terrified. He's long-since dropped the War of Salgrum and taken up clutching the sides of the boat for dear life.

Believe it or not, Big Bad Todd is *whimpering*.

"You're supposed to row into the waves, aren't you?" he says. "At a 45-degree angle or whatever, so we don't capsize!"

Every swing of the oars feels like I'm bench-pressing an elephant. I grit my teeth and remind Todd that 45 degrees into the waves means rowing back into the lake—and we want to get Dogbone Spit because if we don't come ashore soon we really *are* going to capsize.

"Just be careful," Todd yells. His pudgy face is red, embarrassed as he adds, "I'm not a very good swimmer!"

Before I get a chance to respond, a sound greets our ears. Low and drawn-out, it echoes across the lake, piercing the chaos of the storm and calling out to us from Dogbone Spit. A shiver runs up the length of my spine. What it is, is howling.

"Did you hear that?" I shout to Todd, wiping water from my face. He doesn't respond. The kid's curled up in the bottom of the boat, trembling as he tries to make himself as small as possible, tries to keep himself from falling overboard as the storm ravages us.

Lightning streaks the sky, and for a brief moment the island is illuminated. The pebble beach, the trees keeled over in the wind, and there—on Big Rock. A shape. A silhouette. Tall, with gangly limbs and sharp ears. My mouth goes dry. My heart blasts my ribcage at a thousand beats per minute.

The Howler.

I lower an oar, shouting to Todd as I point toward Big Rock. I'm shouting at Todd to just turn his head and look—to get ready because once we get to that island we're going to have to defend ourselves against a fucking monster, but Todd is cradling himself in the boat. He's out of it. Scared to death.

Then something strikes us from the side. A wave. A big one. It crashes over me and, even though I'm already soaked from the rain, I feel *cold* now and Todd is shouting and then, just when I think the night can't get any worse, I realize that the boat is lurching a little too much. The angle is all wrong. It's too steep.

My vision goes dark as we tumble into the lake. Something hits my head and I realize it's the hull of the boat, upside down and quickly falling beneath the waves. Freezing and disoriented, I feel around the bottom of the capsized boat, maneuvering myself around it and gasping for air as my head breaches the dark lake.

Todd.

He said he couldn't swim very well. I look around, throwing my sopping hair from my eyes and calling out, sputtering Todd's name. No response. Then, I hear gurgling. I hear the sound of Todd drowning to death a short distance away, and I swim to him, blind in the dark chaos of the storm, and I feel his hoodie and grip his arm and get him into a position where I can maybe save him.

Then lightning flashes, and once again I see it, out there on Big Rock. The Howler. Waiting for us on Dogbone. Heart hammering, I start swimming for the island.

Sometimes you really don't have a choice.

***

I said rowing in a storm was difficult, but it's really nothing compared to dragging Todd's unconscious body onto shore. The kid's heavy. Big. I'm not weak, I'm actually pretty fit, but I'm not a weight-lifter.

I'm run-a-long time fit.

I'm bikes-to-school fit.

I'm not drag-Todd-through-a-storm-and-up-a-beach fit.

Still, I manage to pull it off. Then I'm even kind enough to give him mouth-to-mouth until he starts coughing up a lungful of water. On top of that, I throw him in the recovery-position free of charge, all so that he won't die and can finish reading his stupid book someday.

I catch my breath while Todd lays there, disoriented but alive. A thin trail of blood is winding down his forehead, no doubt a souvenir from the boat bashing his lights out. I want to give him better help, but I don't have any bandages, and besides that, the lightning is flashing again, and I'm reminded that we're not alone on this island.

My eyes drift up to Big Rock, looming before us. Framed in the brightness of the storm is the legend of Dogbone Spit. The Howler.

Except... It's just some trees. In fact, from this angle, it doesn't look like *anything*. I stumble to my feet and investigate the waving branches, squinting in the downpour. Sure enough, if I position myself in front of the branches, it looks just like a wolf-man brooding in the darkness. But once you step to the side... it's just a couple of pine trees waving in the wind.

"I knew it," I say aloud, shaking my head. "I fucking knew it."

Then, something rises from the forest. A sound. It's long and low, echoing through the storm like a siren call, or perhaps a warning to steer clear.

A howl.

***

Todd's sitting up and rubbing his head.

"Listen," I tell him, jogging over. "Do you hear that? It's howling, and it's coming from the woods."

"Don't care..." he groans. The kid looks in rough shape, and I don't blame him. Not ten minutes ago he very nearly died. "Howl-er not... real. Remember?"

Sure, that's what I said. That's what I even thought after I saw those pine trees masquerading as a werewolf, but then who was howling? Was there a wolf on the island? A stray that had gotten separated from the pack?

"You should get under the trees," I tell him, covering my eyes from the rainfall. "You'll freeze to death if you sit out here."

"Yeah... In a second. Just need to catch my breath."

The howl erupts, even louder now. It's everywhere. All around us. Curiosity takes my reins and I find myself stepping off the beach and into the forest. "Take whatever time you need," I tell him. "I'm going to check out this howling."

It's a stupid idea, maybe, to go into a dark forest—however small that forest may be—to investigate the sound of an animal howling. Generally speaking, animals that howl are not herbivores. In fact, one might even call them predators. Dangerous.

Still, I need to know. What is the Howler of Dogbone Spit? Is it really a stray wolf? If it is, is it plucking wayward children from outhouses and dragging them away for a snack? Wouldn't somebody have heard their screams?

I step through the forest carefully, guiding myself by errant flashes of lightning and the sound of howling in the trees. The closer I get, the stranger the sound becomes. It becomes almost… constant. Like the damn animal never needs to take a breath. High and low. Loud and soft.

It's a minute later that I reach the foot of a small hill. At the top of it, I hear the howling clear-as-day. Steeling myself, I set to work at clambering up the thing—it's steep and wet, and my sneakers slip like I'm climbing a glacier, but I get to the top.

I get to the top, and I see it. The Howler of Dogbone Spit.

No lycan. No rabid dog. No rogue wolf. It's just a couple of boulders sitting tightly together with a small slit between them. I gaze at it, listening as the howling fills the air. It takes me a second, but I realize the 'Howler' is just the wind passing through the tiny opening, almost like whistling lips.

Turns out, the legendary Howler of Dogbone Spit is nothing but some pine trees on the beach, and a couple of rocks in the woods.

Go figure.

***

Trekking back through the woods, ready to tell Todd about my triumphant discovery, I catch sight of something in the glow of the storm. A bundle of sticks. A sort of home-made shelter? Probably a fort some kids made the previous summer.

Whatever it is, it makes for decent cover from the rain. We could stay the night, I figure, then Todd and I would row back ashore with our tails tucked between our legs, get a good reaming-out from senior camp staff, and probably lose our jobs as junior counselors.

But hey, at least we survived.

Before I head back to give Todd the good news—that I've solved the mystery *and* found a shelter, I pause. There's something familiar in the fort. I bend low beneath the twig roof and brush aside some dead leaves.

It's a candy bar wrapper for a Giant*Chew*. Beside it is a faded paperback book, with soggy pages wrinkled from exposure to the elements. It looks like it's been there for months. Maybe years. It's *The War of Salgrum: Book One.*

I chuckle, realizing I probably just found Todd's secret fort. His little getaway. I wonder if he comes out here to let the mask slip for a while, and give himself permission to not always have to be such a tough guy asshole.

Turning to leave, my foot catches on something soggy. I curse, already feeling disgusted by the thought of the Giant*Chew* candy bar, let alone some sweaty old hoodie that used to belong to Todd—and then I realize it isn't a hoodie at all.

And it definitely doesn't belong to Todd.

What it is, is a dress. A small one, maybe for a girl five or six years old. Pieces of it are cut open, the fabric slashed, and red streaks of tie-dye cover its blossom front. I swallow, stepping away. The dress looks familiar. Horribly, awfully familiar. And those red splotches don't look so much like tie-dye. Not really.

They look like blood.

"Whatcha lookin' at?" Todd whispers.

I wheel around. Todd stands a couple meters away, rain pouring down his face, eyes detached. Empty. "Find anything cool?"

"I uh," I stammer. "Yeah, actually. I figured out what was causing the howling."

"Oh, that?" Todd says, emotionless. His eyes drift around the fort, from the Giant*Chew* wrapper, to the War of Salgrum, to the bloody dress lying in a crumpled heap. "It's those two big rocks over there. It happens any time it gets windy enough."

I swallow, stepping backwards from Todd. "Yeah. Exactly yeah," I laugh, nervously. "I was just thinking we could use this fort as a shelter tonight. Crash here. I, um, I haven't had a chance to look around but—"

"You haven't?" Todd says, bending down and picking up the bloody dress. He lifts it to his face and puts the bloodstained fabric into his mouth, sucking on it. "You can hardly taste anything anymore—it's a real shame. If it just lasted long enough I wouldn't need to do this so often... I could just use my memories to make me feel better."

"This was you," I say, disgust mingling with fear mingling with hatred in my voice. "Those kids that went missing, you—"

"I had to do it," Todd says, tossing the dress down and stepping toward me. "You don't get it, Derrick, I feel so... empty inside. I can't feel things. Not like you. The only time I feel anything is when I'm *afraid*, or when I see other people *afraid*. Did you know we all have a spark in our eyes? You can watch it go out if you look closely, right at the moment you kill them."

"Jesus Christ, Todd. You're a fucking maniac." My back bumps up against a tree and I scramble around it, keeping my eyes on Todd as I continue to put space between us. "Is that why you fed them that dribble about the Howler? Not as some fun urban legend, but as a cover?"

"It made it easier, yeah. There's so many of those kids that I figure they'd be bound to notice something sooner or later, but if you can convince them the Howler is the one after them—well, they don't think twice about going anywhere with *you*. It's easy that way."

To think I actually thought Todd might have been half-decent beneath all his maliciousness. It makes me sick to my stomach. I wonder how many other kids Todd's buried his evil for? How many people has he manipulated to get their guards down?

"And me?" I ask, trying to keep my voice steady. "You didn't come out all this way with me for a photo op, did you?"

He shakes his head, then takes a couple quick steps toward me, causing me to skitter backward. Todd throws back his head and laughs. "You're such a fucking pussy, Derrick. Really. I'd only ever chanced killing kids—younger ones cause they were dumb enough to trust me, but then I saw the chance to get you out here, and I *had* to take it."

Todd's tongue slips across his lips. "It was the perfect setting. Incoming storm. Shitty rowboat. I'd bash your stupid face in with a rock, then toss you into the lake and flip the boat over and say you hit your head when we capsized. Everybody would buy it. Why wouldn't they?"

"You're actually insane," I say, realizing with mounting dread that I have no way to escape this psycho. The storm actually did capsize our boat, and there's no way I'm swimming to shore in this weather. "I should have let you drown out there."

"Should, coulda, didn't," Todd says, rushing me.

I twist around to bolt, slipping on a wet slosh of leaves. My face hits the ground hard and I get a mouthful of dirt. Todd's footsteps thunder toward me, and I spin around, but he's already on top of me, slamming his fists into my face. My ears ring and my vision blurs.

Fuck. He's killing me.

I kick out and manage to catch him between the legs. He groans, relenting just long enough for me to get back to my feet and dash away. My world spins. The storm is raging, Dogbone is howling, and the rain is coming down in sheets. As I clear the forest, I'm greeted with the sight of large waves crashing perilously against Big Rock.

"I'll... fucking... get you for that!" Todd's voice roars. He's barreling through the forest, and for a guy as big as he is, he's moving *fast*. Fuck. I clamber up Big Rock, hoping maybe it's just slick enough that Todd's weight will keep him from following me.

He explodes through the treeline, eyes wild. Stones kick up behind him as he charges toward Big Rock, jumping at it, his fat fingers slapping against the wet stone as he tries to grab purchase.

He's struggling. He can't make it up.

Good. I watch him slide helplessly down the slick face of the rock again and again, figuring I can wait it out here for a little while, maybe catch somebody's attention ashore while Todd tires himself out.

Then he vanishes, and I see him near the trees again. He's running his hands along the bark, and I'm confused, mouth gaping as I watch him stick a fist into a tree hollow and pull it out. Then shove another fist inside. "What the hell..." I mutter.

"Think you're so smart, Derrick," Todd yells, walking back to me, chest heaving. "But I know a thing or two about using nature to my advantage too."

He reaches the bottom of Big Rock, there beneath its smooth, slick stone face, and he shows me his hands. They're covered in something. Something brown-yellow. It's not until he slaps them together and then grips the rock that I realize what it is.

Tree sap. Sticky, thick tree sap.

He heaves himself up, bit by bit. Clambering up the face of the rock. Clambering up toward me—now officially cornered on this slab of earth jutting out in the roaring lake. "Todd!" I shout. "Don't do this! You can get help!"

"You think I'll get help after this?" he snarls, his head clearing the peak. "If I don't kill you, you'll tell everybody and then my life will be over. You don't get it, Derrick. I *have* to do this." With that, he pulls himself onto the rock, panting for breath. "Wish I could say it wasn't personal. But it really is."

Todd lunges.

I dive. It's suicide, but it's my only choice. I crash into the roaring water, swimming against the waves. Todd's twice my size and already made his intentions clear—the lake might be a death trap, but I've still got a better chance in here than up there. I kick myself over a wave and then hear something behind me.

A splash.

Hands grab onto me, while a gurgling voice curses me by my ear. "Make me... water... fucking hate... so much.... Deserve this." Fat fists pummel into the side of my skull, and I thrash. He's in the water with me, I realize. He's trying to drown me. Todd's fingernails tears at my face as I push myself away from him, too slick in the water for him to keep hold of.

I take one stroke, two strokes away, and his hand snaps hold of my foot. He drags me backward, even as he sputters in the waves. "Not... letting you... get away," he says. I spin in the water like a crocodile, trying to free myself of his grip, but it's ironclad. "Gonna... bash your head in!"

My foot shoots backward. It shoots backward as hard as I can, right against Todd's face, and I hear something *crack* like a bone splitting in two. I hear Todd shriek, and his hands let go, pressed to his now bloody face as he chokes and sputters in the water—me no longer there to act as a makeshift floatation device.

I don't stick around to watch him struggle. Seizing my chance, I swim away from him as hard and fast as I can. Behind me, I see him paddling after me, splashing against the water, his head dipping below and then back up. He's chasing me, but he's too slow. Too ineffective of a swimmer.

A minute later, and his voice is gone. He's gone. Vanished beneath the waves. Now though, I'm tired. Exhausted, and the storm is beating the shit out of me, and I don't even know if I can make it back to the island. My arms are heavy.

Damn it, they're too heavy.

"Over there!" a voice shouts. "I think I see one of them!"

I turn, treading water in the waves, and see a light in the darkness. It's a boat—a bigger one, with a proper motor. It's bouncing in the waves, but it's not a slave to them like the tiny rowboat or me and my out-of-gas arms. It's coming my way.

I swim toward the light.

***

The camp staff, it turns out, caught word of where Todd and I were because of the younger kids, the very ones who were crying about Todd's legend of the Howler.

Once the storm kicked in and they heard the howling, they figured Todd and I were probably gonna end up as a werewolf snack. Concerned (and unable to live with that on their conscience), they woke up the camp staff and informed them that we'd taken a little midnight jaunt into the storm.

And thank god they did.

After the staff pulled me into the boat, I told them everything. I told them about the kids, about the so-called 'Howler' and about how Todd had been luring his victims under the guise of keeping them 'safe' from the Howler.

We didn't find Todd that night, but his body washed ashore the next morning. The police linked his DNA to the bloody dress, and then several more articles of clothing they found buried in the dirt nearby. With my testimony to fill in the gaps, it was an open-and-shut case. The end of a nightmare.

As for me?

It's been a long time now—decades really, but I still go back to Dogbone Spit every year. Not for Todd, but for the kids that he stole. I go back to be with them. To tell them that I got the Howler, and that he won't hurt anybody ever again.

Mostly though, I go back to tell them sorry.

Sorry that I didn't realize sooner.

MONSTERCALL.ONION

The Dark Web.

The name itself is a meme. It's become the boomer boogey-man, the back alley of the internet where you go to get your kidneys harvested and sold off to a billionaire's all-you-can-torture buffet. It's the skeezy part of town. The no-man's-land of the digital world, chock-full of society's most vile scum.

It's also pretty boring.

See, the dark web isn't much different from the surface web. Sure, it has a cooler name and better privacy, but most people use it for the same shit. Social media? Check. Shopping? Check. Pirating movies? Duh. Did you know Facebook exists on the dark web? You do now.

My parents are *terrified* of the dark web. They speak about it in hushed breaths, sort of like Ron Weasley talks about Lord Voldemort. It's as though they think uttering its name too loudly will invoke the wrath of some serial hacker, just waiting in the wings to delete their bank accounts.

Ridiculous, right? I told them they were paranoid. To prove them wrong, I even downloaded the Tor browser and uninstalled Chrome. There's nothing to fear on the dark web, I said, so long as you've got half a brain's worth of sense in you.

Now, I'm not so sure.

Now, I wish I could take it all back.

I stumbled across the website after a night of drinking. I'd been out with Jared, my best friend since childhood, reminiscing about the good old days of driving Mrs. Crabtree up the wall. When I got home, I felt a bit nostalgic, so I went digging for old pictures on Facebook. Like most drunk missions, one thing led to another, and I landed on an old thread listing the most *exciting websites on the dark web*.

Spooky, right?

Well, most were fairly vanilla. Some free textbooks here, a bit of hacked video games there. I scrolled down through the responses until I found one buried beneath the others. It had just a single upvote.

http://MonsterCall143d1௸௸௸.onion

I stared at the link for a few seconds, then cracked a fresh beer and said fuck it.

The website was plain, mostly white text on a black background. Across the top was a banner emblazoned with the words *CALL YOUR MONSTERS*. I cracked a grin. It was kind of cute, in an edgelord, emo kid sort of way.

After clicking through a few menu links, I landed on the *ORDER A MONSTER* page. It said that, for $99, they would deliver a personalized monster to a doorstep of my choice. Free shipping, too. The flavor text read:

Perfect for getting even with terrible bosses, backstabbing friends, and childhood enemies!

I laughed. The idea was absolute gold. They even had a Monster Call Guarantee of same-day shipping. How they managed to pull that off, I had no idea. Maybe they had a network of paid actors, patiently waiting to dress up in Halloween costumes and say a few canned lines on somebody's doorstep? Or maybe it was like Build-a-Bear, where you got to design your own stuffed version of ghouls like Dracula and the Wolfman?

Who knows?

Whatever it was, I decided I was far too drunk to give a shit about how they made it happen. All I knew was a hundred bucks was a damn steal. I smashed the order button and it brought me to a follow-up page titled DESIGN YOUR MONSTER.

I practically licked my lips. This was the juicy bit! The website gave me a drop-down list of selectable options based on modifiable body parts. The mouth, for instance, had FANGS, BROKEN TEETH, NO MOUTH, MULTIPLE MOUTHS, and TOO MANY TEETH.

I thought the idea of too many teeth sounded ridiculous enough to be awesome, so I picked that and went down the list and selected the rest of the monster's attributes, including its body type, its subspecies, and finally its 'power'.

The next page said LEAVE A MESSAGE. I mulled it over for a few minutes before deciding to keep it simple. I typed *'boo'* into the text field.

Once I was finished, I clicked COMPLETE, and it brought me to a new screen that made me jump. It was a webcam video of me, staring shocked at my laptop. The stream was live. At the top of the page, a red text banner proclaimed PERFORM THE BLOOD SACRIFICE.

Uh, what? I cocked an eyebrow. As if in answer to my confusion, a list of instructions faded into view on the bottom of the screen.

1. UTTER THE NAME OF YOUR RECIPIENT
2. PIERCE YOUR SKIN
3. CONSUME YOUR BLOOD

I burst out laughing. This was too wild! Not only were they gonna deliver a 'monster' to somebody's doorstep, but they were gonna include a goofy ritual video, too.

Alright, I decided, I'm game. I went downstairs, grabbed a knife from the kitchen drawer, and headed back up to my room. Holding my hand up with a coy grin, I pricked my thumb with the tip of the blade.

"Jared Mayhew!" I announced dramatically, stuffing my bleeding thumb into my mouth and sucking it clean. Once I'd finished, I held it up, drunk and proud, as evidence of my dark ritual complete. Seconds passed and nothing happened. Then, the screen went black and a new page appeared.

ORDER COMPLETE! DELIVERY IN PROGRESS.

I sipped my beer, wondering how Jared would react to my spooky surprise landing on his doorstep tomorrow. I really hoped they included the blood sacrifice bit. Jared and his wife, Alyssa, both *hated* blood, so they'd never let me live it down—and that was exactly what I wanted.

A couple of seconds later, a new screen popped up.

DELIVERY COMPLETE. STANDBY FOR RESULTS.

Already? That didn't make any sense. How did they manage to create my order and ship it across the country, all in the span of five minutes?

A depressing realization swept over me. My drunk ass had been duped. There was no way they'd be able to ship something that quickly, so the only explanation was

A) it was a scam, or

B) it was just some lame video-mail jump-scare.

Fuck.

Now the $99 made more sense. There was no way a tiny start-up could offer same-day delivery and a compelling product for so little money. It was a pipedream logistically. Who the fuck did they think they were? Amazon?

Defeated, I decided that was enough dark web shopping for one night. Time to pack it in. I closed my laptop, brushed my teeth, and hopped into bed.

My phone vibrated.

I stared at it, wondering who would be messaging me at this hour. Jared, maybe? He was just as drunk as I was and probably high as a kite by now, too. I chuckled, picking up my phone. The screen indicated one new email—from MONSTERCALL. That was odd. I'd never given them my email.

ORDER DELIVERED!
CLICK HERE TO VIEW RESULTS.

View results? I heaved a sigh. This was either a virus or some guarantee that Jared got a corny 'spooky' email. Still drunk, still making poor decisions, I clicked the link, and it opened a video feed.

Of Jared's house.

I sat up, my tiredness vanishing in a tidal wave of what the fuck. The video was dimly lit, and the way it bobbed up and down looked like it was being recorded off of somebody's cell phone. Jared's small, two-bedroom home was there in all of its suburban glory. Something about the video felt off, though. Wrong.

I told myself to relax. This was just some prank or gag. The company probably put out a call for a fraction of the money to any locals, and somebody pulled the contract. No doubt they were going to walk up the front steps, knock on his door, and then say *boo* and run off or some shit. It wasn't a big deal.

So why was my heart racing?

The video neared the house, the footsteps going slowly. In the silence of the night, I heard the person behind the camera breathing. They sounded frightened. Scared. Why?

Lights went on inside the house, painting the windows in a dull, yellow glow. I squinted, seeing dark shapes darting behind the curtains.

Thoroughly confused, I decided to message Jared and ask if he got my surprise.

TERRANCE: suuup dude, you get my special delivery?? haha
JARED: HE,P
JARED: SKMWTHING
JARED: INSIDE THE HOUSE

Dark splotches splattered against the glass. A moment later, a woman's scream rang out, and the window shattered. Two hands reached out from behind billowing curtains, gripping the side of the windowsill. Then two more gripped the top. A figure emerged, lurching out of the opening and into the yard.

It looked familiar.

Jesus Christ, it looked familiar.

It stood eight feet tall, with large bat wings flared out behind it, and four crooked, muscular arms clenching in and out of fists. The person behind the camera stumbled backward, muttering something incoherent. The creature swiveled its head toward them.

The video feed shifted. Images of the sidewalk flew up and down as the cameraman ran full-tilt from Jared's house, heaving panicked gasps. I caught muffled fragments of prayers. Then a shriek sounded, followed by the flap of powerful wings.

The video crashed, tumbling in a blur of pixels. A man's voice shouted for help, and then something heavy crunched, and his voice died with a wheeze. Another shriek filled the night, and a shadow appeared, gazing down toward the discarded cell phone. It had four arms, a pair of wings, and a mouth filled with rows and rows of teeth.

Too many teeth.

I lurched forward, swallowing the vomit in my throat. In one of the creature's arms was a thirty-something man, struggling wordlessly against the monster's might. His chest looked like it'd been caved in. The creature leaned towards him, pressed its teeth against his face, and slowly bit down. The man's legs kicked and jolted as the beast's teeth began rotating like a blender, tearing his flesh from his skull.

It dropped him there, convulsing and dying, then beat its great wings and took off into the sky. Moments later, I heard confused shouts. Footsteps pounded against the pavement. More hollers. People called for the police, other neighbors told children to get back inside.

I put my phone down, horrified. It had to have been a joke. There simply was no way that had actually happened. It couldn't have. It was too gruesome—too violent. That was digital effects all the way. It had to be. Apps were great at that these days.

Weren't they?

***

The next day, I got a call from Jared's parents. His mother tried to talk, but she couldn't get past the tears, so she put his father, Roger, on the line. He explained that something terrible happened last night.

My breath caught in my chest.

I told myself to relax, that there was nothing to worry about. Monsters didn't exist. I knew that. "What happened?" I asked, as calmly as I could.

"Terrance," Roger said quietly. "This isn't easy to talk about, and god knows it's going to be harder to hear, but last night somebody broke into Jared's home. Police think it was around two in the morning."

My jaw hung limp, my hand trembling as I held the phone to my ear. A terrible coincidence. That's all it was. A terrible, horrible coincidence.

"I don't know how to say this," he continued, "so I'm just going to come right out with it." Roger took a deep, shuddering breath, the kind I'd never heard a man like him take in all his life. When he spoke again, his voice was as fragile as glass. "The intruder that broke in mutilated them. Jared and Alyssa."

"Mutilated?" I said in a small voice. The sound of Roger's voice on the phone felt distant suddenly, like the world was falling away from me at a hundred miles an hour. This couldn't be real. It couldn't. These things just didn't happen to people.

"Yes," Roger said. "God, Terrance. I hate to give you this news, I do. But you've always been Jared's closest friend, and I didn't want you hearing about it in the newspaper. It wouldn't be fair to you."

He paused. "The police," he began, pushing the words out. "They said the psychopath ate pieces of them. They say that the monster chewed their faces clean off their skulls."

I held the phone to my chest as I vomited all over my bedroom floor. I hurled again. Then once more.

"Terrance?" Roger's voice said from the receiver. "Are you alright?"

"Yes," I said, wiping puke from my mouth. "I mean, Jesus, no Roger. I'm so sorry. Holy shit." My hand slipped through my hair and I gripped it painfully, praying that maybe if I just pulled hard enough, the pain would wake me from this nightmare.

"It's—"

"The funeral preparations," I said, guilt pooling inside of me. "I'll handle them. I'll handle everything. You and Charlene need to take this time to grieve for your son. It's the—"

"There won't be a funeral," Roger said, voice trembling.

"What? Why not?"

A sound reached my ears, a sound I'd never heard in my life. I listened as Roger broke down sobbing. This man, this construction foreman who'd never so much as wiped a tear from his eye in the twenty years I'd known him, was crying his eyes out.

"Jared and Alyssa... they're alive," he said. "Hooked up to tubes in the hospital. The sick fuck left them, my baby and his wife, mangled on their living room floor. Can you believe that?" He wheezed, and I heard Jared's mother weeping in the background. "The monster didn't even have the humanity to put them out of their misery."

My mouth hung limp. What was there to say to that? What words could alleviate that sort of pain? "I..."

"You need to be careful," Roger said, and his voice evened out a little. "You've gotta be careful, Terrance, alright? You might not be my son, but you were over enough that I practically raised you. Pretty soon you might be all I've got left. The cops... Well, they told me they haven't caught the bastard that did this. He's still out there. So keep your doors and windows locked, you hear? And don't let anybody inside you don't know."

"Wait—" I said. "They don't have anything? No leads at all?"

"They've got something," Roger said. "It's... not much. A crumpled up note they found on Jared's doorstep."

"A note?" My heart thrummed.

"Yeah. But it was just one word. Practically useless."

A lump formed in my throat. "What did it say?"

"... Boo."

THE KNIFE

Too long ago, there was a knife.

I say 'too long' because most people have forgotten about it. They have moved on to newer mysteries, amused themselves with older legends, and fallen into deeper fables. But this was an extraordinary knife, and as we well know, extraordinary things should never be forgotten—no matter how mundane they might appear.

This story begins in a village.

It's a little thing that sits by a river, with houses of wood and wicker, and is rarely subject to much excitement. An old woman lives there. She has a name, but I do not know it, and perhaps that is for the best, for her tale is one of grave misfortune.

She leads an empty life, which is to say she is neither happy nor sad. Her days are spent tending to her garden, while her evenings are lost to her dreams. She ponders about other lifetimes and other destinies, and whether there is some great magic out there that can extinguish her apathy and ignite her wonder.

Her cottage is tucked neatly next to the river, and it is surrounded by a towering wall of stone and ivy. Her husband built the wall before the plague claimed him, hoping it would keep away looters and thieves. Sometimes when she looks at it, she thinks of him, but the memory dies a little each time she does, so instead she focuses on the soil.

Every night she prepares supper by chopping the day's harvest into a stew. One terrible evening, her rusty knife snaps cleanly in two. Unable to finish preparing her meal, she reluctantly sets out through her iron gate to visit the blacksmith in town.

When she arrives, a young man shows her an array of finely forged knives. Most are well beyond what she can afford, as all she has is an old necklace and a small purse of coins.

The young man tells her not to worry. I have a knife, he says, more affordable than any you've seen. He leads her into his forge, where a blade glimmers in the red light of the furnace. Its steel is a faded blue, and upon its face is an inscription that reads *A Promise to Keep.*

"How much?" she asks.

"It is yours for a promise," the blacksmith replies. "No more, and no less. All you must do is swear that you'll use it each day. Such a fine blade demands it."

A peculiar bargain, she thinks. She has little else to offer, however, and promises are cheap. She agrees. "I'll take that knife," she says.

Upon her return, she resumes preparing her stew. She slices into a potato, and it's almost as though the spud is made of nothing but air. The knife slips through it by the force of its weight alone. The woman is astonished. How satisfying, she thinks to herself. She cuts a carrot next, and then a tomato and then finally an onion.

When she's finished, she's smiling. What a lovely knife.

The next day, she can hardly wait to start on her stew. She spends long hours walking through her garden, selecting the sturdiest vegetables she can find. This time, she thinks, I'll see just how sharp that knife is. When she sets to cutting, the blade glides through them like they were hardly even there.

Again, the feeling of wonder and satisfaction returns. It's the first time in years she's felt much of anything, and she resolves to use the knife every chance she gets. Potatoes. Carrots. Lettuce. Tomatoes. None are safe from the edge of her blade. Each time one's sliced, diced, or chopped, she feels the emptiness inside of her shrink.

Soon though, the feeling dulls.

The emptiness begins to lurch back, extinguishing the embers of joy that once smoldered within. She grows depressed. Desperate for her spark, she harvests every vegetable in the garden, mincing them into tiny cubes. And it helps, at first. Then, she finds each cut less satisfying than the last.

The colors of her life begin to wash away, and now not even the knife can bring them back. That evening, she goes to bed and wishes that the plague had never spared her—she wishes that it killed her too, instead of simply ending her life.

***

The woman stirs, but the sun has not yet risen.

How strange, she thinks. *Usually, I sleep until dawn.* She peers out her window and sees little more than darkness, the great walls surrounding her cottage blotting out the moon.

Then, there comes a clatter.

She narrows her eyes. The sound, she realizes, is coming from high upon the walls. *Clang. Clang.* She studies the darkness, searching for the source of the noise, and then she spots something peculiar: two children atop the wall, with a hook fashioned onto a rope.

She hears their voices.

"Hurry up and get down, the boy says. I'm hungry!"

"We're all hungry!" the girl hisses back.

There's movement on the wall. *Clang.* The steel hook nestles itself into the stone, and then children clamber down the rope toward the garden. The woman watches them as they descend. Two silhouettes in the night. Invaders. Thieves.

"What gives?" the boy says as he reaches the ground. "Where's all the vegetables?"

"There's no way she ate 'em all," the girl replies. "There were plenty here yesterday!"

The dark shapes steal through her garden, searching desperately for a harvest that isn't theirs to reap. They bicker relentlessly. One proposes that they should leave, while the other says they ought to knock on the door and at least ask for a cabbage.

In their distraction though, they don't notice the old woman in the window, slinking away toward the kitchen. They don't know that she lives an empty life. Or that she made a promise to keep.

Most importantly, they don't realize there's nothing left in the garden but them.

CROOKED ANTLERS

I sit down, pop a piece of spearmint gum, and watch the woman across from me. She's nervous, her hands are fretting in her lap and her eyes are bloodshot.

"Long night?" I ask.

She looks up, timidly. Her face is awash in anxiety. She doesn't understand what's going on here. She doesn't understand what she's doing sitting inside an abandoned warehouse with an asshole twice her age.

It's fine. I've seen it before.

"Look," I say, loosening the tie around my neck. "It's just like I said. I only want to ask you a few questions, then you can go."

"Why here?" she says, in a small voice. "This looks like the kind of place you'd take me to... I don't know, murder me."

I crack a smile. She isn't wrong. "You don't like it? It's private. Besides that, it's probably the safest place in the world for you."

"Why? Do you have snipers on the rafters?" There's sarcasm in her voice, but her eyes flick to the steel walkways lining the walls. She pulls her sweater tighter around her, shivering at the draft. "Or is this some secret government fortress?"

"No, and no." I lean back in the wooden chair, and it groans under my weight. Damn. Not as slim as I used to be. "It's much simpler," I say. "This warehouse is the safest place for you, because I'm inside of it."

It's not a lie. At least, not entirely. Still, she gives me an incredulous look. It's the sort of look one reserves for blowhards and narcissists, and I probably deserve it. Time to change gears. "Tell me about the Event."

She studies me for several moments and then shakes her head. "On second thought," she says, picking up her purse. "I think I'd prefer talking to the police."

She stands up, makes to leave and I don't stop her. Her footfalls echo across the empty warehouse, the haphazard lighting casting her shadow in every direction. I hear her mutter something beneath her breath, but I can't make out the words. I probably don't want to.

Then she stops. They always do.

"What's an Event?" she asks.

I click my pen and reach down for my clipboard with a groan. The last job did a number on my ribs. "An Event," I explain. "Is a paranormal phenomenon, most commonly characterized by contact with a sentient entity. To use a more common turn of phrase, it means you stumbled across an urban legend."

She swallows. At this distance, I can just barely make out her expression, but I already know I have her. I bring my pen to my clipboard and clear my throat. "You said your name was Amanda Haynes, correct?"

"Yes."

I scribble it down. "And the Event occurred two nights ago, just outside city limits in the Cascade Mountains?"

Her sneakers patter across the concrete floor as she returns to her chair. Her expression shifts; gone is the nervous shyness, the small posture and the darting eyes. She's staring at me now. She's deciding whether she's in or out.

"Yes," she says at length. "It was in the woods. We were camping."

I check three more boxes on my clipboard. "Stupendous." So far, the location matches up with previous sightings of the beast. I sigh, resting the clipboard on my lap, and place my pen on top of it. "Why don't we start from the top?"

"Before we do," she says, narrowing her eyes. "How do I know I can trust you? This feels so…"

"Bizarre?" I offer.

"Dramatic. Like I'm in an episode of the X-Files."

"Fair point. You've seen my badge."

"Badges can be faked."

I bring a hand to my face, tracing along deep scars. "How about these? You don't get these working for television."

She's quiet, skeptical, and her eyes drift down to the clipboard on my lap. She's analyzing it. Determining if it's a real government form or not. All things I've seen before. She wants to believe, but she isn't ready yet.

"Let me ask you this," I say, handing her the clipboard. She begins looking it over. "When you told the search and rescue team a monster attacked you, did they believe you?"

Her eyes meet mine, and I see it: the surrender. She knows as well as I do that I'm her only shot. What she doesn't know is she's my only shot too. I've been looking for this legend for close to forty years now.

One might say it's been my life's work.

"I see your point," she concedes. "Let's get this over with."

She passes the clipboard back to me and I click my pen, bringing it to the box labeled ENCOUNTER. "Alright. You said that you were camping. Who was with you?"

"Just Rachel," she says. Her eyes are filled with something. Guilt, maybe. "We'd been friends since elementary school. We hiked together pretty often."

"Ah," I say, noting her name on my clipboard. "Rachel Tully, correct?"

The victim.

Amanda nods. "We went up to get a break from the doldrums of city life. Rachel just got out of a pretty serious relationship, and I didn't want her cooped up in that apartment, stuck with all those memories."

Her voice cracks. Emotion spills into her words. "I suggested we take the weekend and go for a hike into the Cascades. There's an old trail we spotted the last time we were up there, just off the main path. I said we could follow that, see where it leads us."

She brings a sleeve to her face, wiping at forming tears. "Rachel didn't want to. She said she was too depressed to shop for groceries, much less go on such a big hike. I convinced her eventually, though."

"I see," I say quietly. "How long was the hike?"

"I don't know. It was a really old trail, overgrown in parts. There weren't any mile markings."

"Ballpark it."

"Eight miles, maybe? We left early that morning, and it took us seven hours to get up there."

I whistle, scratching at my gut. "That's quite the walk."

"It's not that bad, honestly. We'd both done longer hikes, on harder trails. We actually didn't go as far as we intended."

"Why's that?"

"We came across an old cabin. It was run down, with shattered windows and it looked like it hadn't been lived in for decades."

My breath catches. I swallow the excitement before it has a chance to leak into my voice.

"A cabin?"

She nods.

I'd gone looking for that cabin a hundred times. It was never there.

"What sort of cabin?"

Her eyes leave mine. They're gazing off at some distant point on the ground, transfixed. She's replaying the memory. "We figure it must have been an old ranger cabin, which would explain the overgrown trail that led us there."

She pauses, her mouth hanging open, words struggling to break free. "Rachel suggests instead of using our tents, we could just stay inside of it. I remind her the windows are busted and it's the middle of November. Plus, it's probably filled with spiders. She says all the better. Let's set up our tents inside the cabin. Double the protection."

Amanda gnaws on her bottom lip, her voice growing smaller and smaller with each passing sentence. "There's dark clouds above us. It was supposed to rain, but it looks worse than that now. A lot worse. It looks like a storm's coming, so I agree and we head inside to check the place out."

"What did it look like on the inside?"

"It looked like... a nest. We spend some time walking around it. It isn't very big, there's only a handful of rooms, but there's... branches and leaves all over the floor. Every step we take, there's a snap of a twig.

"The entrance leads through a small kitchen alcove with a wood stove and dining table. Past that, it opens up to a living area with some rotting chairs, and at the very end is a bedroom filled with splinters from a broken bed frame. The place is a mess."

The layout sounds familiar. I can almost smell the cedar and feel the toasty warmth of the wood stove burning during cold December evenings.

"I check out the bedroom first," she says. "I spot a couple of shattered picture frames. Call it the millennial blogger in me, or call it dumb curiosity, but I'm drawn to them. One is old, yellowed and faded. It looks like it could be from the thirties. It's a picture of a young man and woman, dressed to the nines. Probably their wedding day."

She smacks her lips and then looks up at me. "Do you have anything to drink?"

I nod. "Of course." I reach down and unclasp my briefcase, opening it up to reveal a stack of documents and three water bottles. Two filled with water, one filled with a black grime. I grab the two filled with water, crack them, and pass one to her. We both take a sip.

"Thanks," she says, wiping her lips. "All this talking works up a thirst."

"Sure," I say. "And the other picture?"

"The other picture is more recent. I mean, still old, but not ancient." She laughs, but it's a nervous, self-conscious laugh. "It's a photo of an older guy, and a young kid with this mess of black hair. The two of them are standing outside the cabin holding rifles."

"Interesting."

"Yeah, I figure it's probably the ranger that lived there, back when the cabin was operational. Before I can check out anything else though, I hear a snap. It sounds like wood cracking in half, and then a crash. I drop the picture frame and Rachel starts screaming from the other room."

"Screaming?" I lean forward, my pen scratching at the clipboard. It feels too early for the Callous Man to appear. Certain criteria haven't been met. Still, if the work of my late colleagues has taught me anything, it's that legends can evolve, and I keep an open mind to that.

Amanda nods. "Yeah, she's screaming bloody murder. I storm in there, my bear mace in hand, expecting to see a wolf or cougar or bear, but I don't see shit. I don't even see Rachel. I call out to her, and she calls back, but she's whimpering. The sound is coming from the pantry, just outside the kitchen alcove."

"I look toward it, but I don't see her there. I jog over, wondering what the fuck is going on, when I catch sight of the floorboards inside of it. They're busted. Splintered and shattered. There's a dark hole in the ground, one big enough for a man to fit through. I almost have a heart attack when her arm reaches out of the blackness."

Amanda closes her eyes, takes a deep breath. "She shouts at me to get her out of there. I tell her to give me a second, and I take off my jacket and put it over the jutting pieces of broken floorboards, because I don't want her getting impaled on the things, and then I reach down and pull her up. She's bawling her eyes out, hyperventilating, and once she's firmly out of the pit, she's pointing to her foot. I ask her if she's hurt, and she tells me thinks she twisted her ankle."

Pieces of Amanda's Event are beginning to connect in my mind. The twisted ankle. The panicked friend. They're all familiar ingredients, and the end dish is anything but delicious.

She keeps talking. "Rachel says we need to get help right now, and I'm a little thrown off by her panic. I mean, it's a twisted ankle, not a death sentence, right? Still, I pull out my phone and check for service. Predictably, there isn't any. I ask Rachel for hers, and she can hardly speak. She's still pointing, but this time it isn't at her foot. It's at the hole in the cabin floor.

"She keeps whimpering about dead things. Over and over. Dead things. Dead things. Dead things. I'm wondering if I just became a party to my best friend having a psychotic break, but I give her the benefit of the doubt and check out the hole. It's dark enough that I can't see the bottom, so I flick on my phone's light."

Her fingers play at the tips of her hair. Tugging at it. "It takes me a bit for my eyes to adjust, but once they do, my blood goes cold. There's bones littering the ground. Deer bones. Rabbit bones. Then there, at the edge of my vision, I catch sight of a human skull.

"I'm swearing up a storm, and my imagination's going haywire. Rachel's hysterical, and I'm feeding into it. Both of us are repeating the words 'what the fuck' like it's a personal mantra."

Amanda takes a breath, holding it for a few moments. Goosebumps line her arms. Even reciting the account is beginning to work her up. "Then I remember I'm not living inside of a horror movie. I remember what I thought Rachel was screaming about in the first place. I tell her to relax, that it's probably just a mountain lion, or a grizzly's dumping ground."

"In the basement?" I ask.

"Sorry," she says, hastily. "I probably should have mentioned it earlier, but the cabin's raised off the ground on these wooden stilts. Where I'm at, it helps things avoid getting trapped beneath snow. There's a crawl space beneath it. I figure an animal was probably using the crawl space as some sort of shelter."

I check a box on my form. The story matches up, so far at least. The cabin is identical to the one in my memories. The question is, did she really encounter the Callous Man, or some rabid wolf? A human skull is a promising detail, but it's not like predators don't occasionally snack on hikers.

"A logical conclusion to draw," I say. "Does it calm your friend down?"

"Yeah," Amanda says with a nod. "Rachel starts to breathe a little slower. She relaxes a little. Eventually, she's ready to try standing, and she can—but just barely. She limps over to a dusty wooden chair near the fireplace and sits down in it, grimacing. She tells me she doesn't think she can make it back down the mountain.

"There's a crack of thunder in the distance. I walk over to the windows and see the sun turning a blood red, setting over the tree line. Storm clouds are rolling in. Rain starts pitter-pattering on the cabin roof. Rachel's groaning in pain, and she shows me her phone. It doesn't have service either."

"You were picked up by a search and rescue team, weren't you?"

"Yes."

"How's that if you had no way of contacting them? You weren't gone longer than anticipated."

Amanda sighs. "I was just about to get to that, actually." There's an undercurrent of annoyance in her tone. She clearly doesn't care for interruptions once she gets going. I lean back in my chair. All the better for me.

"Like I said, Rachel and I go on this sort of hike pretty often. Me more than her, but still. I come prepared. All-weather clothing, bear mace, flint and steel. You name it, I got it. I don't cut corners, so I made sure to pack my GPS locator beacon. It sends a one-way distress signal."

"Ah," I say, noting it in the report. "A survivalist."

The fire in her eyes falters, and she pauses. A moment of silence stretches between us, and when she starts talking again her voice cracks. "Not as much of a survivalist as I should have been. Rachel wants me to use it, but I tell her no."

Odd.

"Hear me out." Amanda's eyes connect with mine, and there's a pleading expression on her face. A desperation to be understood. "Rachel wasn't in any immediate danger. Not then. Neither of us were. Plus, a storm was rolling in, and it looked like a big one."

She takes a shuddering breath. I know the look. Memories are clawing at her mind. "My father was a search and rescue technician. He was killed trying to rescue a couple of teenagers who got themselves trapped in a cave."

Ah, there it is.

The tragic backstory. I was wondering when it'd squirm its way out of her mouth. Somehow, all the human stupidity in the world can be traced back to our emotions overriding our will to survive. I scratch her reasoning down on the clipboard.

"I didn't want anybody risking their lives when we had food, shelter, and weren't in danger. I told her no. No way. I—I couldn't have that blood on my hands if something went wrong and…" She trails off.

"… And Rachel understood."

Amanda gets quiet. She's staring at me, and there's that same look I've seen a thousand times before.

I want to roll my eyes. I want to spit in her face for being such a naïve idealist, but I hold it down. Instead, I plaster an understanding smile on my lips and nod my head sagely. "You made the right choice. It was the only choice you could have made, knowing what you knew in that moment."

It works. She perks up. "Yeah, I suppose."

"So the two of you decide to stay inside the cabin then? You're not worried about the bear or cougar using it as a snack bar might swing by?"

"At that point, we don't really have another choice. I'm the outdoorsy type. I've seen storms, and I know that the one coming our way is going to be a big one. We decide the cabin's our best bet, but we take precautions. I keep my bear mace close by, and we close all the doors. A cougar isn't going to open a door, and a bear might break it down, but only if it feels it needs to. It's far more likely to wander into the crawl space, safely away from us."

"Sure. Makes sense."

"I decide to put an extra layer between us and the front door though. Just in case. I clear out the busted bed frame and sweep the splinters from the bedroom floor, then I get to work setting up the tent." Her voice dies. Memories are calling to her again. Difficult memories.

"What happened?" I ask, the hairs on my arms rising. "Did you see something?"

She nods. "Yes. Animals were running through the clearing outside of the window. They were running past the cabin. Deers. Rabbits. Then a whole flock of birds burst through the treetops and started flying over us."

I lick my lips. Yes. This is very promising. My pen scratches at the clipboard in excitement. The Callous Man has a defining characteristic, one unique to him in the realm of legends. He always comes from the same direction. Always.

"Which way were the animals running?" I ask.

Her voice is small. Brittle. I barely hear it over the sound of my pounding heart. "South," she says.

I write the word, and underline it three times. My fingers are shaking with excitement. My mind's racing. After so many dead ends and broken threads, so many killed and missing, it's finally coming together. I've found one. A survivor, and not only that, but one that might still have the Link.

"How many animals were running?" I ask. I know the answer, but I need to hear her say it.

It takes her a second to get the words out. They're uncomfortable for her. Disturbing. "All of them," she whispers. "It was like… an exodus of life."

My heart hammers. My breath quickens. All of it, each detail of her story, means one thing.

The Callous Man is coming.

I take a breath and stand up from the chair, stretching my legs. My back feels like it's been crushed between two boulders, and sitting for any length of time always turns it into a pin cushion. Still, I couldn't be happier.

"Everything alright?" she asks.

"Peachy." I pick up the clipboard and clear my throat. "What happens after the animals flee the tree line?"

She opens her mouth to speak, but stops. Her eyes glance down to my open briefcase, staring at the manila folders and the crinkled old water bottle, filled with grimy black fluid. "Why do you have that?" she says, wrinkling her nose. "Its label is... yellow. It looks like it's twenty years old. What's that gunk inside?"

I scowl, kicking my briefcase closed. "An experiment. It's nothing to concern yourself with. Now then, if you wouldn't mind continuing, I'd like to hear what happened following the exodus."

There's a moment of shared disdain between us. She feels like I'm hiding something from her, and I feel like she's putting her nose in places it doesn't belong. Thankfully, it doesn't last long, and she continues her account.

"Rachel calls my name from the main area, then she limps into the bedroom, leaning against the doorway. She looks really shaken up. She asks if I saw all the animals taking off, and I tell her I did. Her eyes are getting wide and I can tell she's throwing herself into another panic attack, so I... I tell her that they're probably just running from the storm."

"Do you believe it?"

"I don't know. Maybe? It seemed like the only logical reason, but at the same time, the whole scene felt so eerie. So wrong." She opens her water bottle and takes a drink. "Either way, it's not like I'm gonna start feeding into Rachel's paranoia. One of us has to be calm, right?"

I shrug. "Sure. You said the sun was setting when the animals made a run for it. Is it dark yet?"

She nods. "Mostly. I mean, the last rays of sunlight are just barely peeking over the treetops. The storm's making it worse. The clouds are blocking a lot of the light. I get a move on with finishing setting up the tent, and we set up this LED lantern that Rachel brought. It... feels weird."

"In what way?"

"The silence." She pauses, shakes her head and then mutters something. "Sorry, that's the wrong word. It isn't silent. The wind is howling and the rain's coming down pretty hard, but there's no sounds of life. No crows cawing, no squirrels chattering. I don't even see any bugs in the cabin, despite a whole shit load of spiderwebs.

"I brush it off, though. I keep telling myself one of us has to be calm. So we close the bedroom door and settle ourselves into the tent. Neither of us have much of an appetite, so we eat a couple of protein bars for supper and pull out our books. We don't talk. I don't even know if we actually read—I know I don't. I stare at the words, but my mind's a million miles away, too wrapped up in the feeling that something is wrong with this place. Something's wrong with this scenario."

She sighs, running a hand through her blond hair. "I chalk it up to the darkness. Things always seem scarier in the dark, you know?"

I nod. The dark has always had a powerful effect on human beings. It makes it more difficult for us to see our enemies, and in my line of work, easier for them to see you. It's a lose/ lose environment. Unfortunately, it's often a necessary one.

"You don't talk at all?" I ask, sitting back down in my chair.

"Not at first," Amanda says. "After ten, maybe twenty minutes, Rachel breaks the silence. She asks if we should use my rescue beacon, since it's getting pretty bad outside. I know that's not why she wants to use it, though. Not the real reason. I remind her that we can weather the storm in here, and call for help in the morning once the storm clears."

Amanda screws up her face like she's holding back a wave of emotions. "I manipulate her. I remind her my dad was killed during a botched search and rescue job, all because some teenagers couldn't exercise a little bit of common sense."

I study her. Perhaps she's more cunning than I thought. Naïve, though. Still so naïve.

"Rachel lets up. She agrees we can call in the morning. I can tell she's scared, and honestly, so am I. And I know what we're both thinking, so I blurt out that there's no such thing as monsters. I tell her we're…. Fucking adults, and we'll deal with this." Amanda chuckles. It's a small sound, full of disbelief and regret. "I promise her we'll laugh about it in the morning."

The woman's not bad with a story. I idly wonder how popular her blog is. Unlike the gum in my mouth, her words have flavor. I dig in my jacket pocket and pull out my pack, popping a fresh piece free. Spearmint. It's not a cigarette, but it's the next best thing.

"Famous last words," I say with a grim smile. "What's Rachel think of your pep talk?"

"She… she's fine with it, at first. I think she might even be on board. She doesn't want to spend the night terrified anymore than I do, so anything that makes that fear a little smaller is a welcome distraction."

Amanda swallows, and her expression goes blank. "It seems like everything's going to be just fine, like it's just another overnight hike. At least, until we hear the footsteps outside."

Here we go.

"There's a creaking sound—like old wood straining under something's weight. It's hard to hear over the roaring wind, but given of our mental states, it's practically unmissable. Something's outside. The footsteps are slow, gradual. Whatever's out there is taking its time, and both of us are frozen in fear.

"Rachel grabs the lamp and turns it off, and I suddenly realize just how dark it really is. It's pitch. I can barely see Rachel, and she's sitting close enough that we're touching. It's just us, the storm, and the sound of footsteps now. I whisper to her that it's probably a deer, or maybe a mountain lion or just some kind of animal looking for shelter from the storm."

Amanda's eyes are glazed, her hands picking at the fabric of her jeans. She's lost in the memory.

"I don't believe it myself. Something inside of me is rioting and telling me that we're not safe. We haven't been safe since the moment we walked into that cabin, and we won't be safe until we're far away. Still, I take a breath. I repeat that stupid internal mantra that one of us needs to be an adult. One of us needs to be rational.

"So we wait. I whisper to her that all the doors are closed. No animals are going to get inside. We're safe. We're safe. I keep repeating it, like if I say it enough, I'll start believing it too. I do my best to reassure her and stave off another panic attack."

Amanda uncaps her water bottle and takes a quick swig. Her hands grip it, squeezing, and the plastic crinkles. "It works. Maybe. I can't see her, but I can't hear her either. She's not screaming. It's good." She swallows. "Then I realize things are bad. Really bad."

"Why?"

"We hear this sharp whining sound—like rusty hinges, and we recognize it. It's the front door of the cabin. Something opened it. The next second, the sharp whining is followed by dull thuds, like heavy footsteps. The floorboards groan, and we hear it, whatever it is, moving through the kitchen and into the main area."

I remind myself to keep writing, but it's hard. This is the moment I've been waiting for, the moment when I can finally determine whether or not she's actually encountered the monster I've been chasing my entire life.

"I'm clutching my can of bear mace to my chest, and Rachel's whimpering beside me. I'm hissing at her to be quiet, to shut the fuck up, because I know that if whatever's out there hears us, it's going to come in here.

"She listens. Neither of us move, we just listen for the footsteps. Thunder's crashing outside, and the weather's screaming through the busted window, but somehow, in spite of it, all those footsteps are clear as day. I couldn't tune them out if I tried."

Her fingers find the armrests of her chair, and she grips them. They scratch against the tattered wood. "I pull the safety tab on my bear mace, ready to blast something if that's what it takes. Rachel grabs my arm, and I feel her hand trembling. Her whole body is. Something smells like piss, and I realize it's her. She's losing it.

"The footsteps get closer. They're halfway through the living area now, and they're approaching the bedroom door. Whatever's out there is close enough that we can hear this... snickering sound. Like really fast, short breaths. Nyeh nyeh nyeh. It doesn't sound human, but it doesn't sound like any animal I've heard either. It sounds like a nightmare."

I circle a box on my clipboard, identifying the sound as COR-RECT. According to more recent eyewitness encounters, the Callous Man snickers before engaging with his prey. An evolution of his mythology. In my memories, I recall only the screaming.

Amanda keeps talking.

"Rachel's squeezing my arm so hard that it hurts. Her nails are digging into me and I can feel her warm piss on the bottom of the tent. It's soaking through my jeans but I don't care. I don't do a damn thing. I can't, because as soon as I make a sound or a move, those footsteps are going to get faster, and something's going to open the bedroom door and then I don't know what happens."

She stops talking. Tears are forming in the corners of her eyes, and she grips her sweater sleeve and dabs at them. "Rachel... Rachel can't take it anymore though. She reaches across me, hissing at me to give her the rescue beacon. She's begging me to activate it, and I'm trying to get my hand over her mouth and shut her up, but she's desperate and she's fighting me."

"The footsteps pick up their pace. They're walking toward us, these heavy thumps on the creaking floor. I whisper to Rachel if we send the distress call, the beacon's going to start beeping."

Tears slip down her cheeks and Amanda stares, transfixed, at the concrete floor. There's something swimming in her eyes, and I think it's self-loathing, but I can't be sure. All I know is it's familiar. "Continue," I say.

"Rachel gets hold of it. She hammers at its buttons, and it works. It starts beeping. The signal's sent." Amanda's voice trembles, her lips quiver with the onset of her next words.

"The bedroom door opens. It's this long, drawn out screech and both of us freeze. It's just the rusty hinges and the beacon beeping. I want to scream. I want to run. I think we both do, but we're too afraid. We're paralyzed."

She swallows. "I get my finger ready on the trigger of the bear mace. I don't want to use it inside. It'll probably fuck us up just as bad as whatever's standing in the doorway, but I'm ready to if I have to. Moments pass, and all we hear is the beacon beeping, and the rain and thunder outside.

"Then, there's that snickering again. Fast and raspy. It's followed by footsteps, and now that it's in the room with us, it sounds big. The tent shakes, the whole room shakes. It's dark enough that we can't see so much as a shadow through the canvas of the tent, but soon we don't need to. The footsteps start circling us, and then a finger presses to the wall of the tent and begins tracing around it.

"Whatever it is, it starts sniffing. Softly at first, then louder and with more intensity. I realize it isn't a man, it's some kind of animal. It sounds beastlike. Feral, and hungry."

Amanda closes her eyes, putting her head in her hands. She takes a moment and groans. When she looks up again, her eyes are hollow. "Rachel can't stand it. She screams. She screams to leave us alone. She screams we have a gun. She turns on the lantern and tells it to fuck off, go to hell, die in a fire, you name it."

"I'm going to assume that didn't go over well."

She rubs her arm anxiously. "I don't know. It didn't seem to hurt things. It left the room—walked into the living area, but then it stopped. It didn't leave the cabin." Her voice trembles.

"What happened after he—after *it* walked into the living area?"

"Rachel hisses at me that we should run," Amanda says. "I remind her that her ankle's fucked. She barely limped into the bedroom, how far does she think she's going to get in the woods, over uneven ground that's slick with rain? She tells me if we stay here, we're both going to die."

Amanda shivers. "I know she's right. I know it, but I can't bring myself to leave. It feels like the tent's the only thing keeping that thing away from us. Like, as long as the canvas is between us, it can't see us and we can't see it. It doesn't exist."

It takes everything I have not to roll my eyes. Still, I flip a page on the clipboard and keep a neutral expression. Her perspective is not unlike a child's. People often approach terror with irrational and sometimes nonsensical methods of survival. Of course, there's nothing magical about her tent. There's nothing about it that will save their lives.

"Continue," I order.

"It starts with a creak of a floorboard. We hear it walking again, but it's not coming toward us. It's pacing back and forth, out there in the living area, and it's snickering faster than before. Soon, the snickering gets heavier. Violent. It starts grunting, then growling." She takes a breath and chokes back a sob. Tears race down her cheeks, and her eyes are alight with terror.

"Then it goes silent. No movement. No grunting. No weird fucking snickering. Just the thunder outside, the howling wind, and the rain on the roof. I'm sitting there, clutching the bear mace and Rachel's crying, and both of us are praying it's gone. We're praying it's just given up. Decided to move on. And… and…"

"And what?" I press.

She meets my gaze with her own, and a hopeless horror swims in her eyes. "… And then the entire cabin shakes. Footsteps pound on the floor, and there's this hateful, agonizing sound, like a hundred human screams mixed together and poured out of a single voice. Rachel and I lose it. We're shouting, crawling over each other, trying to unzip the door of the tent and get the hell out of there, and then our world turns upside down.

"It's like we've been thrown in a washing machine. My head cracks off her knee and we're rolling around, bouncing in this cacophony of sound and fabric, and then I realize the tent's been lifted off the ground. Above me, in the light of the LED lantern, I see two crooked, broken antlers piercing through the canvas. That monster's throwing us around, bucking like a damn deer.

"Soon the tent canvas tears and we fall free, crumpling to the ground in a painful heap. Rachel's scrambling over me, holding the lantern in her hand, and in the madness of it all I see her make a break for it toward the window. As she does, the light passes over that… that fucking monster."

Amanda chokes back tears and sniffles. "I'm sorry," she says. "I just need one second."

"Of course." I reach into my jacket pocket and retrieve a set of tissues. I pass them to her. "Here, blow your nose."

She does. When she's finished, both of us sit in silence for a moment. Her bottom lip quivers. "It must have been eight feet tall. It was crouched over, humanoid except its chest was covered in fur and its legs were scaly, like a bird's. It had a long tangle of black hair and… and its antlers jutted out from its eye sockets."

I mark the details down in excitement. Yes. Good. It's a near-perfect description. It's missing only a few key things. "The antlers," I press. "Can you describe them?"

"They were crooked," she says, slowly. "They came out at odd angles, both different, and around them was a halo of eyes. Tiny black ones." She closes her own eyes and takes a stuttering breath. "I almost missed them except they all blinked in unison, and I remember thinking it was the most terrifying thing I'd ever seen."

"The fact that all of them blinked?" I ask.

"No. The fact that all of them were looking at me."

"Did it attack you?" I have to know. The defining characteristic of the Callous Man is his method of attack. If she nails it, then I've got her. I've got my Link, and I've got him.

She shakes her head. "No. I thought he might, but then Rachel makes a racket. She's throwing herself up onto the window ledge, and then she falls over the other side. The creature turns toward her, snickers, and launches itself at the window. It seems like it should be too big to fit, whatever it is, but it isn't. It's like a snake, the way its body contorts to fit itself into the window frame. It perches there, and I see at the bottom of its scaly feet are these thick claws, and the hands it uses to grip the window have thin, impossibly long fingers. It drums them on the wall, before it launches itself after Rachel."

My pen races across the form, filling in details and circling boxes as the information presents itself. This is *very* good. I've waited my entire life for this moment.

"I sit there for a second, in too much shock to move, and then I realize my friend is out there being chased by some... some fucking monster. I get to my feet and turn my phone's light on, and in the distance, through the rain and swaying trees, I can see Rachel's light bobbing in the darkness.

"I call out to her. I shout her name, but she either doesn't hear me or she doesn't care. I scan the area for the monster, but I don't see a thing. I lean out the window, looking around the cabin, using my phone's light to illuminate as much as I can, but it's not there. The monster's vanished."

"I'm surprised you didn't take your opportunity and run," I say. "The creature was clearly more interested in Rachel."

Amanda glares at me. There's a stubborn defiance in her eyes, and I have to remind myself that most humans have a perverse obsession with self sacrifice. Maybe it's the Hollywood brainwashing, maybe it's the fact that they just haven't suffered enough, but they can't get enough of it. Before she even speaks, I see it in her too.

"I couldn't leave her," Amanda snaps. "I was the one who dragged her out there on that hike. I was the one who suggested we follow that stupid, overgrown trail. I was the one who refused to use my locator beacon before it was too late. All of this was my fault. If I walked away from her then, I could never forgive myself." Her voice breaks. "I still can't."

Time to get a move on. "You went after her then?"

"Yeah... I clambered through the window and took off, following her light as best I could. I had the bear mace in one hand and my phone in the other. The light from my phone wasn't much, but it was enough to keep me from tripping on roots or running into trees. I kept calling Rachel's name. Kept telling her I was coming."

"She can't have gotten far with a twisted ankle," I say. "Then again, adrenaline can do incredible things."

Amanda shakes her head. "She wasn't moving that fast, at least compared to me. I was gaining on her. I could just barely see her silhouette ahead of me, and the LED lantern bobbing up and down as she limped away. Then the light drops. Rachel's silhouette vanishes, and I hear her scream.

"I double over, running with everything I have. My lungs are burning and my feet are slipping on the mud, but I don't care. I'm not thinking anymore. I'm acting on pure instinct, and my instincts are telling me that if I don't get to Rachel soon, that creature's going to kill her."

The words stop. Amanda's body trembles, and she breaks down. She can't hold it in anymore. The torrent falls out of her, and her face gets ugly as she sobs into her hands. It doesn't take long before her palms are glistening with wetness, but to the girl's credit, she forces herself to keep going. She doesn't quit.

"Rachel's screams stop. I can't see anything, really. The lantern's on its side far ahead of me, and I can just barely make out a shape in the darkness. It's the sound that still haunts me, though. I think it always will."

"What sound?"

"This wet, tearing sound. Like skin being ripped, and blood splattering the ground. It's followed by a dull crunch, and then I hear slurping. Swallowing. I charge forward and I'm basically just adrenaline at this point. I hold my phone up as I close the distance and I see… I see it."

She takes a sobbing breath. "I see the man with crooked antlers. He's crouched over Rachel's corpse, and one of her arms has been torn in half, dangling by a thin strip of flesh. It's missing her hand. Blood is everywhere, and it's still spurting out of her torn limb. I'm too stunned to move. Too shocked at seeing my friend, dead on the ground in front of me, being eaten by this thing."

Her voice trembles, and she launches into another fit of tears. She brings a tissue to her nose and blows a thick wad of mucus into it before throwing it unceremoniously onto the warehouse floor. She wipes her face with the back of her sleeve. "Then the thing rears back its head, and it tears what's left of Rachel's arm off. It starts to chew it.

"It's… it's more gruesome than anything I've ever seen. I don't think we're wired to deal with seeing that shit, as human beings, you know? Like nothing in my programming knew how to deal with that. Once it finishes chewing, it swallows the arm, and it opens its mouth again.

"Its bottom jaw falls all the way to the forest floor, its gaping maw large enough for a grown man to walk straight into. It sits there in front of her corpse for a second, and then that uproar of screaming starts again, like a hundred anguished voices stitched together.

"A flurry of human arms reach out of its mouth, clawing toward Rachel's limp body. They clutch at what's left of her torn limb, her hair, her jacket. They clutch at anything they can reach. Then they start dragging her into the monster's mouth."

There it is. It's just as I remember.

Amanda loudly blows into the tissue again. "Then… I hear Rachel whimper, and my fucking blood goes cold. I realize the entire time I've been standing there, watching this thing eat her, she's been alive. I was watching her get eaten alive."

"My mind goes blank. I point the bear mace and let loose a blast toward the monster, shouting at it to get the fuck away from her. It recoils, howling in that symphony of screams and shuffling back into the bushes. I take my chance and press the lantern into Rachel's hand. I tell her she needs to hold that for us, and she nods weakly. Her face has lost all of its color, and I know she's not long for this world.

"I get her good arm over my shoulder, and keeping a grip on the bear mace, begin putting some distance between us and that monster. She's groaning. She keeps saying my name. 'Mandy.' Over and over again, but I tell her to be quiet. She needs to save her energy, and I need to hear that *thing*.

"We don't get far before I hear its thunderous footfalls pound against the forest floor. It's running at us. I wheel around, and Rachel's lantern illuminates the monster for only a split second before I let loose another round of the mace. It snickers in pain and brings those long-fingered hands to its eyes.

"I don't wait around for it to recover. I keep going. I don't know where. All I know is I need to get away from this thing, because it isn't going to stop until it finishes what it started. Again, I hear its footsteps pound and the dirt, and again I wheel around and blast the monster. It shrieks in pain and shies away, but only a few moments later it charges again."

Amanda keels over and starts bawling. She grips her hair, then starts pulling on it so hard I half-expect her to tear a chunk from her scalp.

"I realize," she says, choking out the words between sobs. "I realize Rachel's too heavy. I can't carry her. I can't get away from this thing because I can feel the can of mace is almost empty and every time I hit it with the mace it affects it less."

She shakes her head, her eyes are bloodshot, her cheeks tear-stained. She sniffles and wipes mucus onto her sleeve. "I have to leave Rachel. I have to. If I don't, it's going to kill us both. You understand, right?"

For the first time in her desperate recollection of the Event, I do understand. "Yes," I say. "Life isn't easy. There aren't any real heroes, just people who pretend to be. You made a difficult choice, but a necessary one."

Amanda stares at me, she stares at me for a long while, like she's searching my expression for something. Finally, she nods, slowly. "Yeah," she says, wiping more snot onto her sleeve. Her voice evens out, the tears no longer coming in torrents.

"I did what I had to do. I put her down, apologizing. I apologized over and over again, and I heard that thing coming and I took off. I ran full tilt into the woods. Behind me, I heard that screaming. All of that awful, horrible screaming."

She swallows, and her voice stutters. "I listened to that familiar sound of tearing flesh, and then the dull crunch of snapping bone. I listened to the creature chew on Rachel. I tried not to. I tried to just focus on running, or the sound of the rain, or the thunder, or the wind, but I couldn't. All I could hear was my friend being eaten alive."

Silence stretches between us. I clear my throat. "Is that it? You got away, ran into the SAR team on your way down the mountain?"

"No," she says, closing her eyes. There's a look of resigned regret in her features. "I hear another sound. I hear a helicopter. A moment later, I catch sight of its searchlight, beaming over the forest. I know this might be my only chance, so I start waving around my phone's light, trying to make as much of a scene as I can.

"It works. The helicopter swings over, and it lowers a ladder with a rescue technician. He straps me to a line and asks me if I'm alone. I'm hysterical, shouting a mile a minute. I shriek that a monster attacked my friend, and I point toward Rachel's lantern, faintly visible in the distance. I tell him it killed her."

Amanda gulps, wiping at her eyes. "He radios in to have me brought up and says he'll go look for Rachel. I tell him not to. I know if he does, he'll die too. It'll kill him just like it killed her, but over the wind and rain he either doesn't hear me, or doesn't care.

"I'm pulled into the helicopter, and a few minutes later I hear the man's voice over the radio. It's desperate. Full of grief. He says he needs a stretcher down there. He says he found the other woman, and that she's still alive."

Jesus.

"Have you spoken to Rachel since?" I ask quietly.

Amanda shakes her head. "No. She um—she's in a coma. Both of her arms are missing, the wounds are infected and she's developed serious pneumonia. Doctors aren't sure if she's going to make it."

She brings a hand to her mouth and chokes back a sob. Her eyes are wide, and her body quakes. "I... I left her there to die. If I had just stayed with her a couple minutes longer then the rescue chopper would have found us. It would have scared that fucking thing away and Rachel..."

"Would still be gravely injured," I finish. "You can't blame yourself. You didn't know the chopper was around the corner. All that you knew was something wanted to kill you, and it was winning the battle for your life."

Her shoulders wrack with silent sobs. "I could've stayed with her." She breaks down all over again, and this time I give her all the time she needs. I've scarcely seen somebody so grief-stricken in all my years of doing this, and it's almost as bizarre to me as the anomalies I've spent my life hunting. To hate yourself for something as simple as wanting to live. It's inhuman.

"I'm sorry," she says finally. "That's... that's everything. Can I go now?"

I lean back in my chair, frowning. It's not that I don't empathize with her, but such messy reactions only serve to get in the way of actually fixing problems. In her case, getting revenge for Rachel.

She stands up, sniffling, then answers her own question. "… I'm gonna head home."

"Wait," I say.

She stops in her tracks. "What?"

"Can you take me there?"

She stares at me with red, puffy eyes. Her face is a mask of confusion. Disbelief. "Excuse me?"

"The cabin, I mean." I lean forward in my chair. "Can you take me to the Callous Man?"

***

I've never been a fan of the woods.

Call it a bad childhood experience. Call it being an out-of-shape asshole. I'm even less of a fan when I'm stuck hiking through them for work, and yet it seems like work has a sick sense of humor, because I find myself in these fortresses of shit and sticks more often than I'd like. Which, for the record, is never.

Well, except for today.

It's a long time before we reach the cabin. The girl said it took her and her friend eight hours. Well, it takes us twelve. My best days are behind me, unfortunately, but luckily I don't need to be very fit for what I'm about to do.

"I still don't understand why you couldn't have just followed the map," Amanda says. "I told you exactly how to get to—"

"Because," I say, still breathless from the hike. "This cabin doesn't exist on a map. You can point it out to me all you want on your iPhone, but unless you're right beside me, I'll never see it. It's just the way the Callous Man works."

She narrows her eyes at me. "You keep saying that name. Why do you call him the Callous Man?"

I pull open the door of the cabin, and instantly it smells like shit and dead animals.

Great.

"I call him the Callous Man," I say, strolling across the creaky floorboards, "because that's his name. It's the name the first person that ever encountered him coined him with, and so it is the name with which I refer to him."

"The first person?"

"Yeah," I say, stepping into the bedroom. "Me."

The floor is a mess, covered in what's left of Amanda's tent. A small device lays a few feet away, and I figure it's probably her locator beacon.

"Hang on," she says, appearing in the doorway behind me. "You're the first person you saw the crea—the Callous Man?"

I nod, bending down and picking up one of the shattered photo frames she'd mentioned. Dusting it off, I hold it up to her. "This is my grandpa and I, showing off our rifles before going deer hunting."

She looks shocked. Stunned. Her eyes gaze at the picture, then back at me. "On second glance, you two really do share a resemblance. You and he look so much alike."

"Yeah, I suppose we do." I toss the frame onto the ground.

"You lived here?"

"Visited. My grandpa lived here."

"You're kidding." She shakes her head, incredulous. "This whole thing is so bizarre. It has to be a nightmare. It can't be real."

I flip the water bottle full of black grime in my hands, catching it with a smile. "You're preaching to the choir, lady. If I had to guess, I probably hope I wake up from this even more than you do."

"Unlike you," she says with a glare. "I don't have any... secret agent training, or whatever."

"Unlike me, you've got my gun. The only training you need is to point and shoot, and not hit me with the bullets."

She taps my revolver, strapped to her thigh. It was the sole condition of her joining me on this little woodland excursion: she gets to carry the gun. I told her that's fine, with one stipulation.

"Remember," I say. "Don't fucking touch that thing unless the Callous Man's already pulling you into his big mouth. I don't need you shooting me before I finish my business."

"What if he's attacking you?" she asks.

"I'll deal with it."

"You'll deal with an eight foot tall monster with nothing but your bare hands?"

The water bottle crinkles in my grip. "Just trust me on this. I'm a professional." I place my hand on the windowsill and look out over the clearing, out past the treeline. The sun's turned a golden red. Soon, it'll be night.

"Nervous?"

"What do you think?" she says. "I hope you're as good as you say you are."

The way she moves, the way she speaks and the way she keeps touching the revolver on her thigh tell me everything I need to know.

She's terrified.

"Relax," I say. "Save the anxiety for when our friend shows up."

Amanda pulls one of the chairs from the living area into the bedroom with me. She sits down on it, rigid and straight. I'm almost proud of her. Sure, she was only willing to accompany me with a revolver strapped to her thigh, but she still chose to do it; she chose to get revenge for what thing did to her.

What it did to Rachel.

"Almost there," I mutter. My eyes follow the sun as it slips behind the treeline. Shadows stretch out, engulfing the cabin in thin strips of darkness. "He'll be here soon."

Seconds pass, then minutes, and then things begin to change. It starts with a crow taking flight, and I already know he's coming. I can feel him. A family of rabbits follows, bounding through the clearing. Soon, the entire forest is fleeing past us, far away from the Callous Man, and the death he represents.

I pop a piece of spearmint gum and start chewing. It helps me focus. "You ready?"

"Why?" she says, shooting up from the chair. "Is he here?"

"Does it make a difference? You're either ready or you're not."

She scowls at me, but her body relaxes. "I'm ready. Are you sure you can kill him?"

A mad mixture of impatience and nervousness flutters in my stomach. I toy with the idea of lying. It'd put her at ease. Then I decide it doesn't matter anymore. Both of us are in too deep. "No."

"No?" she repeats, hysterical. She rises from her chair, rounding on me. "You said you were professional!"

"I am."

"You told me you've dealt with a hundred different monsters!"

"I have."

Her mouth opens, but no words come out. She stares at me with something between stunned disbelief and absolute loathing. She thinks I've signed our death warrants.

"I'm not going to lie to you," I say. "I've dealt with a lot of creatures. Some bad, some worse. I know this job inside and out, and I don't plan on dying today, but the Callous Man is different."

"How?"

"He's—" I catch myself. We're on the precipice, and there's no going back, but there are still words that can upset the operation. I exercise some tact. "He's powerful. He can distort this world and manipulate dimensions. It's why I needed you here, it's why I needed your Link. He chose you. The Callous Man gave you the key to his world, and only you—but he never said you couldn't bring visitors."

She shakes her head. She's trying to piece it together—bless her heart, she's trying her best, but there aren't enough pieces to make sense of it, and that's intentional. It's by design. I need her obedient, not unruly. Everything hinges on her cooperation.

"I don't understand. Why did he choose me?"

The sun finishes its descent, its red-orange rays fading to darkness. I flick my flashlight on, holding it up to the window and watching the clearing with bated breath. The Callous Man is coming.

"He chose you because of the life you live," I explain. "The values you represent. It means something to him."

"Values I represent? What, like honesty and integrity?" She snorts. "What do *values* mean to a monster like that?"

I smirk. "They mean you taste good."

The night is still. Silent. Just as she earlier described, there's no sound of life, except this time there's no storm either. It's a cloudless sky, without so much as a breeze, and I can almost hear Amanda's heart beating out of her chest.

"Ha ha," she says sarcastically. She's close enough behind me now that I can feel her breath on my neck. She really is terrified. "What do those values actually mean to it?"

"To him," I correct. "Believe it or not, that monster really is a man. When you become as powerful as he is though, food stops meaning what it means to you and I. It's less about calories and more about filling a void. It's trying to supplement its diet with concepts, ideas that it's missing."

"Why?"

"To become better. To cure itself."

There's movement in the clearing, and my breath catches as I see it: a set of crooked antlers. They rise from the bramble, soon revealing a face covered by matted black hair, one with a tiny snout and a halo of dark, beady eyes. The dots glimmer in the beam of my flashlight.

"It wants to stop being a monster?" she asks, her voice thick with disbelief. "It's eating people to save itself?"

"Shh!" I hiss. My eyes are wide, and my mouth is split into the largest grin I've worn in years. "He's here."

I sense her tense up behind me, but to her credit she doesn't unholster the revolver on her thigh. She keeps her cool. I grip the water bottle tighter, reaching a hand to its cap.

No.

I pull my hand away, reminding myself that I need to keep *my* cool too. It's still too soon. The Callous Man can still make his escape. Fade away. I need him committed.

At the edge of the clearing, the man rises to his full height. I can see clearly now his dark fur chest, and his long, thin fingers resting on the ground. His bird-like legs begin a slow march forward, their claws digging at the loamy earth.

"He's coming," I say, taking a step back. "Stay behind me. Directly behind me."

She doesn't speak, but I know she's nodding. I hear her feet creak on the floorboards in concert with my own. My fingers play at the cap of the water bottle. Everything comes down to this. Forty years of horror and misery have led me to this moment.

A snickering sound pierces the air. The man's moving faster now, each footstep coming at the pace of a light jog. There's hardly any time left, but still I wait.

"He's coming," Amanda hisses from behind me. She's panicking. Her hand clutches at my shoulder and I grunt, shaking her off.

"Don't," I tell her. "Relax. We're almost done here." My heart races. Seeing the monster again after all these years is dredging up old memories, and the little boy threatens to take hold inside of me. My palms are thick with sweat.

It doubles over, sprinting on all fours. Its armada of eyes connects with my own, while its crooked antlers sway in concert with its powerful body. Clouds of earth burst out from behind it, its long fingers tearing at the ground with each stride. "Nyeh nyeh nyeh," it snickers. "NYEH NYEH!"

It leaps at the window.

For a moment, time seems to stop. I stare, transfixed by the creature I used to know so well. It's horrifying, inhuman face gazes back at me and inside of it I see an insatiable hunger. A need to feed.

My body freezes, my blood goes cold. Terror grips me as its fingers reach outward, passing through the window while its vocal chords chitter in anticipation. It wants me.

I lunge to the side.

It collides with Amanda, its antlers piercing her stomach and showering the bedroom in blood. Her body crashes against the wall with a sickening crunch, and lays there in a broken, whimpering heap.

I stay as quiet as I can. The Callous Man shakes his tangle of black hair and looks around, reorienting himself. First to me, then to her.

Then back to me.

Fuck. My fingers begin untwisting the cap of the water bottle. It's too soon. I need him distracted. I need him feeding and committed, but I don't think I have an option anymore. It steps toward me. The floor groans. My mouth feels dry, my limbs twitchy. Fear takes root in my chest, and the little boy inside threatens to take hold.

No. I have to hang on. I open the water bottle, and my mouth begins stuttering the words. "T-Thu Val Nolar..."

The Callous Man lowers himself. His back arches, and his tiny snout begins to open, growing larger and larger. Screams of a hundred souls echo from the void inside of him, their arms reaching toward me, desperate to draw another into their nightmare.

"Gal Nush Alza..."

I continue the words, but there's no time. They're so close. He's so close. I press myself as far against the corner as I can, but still I feel their cold grip on my leg. They pull. They're strong. My balance goes out from under me, and I fall on my ass. "Yust val kulna…"

It wasn't supposed to happen like this. She held the values he needed. Her. Not me.

I keep speaking the incantation. I keep moving my lips, but now my body's acting on instinct, on learned behavior. I can't so much as think as I slip further and further into the abyssal darkness of the Callous Man's jaws. I keep speaking the words, but my voice is drowned by the pleas of the dead. Screaming. Howling. Begging. The incantation is all I have left. It's not enough. It's taking too long.

A deafening bang rings out, interrupting the chorus of screaming souls. The Callous Man recoils, its jaw sliding across the floor and its body writhing in agony. It stumbles to the side and then two more gunshots pierce the night. It falls to its knees.

I can see behind him now. I can see Amanda's bloody, mangled heap. One of her legs is snapped backwards, and her white shirt is torn at her stomach, with pieces of her falling out of the hole. Blood spills from her mouth like a fountain, and in her trembling hands she holds the revolver.

"Thank you," I breathe, rising to my feet on shaky legs. "Thank you, Amand—"

Another blast of the hand gun, and this time my ears are ringing like church bells. I stumble to the side, and in the dim light of my lantern, I see a bullet hole in the wall beside me. I barely have time to look back at her before agony rips through my thigh, and I collapse onto the bedroom floor.

Fucking bitch! My hands clutch the wound instinctively. I don't need to look at it to feel the warm wetness of blood seeping through my fingers. I gaze up at her, and she steadies the gun at me. I was so close. So goddamn close. Forty years of this shit and I'm undone by a blogger.

"Do it," I growl. Death by a bullet isn't a bad way to go, all things considered. "Do it before he takes us both!"

She lowers the revolver and tears fall from her eyes. She's choking on a word, but all that's coming out is a torrent of blood. It's fine. I know what she wants to say.

"I did it because it was the only way," I explain through gritted teeth. "One of us always had to die, but if it was me, then it meant we both did."

Her body's twitching in shock. She's still moving her mouth, but it's just blood now. No words. Only blood. Her face is pale and glassy eyed, but I only see it for another moment before the Callous Man begins to rise. Nyeh nyeh nyeh. He's snickering, but it's violent. Angry.

His eyes gaze at me. The antlers are casting twisted shadows in the light of my lantern, and it's making him seem even more unnatural. More inhuman. Nyeh Nyeh. He turns away from me. He turns to Amanda.

"Fel guz rea…" I whisper. "Morath un gre' shan."

His footsteps groan on the rotting cabin floorboards. I don't see Amanda, but I hear the gurgle of blood. I hear the desperate shuffle of her body, pushing itself against the wall. I hear a gunshot ring out. Then another.

The footsteps march forward, and so does my incantation. The water bottle's shaking in my grip now, the grimy fluid swirling in a murky maelstrom. "Grea yulia."

Another shot.

"Thel ra dua."

A cacophony of screams.

"Set kil ona."

Amanda lets loose on the hand gun twice more, and then the firearm clicks impotently. She's burned through every round that it has. It wasn't enough. It never could be. My lips keep moving even as I hear her body being dragged across the floor.

The ancient language flows out of me, and I'm deaf to the sounds of her flesh being ripped and torn, her limbs being devoured inch by inch. She needs to hang on. Her role in this isn't over yet.

I speak the final words.

"Set rindas!" The water bottle jolts from my grip, the murky fluid inside exploding into a dark cloud, twisting around the room like a tornado of smoke. I hear the screaming falter, then I hear the Callous Man lurch around, snickering in confusion. I hear Amanda groan.

She's a fighter. Good.

It takes the cloud only a handful of seconds to coalesce into the greatest monster I've ever seen. But in that moment, it feels like a lifetime. Its form snaps and cracks with bolts of electricity. Its twelve eyes glow an impossible blue. Upon its six muscled arms are heavy chains linking to a choker on its neck, and it roars in fury.

"This time I'll have your soul, little man. I'll enjoy it over a glass of your misery!"

I let a grin slip across my lips. For the first time since the Callous Man appeared, I feel my sense of humor returning. "Sorry to disappoint, Dreighar, but I summon you by means of an offering."

The genie's brows furrow and his mouth opens to reveal a row of jagged teeth. "I see no living humans here, save for one." He's smiling. He reaches an arm out to grab me, but as soon as his fingers brush my throat, they hiss and steam. He recoils, snarling.

"She's your offering," I say, pointing past the Callous Man to Amanda's mangled body. "Now obey my command."

A legion of screams interrupt us. The Callous Man's jaws have opened, and once more a hundred arms reach from the maw—this time toward the newcomer. They grasp at the genie, phasing through the gaseous image.

Dreighar scowls, his voice dropping to a low growl. "Very well. The words are spoken. A soul for a soul." His body splits in two, circumventing the Callous Man and reforming in front of Amanda. She's nearly dead. She's confused. She doesn't understand what's happening.

I've given her a mercy. Dreighar will treat her soul better than the Callous Man ever would. The genie's hand reaches out to touch her, and in the next instant, her body is gone. Only the bloodstains remain.

The Callous Man looks back to me, its jaw scraping along the floor. It recognizes there's nothing in the genie to consume. It wants what's inside of me, though. It wants the memories of its humanity. Revenge.

It takes a heavy step toward me. Then another. The screams are deafening, but I know I don't need my voice to be heard. A command is a command.

"For her soul, I want His."

The pale hands reach out from the abyssal maw, grasping my legs, and I let them. My body falls to the floor. It inches toward the jaws of the beast. Toward damnation.

Then, light fills the room, and the cabin shakes with the low bass of eternity itself. The screaming fades to a whimper. Then, after a loud pop, it's gone.

Everything's gone.

The Callous Man. The cabin. I'm alone, laying in a dark field, my lantern illuminating a clearing of grass, with tall trees surrounding it. My thigh aches, my mouth is parched, and my conscience is in tatters. But I'm alive.

I'm always alive.

"Soon you'll have fulfilled our contract," says a hissing voice, scraping along my inner ear. It's everywhere and nowhere. "I've taken ninety three souls for you. Only seven more to go."

"Yeah, yeah. I've heard it before," I say with a groan. "Now, hand over my soul."

There's a swirl of smoke, and the frowning genie appears before me. He snaps a finger on one of his six arms and produces a vial filled with murky purple fluid. "The man never deserved this," he says. "He was your own blood."

"Don't lecture me," I say, reaching for the vial. "You and I both know he was never supposed to turn into that."

The genie pulls back, gazing at the vial. "What is meant to be and what comes to pass are two different things. You shield yourself in the delusion of intention."

He encircles me in a snaking ribbon of smoke, his face materializing near my ear. "You forced that destiny on the man. He had no desire to participate in your war."

"Yeah, well none of us do. And yet it's coming anyway." Something takes a seat in my gut. Regret, maybe? Remorse? It's an ugly feeling, whatever it is. I blame it on the woman. Why didn't she just kill me?

No, I think to myself. Shake it off. I've got more important things to worry about.

"The vial," I growl, holding my hand out.

"I think I may have miscalculated," Dreighar mutters, staring at the vial with curiosity. "A soul for a soul, such are the terms of our contract, and yet…"

I swallow and it feels like sandpaper. When's the last time I had something to drink? "You got your soul, now give me mine." My voice cracks. Fuck. My voice *cracks*.

The genie's twelve eyes swivel their gaze to me. A smile slips across its lips. When he speaks, his voice is quiet. Unsettling. "I count over a hundred souls in this vial."

My heart slams against my ribcage. Damn it. "That's not fair!" I shout, trying to rise to my feet, but my thigh screams in pain and I fall back to earth. "I only asked for his soul! I never asked for the souls he devoured."

"And yet, they are still a part of him."

"Please…" It can't end here. "Be reasonable."

"Reasonable?" the genie roars, and his form becomes massive. Lightning sparks around him, and the wind whips into a gale threatening to unseat me from the ground.

"You chain me to this earth for decades, turn me into a common reaper for your own ends, and you confine me to a *plastic bottle*! You speak of reason to me?"

"I did what I had to!" I bellow. "A war is coming, and we need these souls! We need an army!"

"Your petty war means nothing to me." Dreighar points a long finger toward me, and a red aura swirls around it. Sparks crackle at its tip. Then slowly, reluctantly, he curls it back into a fist. "I am, however, a reasonable being."

My breath hitches in my chest as I hang on the monster's every word.

"You have broken the terms of our contract, but I have also willingly fulfilled your wish. For that, I will give you a compromise, little human."

Compromise? That's good. Better than nothing, at least.

Dreighar's eyes glint. "One month."

"One month?"

"Settle your affairs. Prepare for your war. One month from now, I'll take the soul I've dreamed of for decades. I'll spend the next century picking you out of my teeth."

I sigh, falling back onto the grass. It's better than I could expect, all things considered. I'm surprised the cosmic asshole didn't just scoop me up right then and there.

Fucking fine print.

"Okay," I say. "Can you get me out of here?"

He smirks, turning into formless smoke. "A soul for a soul. No more, no less." He begins swirling like a mad tornado of shadow, howling and roaring, and a moment later he's gone, vacuumed back into the water bottle.

Asshole.

Looks like I'm finding my own way down. Once more, I try to rise to my feet, and once more I wince in pain and fall to the earth. Damn. The revolver did good work on my thigh.

No, *she* did.

The woman tugs at my thoughts. Her resolve. Her strength. Her blog. She could tell a story, Amanda Haynes. She's gone now, but there's still a story that needs to be told, and I'm running out of time to tell it.

I spot a mess in the corner of my eye. A pile of canvas, torn and bloody, with tent poles poking out.

That should do.

I crawl toward it, and a moment later I find what I'm looking for: a black device laying a few feet away—just like it'd been in the cabin.

The beacon.

I reach out and grab it and click the button. It beeps.

Good.

It beeps.

***

You don't need me to tell you that the search team located me, and you don't need me to tell you that they had a lot of questions, but that the Facility stepped in and took care of it. You also don't need me to tell you that I'll be walking with crutches for the rest of my short life.

What you need me to tell you is why I'm sharing this. You need to know why I'm telling you this story, and why I need you to tell it to others. Your friends. Your family. Everybody.

The reality is, a war is coming. It's a war that humanity isn't outfitted for, but we're doing the best we can. Strictly speaking, everything I've just said is classified, and yet it's critical this information be spread far and wide. What's coming for us can't be stopped by missiles and guns. It can't be overcome by men and women. It has to be through other means.

Legendary means.

The folks at the top don't want to admit that. They don't want to sow chaos and uncertainty and admit our hourglass is danger-ously low on sand, but it is, and chaos is coming one way or another.

We're doing what we can at the Facility, but it isn't enough. Not even close. They'd skin me alive for telling you this, but my time's already up, so fuck 'em.

I'm asking you—all of you, if you see a creature that defies explanation, or a certain something that goes bump in the night, share your experience. Make it known. Against the eldritch abominations coming our way, those monsters might be our only chance.

And honestly? We need all the help we can get.

THE SITTER

The girl was odd.

Cross-eyed and snaggle-toothed, she looked a bit like she'd spun the Wheel of Misfortune six times too many. She spoke with a wheezing voice, like every word was some great effort. Asthma, maybe? Hard to say. Her parents, Mr. and Mrs. Thomas, never mentioned any medical conditions.

All they said was Madeline was different.

Oh, and that I should lock the bedroom door.

Of course, I didn't bother with that last one, mostly because I'm a full grown man and six-year-old girls are not at all terrifying to me. Still, when I opened my eyes that night and saw Madeline standing next to my bed, I confess I was spooked. Her expression was manic. Her eyes, cross-eyed as usual, stared at me and the roof with equal intensity. It would have almost been comical if it wasn't for the bizarre, nonsensical words she was muttering, and the long, gleaming object in her hand.

"Madeline," I said, swallowing. "Is that a kitchen knife?"

She nodded, though her expression didn't change. "It's okay," she wheezed. She lifted the knife and pressed her thumb to the blade, where a bead of blood slid across her skin. "It's sharp, see?"

"Stop that!" I said, reaching for the blade.

She recoiled, clutching it close to her chest, her face twisting into a snarl. "You didn't lock the door like mummy and daddy told you to."

"I'm a grown man," I said, feeling foolish for arguing with a child. "I don't need to explain myself to you. Now, what are you doing with that knife?"

Madeline raised the knife. She looked at it with a sort of detached fascination, her lazy eye rolling up in her head. "This is so you can sleep."

"Give it to me," I said, holding out my hand. "Now."

Her bottom lip quivered. She gave a wheeze of defiance.

"Madeline!" I shouted, louder than I intended. It seemed to serve its purpose though, because she quickly handed the knife to me. I slipped it behind me on the bed, far from her reach. "Thank you," I breathed. "Now, go back to your room and this time stay in bed, understood?"

She nodded, despondent. I thought my little nightmare was over, but then she stopped halfway across the room. She faced me again with a snarl, again with her lazy eye rolled upward like some twisted, demon-possessed asylum subject. "Get out of this house," she spat.

A chill swept over me. The way she spoke, the malice in her voice was like nothing I'd ever heard of from a child. "No, Madeline," I said, hoping I sounded much braver than I felt. "I'm the adult, and I'm telling you to get back to bed. Understand? I don't want to hear another word from you!"

"If I were you," Madeline said. "I wouldn't close my eyes tonight." Then she turned and slipped out of the room, leaving the door wide open in the process. Needless to say, I jumped out of bed and slammed the thing shut, triple-checking to make sure that it was securely locked.

Catching my breath after the whole scenario, I stalked back to bed and crawled onto the mattress. I grabbed a fistful of covers and pulled them onto me, rolling over onto my back.

Then I froze.

Somehow, I'd never noticed it before. The Thompsons had a strange art piece on the ceiling, one that looked almost as though it were moving in the dark of the room. Four long, twisting lines sprouting from a bulbous sphere.

No.

Not lines, I realized.

Legs. Legs that were clicking along the ceiling now while something small and hairy unfurled itself from the dark sphere. It lowered itself toward me.

A head.

181

"Finally," it whispered. *"Alone at last."*

HOUSE OF THE HOLY

It's a scary thing, being apart from yourself—being a tool. Have you ever been possessed? I'm guessing not. Most haven't. And they can thank their lucky stars for that.

I have, though.

I've felt the suffocating grip of something closing around my mind, squeezing it until every last ounce of me was gone. I've felt the horror of knowing I'm not alone. The horror of knowing I might never be alone again.

Three days after I turned six, my life turned into confetti. It tore itself into little pieces, each less recognizable than the last. That night, my foster parents locked me in the attic. They told me that a monster was coming to eat me—a werewolf.

"We'll let you out in an hour," they laughed. "If there's anything left to let out."

It wasn't real. Of course it wasn't real. The whole thing was just a twisted power play, a means to scare me into obeying their overbearing rules. I was young, though. Naïve. And the thing about being young and naïve is sometimes you say and do things that you live to regret, and I'd done exactly that.

I'd confided in them my greatest fear: men that turned into beasts. Werewolves.

I gave them my vulnerability, openness. They gave me psychological warfare.

Betrayal cuts deep, but the betrayal of a parent—the person meant to protect you when the whole world turns its back on you—that cuts deeper than skin.

Those scars don't fade.

I spent my first minutes in the attic screaming and crying, beating my fist against the door. They answered this with a volley of threats, beginning and ending with three hours standing in the corner, balanced on my tippy-toes, if I so much as dared to open that hatch.

"You deserve this," Papa Joey told me. "You knew damn well to keep your eyes closed during that Sunday prayer, but you opened 'em anyway. You embarrassed us. Humiliated us, not just in front of the church, but Father Andrews too. People are gonna think we don't know how to raise a child, or that we can't keep a little boy in line. You think that's funny? You think that's fair to us?"

"Shame on you," Mama Sharon said.

They weren't lying—at least, not about me opening my eyes. I was a distractible child. Later, I'd be diagnosed with attention deficit disorder, so what was I supposed to do? That didn't matter to them, though.

In their eyes, not only had I disrespected the law of the house, I'd disrespected the law of the Lord. That made punishing me easy. Necessary. It made punishing me an act of God.

"Do I really have to stay up here a whole hour?" I whimpered, gazing warily across the sea of darkness. The light in the attic hadn't worked for as long as I'd lived there.

"That depends," Mama Sharon replied. "If the werewolf gets you first, you might only be in there for ten or twenty minutes."

"Who knows?" Papa Joey called as they left down the hallway. "You might just get lucky."

They descended the steps, chuckling to themselves.

The thought of opening the hatch and slipping out of there crossed my mind. It crossed my mind over and over again, as a matter of fact, but I knew it wouldn't be worth it. As scared as I was, I'd lived with Mama and Papa for eight months by then, and I knew well what kind of punishment they were capable of doling out.

For this, I'd be in the corner for certain. On my tippy toes.

If they saw me resting my feet—even for a moment, they'd get out the wooden board with the nails in it. They'd slip that under my heels. I'd been there before.

I never, ever wanted to be there again.

So I did my best to swallow my fear. I took a deep breath and braced myself against the nightmare of the attic. "I'm not afraid of you!" I said to the shadows. "I'm a monster too, you know!"

It was a lie. I was no more a monster than I was an astronaut, or a dinosaur. I was just a scrawny kid who missed his mom, sitting in an attic that seemed to press upon you from all sides. But it was all that I had. See, the only thing I knew capable of harming a werewolf was a silver bullet, and I was fresh out of those, so I went with the next best thing: convincing the werewolf I wasn't prey.

I began my punishment sitting near the hatch. It seemed the safest option, and vibrating with adrenaline and panic, safety was at the top of my mind. I waited silently, eyes closed, heart fluttering, listening for a growl or howl to meet my ears, for the sounds of my doom to rush out and greet me. But they never did.

Once I'd made it ten minutes without being eaten, I started to calm down. Maybe there weren't any monsters up there, after all. Maybe I was just afraid of the dark. If that was the case, then that was a problem I could solve.

The broken light switch was far beyond my ability to repair, but I knew for a fact there were a couple of flashlights lying around here somewhere. I'd used them while helping Papa Joey put out mouse traps. Trouble was, there was enough junk in the attic to fill a small museum, so finding which teetering box those flashlights were in might take some time.

Still, time was one of the few things not in short supply up there.

Closing my eyes, I took a breath, steeling myself against the darkness ahead. Then I stepped off into the unknown.

My footsteps groaned as I crept through the attic. Much of my movement consisted of stumbling around blindly, holding my arms out like Frankenstein's monster and praying I didn't encounter anything with fur. A few steps into my journey I bumped into something. My heart jumped, but it was just an old table.

I felt its surface, figuring if there was a flashlight up here, then it was probably somewhere on th—

Eight tiny legs skittered across my hand. I flailed, falling backward and knocking the spider off of my skin. Heart pounding, I sat there and caught my breath.

"You're kidding, Franky!" The television echoed from below the floorboards. "Keep that up, and you won't just be outta a job—you'll be out of a *wife!*" A laugh track kicked in, joined by Mama Sharon shrieking in amusement and clapping her hands. From the sounds of it, they were watching their favorite sitcom again. I'd never seen it since I wasn't allowed to watch TV, but I always wondered if it was as funny as they made it seem.

"It's not."

I jumped, startled by the voice. "What?"

"You deaf, kid? I said it's *not*. It ain't that funny."

My heart struck my ribcage like a hammer. No, no, no. This wasn't happening. It's just the dark, that's all. There's nothing to be afraid of in the dark because I'm all alone and there's *no* such thing as monsters and it's *just* the TV that I'm hearing and—

"You're not alone, kid. And I ain't Will or Grace, either."

I scrambled backward, away from the voice as quickly as I could. Too quickly. My head found the downward slope of the attic's roof and hit it with a *crack*. Pain exploded across my skull. "Stay back," I groaned, my vision swimming. "If you don't, I'll—"

"You'll do nothing!" the voice sneered.

"I—I'm a werewolf," I warned, my voice shaking with counterfeit authority. "Stay back. It's a full moon tonight and—"

"Ain't no full moon, and you ain't no werewolf."

Something thumped a short way from me, and my mouth went dry. Another thump. *Thump. Thump. Thump.* The floorboards trembled. My eyes swiveled to the thin square of light that outlined the attic hatch. It was rattling. Somebody was knocking on it from below.

"You breaking things up there?" Poppa Joey shouted. "You better not be! Any more banging around and you can forget the werewolf. I'll come up there and beat your ass myself!"

Even then, I could hear the voice whispering all around me, moving around the attic like an unholy breeze. "Please," I said quietly, making myself small in the corner. "There's something up here! I need you."

"You think I'm stupid, boy?"

My mouth trembled, my entire body quaked. I recognized the tone in Papa Joey's voice.

"I asked you a fucking question, didn't I?" he bellowed. "Answer me when I speak to you!"

"N-no sir," I said, tears welling in my eyes. "I don't think you're stupid, Papa."

"Then why are you lying to me?" Something struck the bottom of the hatch and made it jump violently—his fist. "You just earned yourself another half hour up there. Keep up this shitty behavior and I'll show you some shitty behavior of my own. Understand?"

I whimpered.

"DO YOU FUCKING UNDERSTAND?"

"Yes, sir!" I called, doing my best to keep the tears in my eyes. "Yes, sir, I understand, sir!"

"Good," he muttered. His footsteps faded as he made his way back downstairs.

"What's he broken?" I heard my Mama ask at the bottom of the steps.

"Nothing," Papa said, raising his voice so I could hear. "If he doesn't want me breaking something of his, it'll stay that way. Lord knows I'll start with the teeth. Ain't nothing out of the ordinary about a young boy missing a tooth."

Laughter rang out around the attic. "You're not safe here," the voice said, right beside me. "Not safe here at all."

I recoiled, terrified, but careful not to make a sound. The voice sounded low, raspy and inhuman. It sounded hungry. "Please," I said. "Leave me alone. I wasn't kidding about being a werewolf, you know."

"Do you want to be safe?" the voice hissed, slithering all around me like a cockroach on my skin. "I can make you safe. I can make all this pain go away. Doesn't that sound... nice? Just say the word and poof, you're home free, back with dear *mommy*."

"What word?" I said, confused.

The voice tutted in my ears, as if it were on both sides of me at once. "Oh, don't play coy. You know the word. The one you say kneeling beside your bed every night, praying to the big cheese in the sky."

"Amen?"

"Amen?" More laughter, this time sardonic, mocking. "Give me a fucking break, kiddo. I mean the other word, the one you whimper with tears in your eyes and fear in your heart—afraid Mama and Papa might hear you say it out loud."

A terrible feeling was beginning to take hold in my gut. The voice sounded suddenly so much worse than a simple werewolf. It sounded sinister. Like it was manipulating me. Testing me. "I don't have tears in my eyes when I pray," I said defiantly. "I don't know what you're talking about!"

The voice—whatever it was—stepped forward then, and the entire attic rattled against its weight. Dust drifted down from the rafters. Floorboards shuddered.

It was loud.

Too loud.

"The fuck did I just tell you, boy?" Papa Joey hollered from below. "So help me God, if I have to get up from this couch you're gonna wish there really was a lock on that fucking hatch!"

I slammed my eyes shut. "Go away," I said quietly. "Please, whatever you are, just go away."

"No."

It took another step forward, and the attic shook again. This time, the frame of the house trembled with it, rumbling as it braced itself against the monster inside.

"I'm not playing around," Papa growled from below, and this time his voice was different. Something had wormed its way inside of it. Something dangerous. Deadly. "One more time, boy. Try me one more time and I swear to you that it'll be the last…"

"He's mad," I whimpered, clutching my hands to my ears. "He's really mad and he's gonna think it's me. Please, you've got to stop. You've got to go!"

"I'm not going anywhere," the voice whispered. "You're stuck with me."

My heart fell. My world was practically spinning. The situation had spiraled so far outside of my control, and I knew that no matter what, once the television episode was over Papa Joey would come up here and show me just how angry he was.

"What's this?" the voice asked, bemused. A sound met my ears; dull and low, like a cardboard box sliding off of a wooden table.

My heart froze.

"Looks expensive."

"No! Don't—"

My plea was cut short, interrupted by a symphony of shattered glass. A half-second later and another box tipped. Something tumbled out of it, obnoxious and heavy, rolling across the creaky floor like a bowling ball.

"I'm going to make you believe," the voice hissed. "No matter what it takes."

I sat, paralyzed with fear, waiting to hear Papa shout my name and tell me that was the last straw. But I didn't hear anything. I didn't hear Papa yelling, or Mama either. I didn't even hear the television.

Something *snapped* from below. "… nothing in him this fucking belt won't fix!"

Footsteps thundered up the stairs.

"Why are you doing this?" I shrieked into the darkness. "Why are you making them hurt me?" Tears poured from my eyes as I trembled in the corner, taking deep, heaving breaths as I prepared myself for the discipline I was soon to receive. For the pain.

"I'm trying to teach you a lesson!" the voice cackled. "Now say the word, boyo! Say the word or you'll *beg* for it later, beaten and bruised!"

"No!" I shouted, shaking my head furiously. Tears stained my cheeks. "I know what you are! I know what evil monsters like you do, but I'm a good kid and I pray every night, so just leave me alone!"

A fist pounded against the underside of the hatch. Then it rattled, like somebody was pulling on the handle, trying to get it open, but it wouldn't budge. "Get your hands off the hatch!" Papa Joey roared.

"Say the word," the voice hissed.

I plugged my ears, curling into a ball. "No! Just leave me alone and go away."

"Do it now, before he gets you! He sounds *so* angry!"

Mama's voice joined the chaos below. "What's he done now? Locked himself up there?"

The hatch rattled, and I heard Joey grunt. "What's it look like, Sharon?"

"Well, just leave him there, then! If he wants to stay up there with the werewolves he can stay there all weekend if he pleases."

"No he damn well can't, Sharon!" Papa shouted. "I've got valuable things in those boxes and the little shitstain's destroying them!" Joey heaved and the attic hatch squealed, sounding as though he were pulling against it with his entire weight.

"Running out of time," the voice said, up against my ear. "Tick tock. Say the word, or you'll pay for this in *blood*. Who knows when he'll stop beating you? Hopefully before you drop dead."

I screamed then, lashing out and throwing out my fists helplessly into the dark, doing anything I could to stop the voice from talking. From tormenting me. "Stop it!" I shrieked. "Stop it!"

In all my life, I'd never felt so helpless. So afraid. There wasn't any escape here. Threats surrounded me. Below, my foster parents were beating down the attic door, while all around me a voice taunted and jeered, goading me to turn away from God, to make me admit I didn't have the faith I claimed to.

I just wanted them both to go away. Forever.

I just wanted to go to my room and play with my action figures and read my story books. I just wanted to be a normal kid again, with a normal family. I wanted to feel safe.

A sharp creak sounded, followed by a snap of wood. Light flooded the attic and I gazed in horror toward the now open hatch, feeling suddenly weak and helpless. Joey had broken the steps clean off of their hinges.

"Obnoxious little shit," Papa snarled, stomping up the stomps.

"Don't kill him, Joey," Mama Sharon said casually. "Just smarten him up. He's been nothing but disobedient since he got here last July."

"Oh, I'll smarten him up," Papa said, face appearing above the floor line with bulging eyes. "I'll teach him a lesson so good he'll wish he was back with that drug addict whore he calls a mother."

"Papa!" I called out, whimpering. "It wasn't me! There was—"

"More lies, boy?" He reached for his waist and unslung his belt, snapping it in his hands. The metal buckle gleamed in the light. "This time," Papa said, stepping forward, "I'm not gonna stop until you bleed."

I recoiled, raising my hands defensively. "Please," I sobbed. "P-please don't, Papa. I'm sorry I—" A crack sounded and pain exploded across my hands. I gasped, instinctively scrambling away, but strong hands grabbed me and dragged me back.

"This time I'll give you the buckle," Papa growled.

Tears gushed from my eyes. Blood leaked from my hands. A word fell from my mouth with all the force of an atomic bomb.

"Well, well," the voice whispered, dripping with violence. "Took you long enough."

***

I woke up in a large, white bed inside of a pale gray room.

"Look who's up," said a familiar voice. I squinted, my eyes adjusting to the brightness of the space. A man in a robe with a crucifix necklace stood at my bedside, staring down at me with cold, calculated eyes. "It only took you four days."

I blinked, bleary-eyed. "Father Andrews?" I mumbled. "I've been asleep for four days?"

"That's what I said."

"Where am I?"

He looked around, as though appraising the setting for the first time himself. "If I had to guess, I'd say we were inside of a hospital, weren't we?" He shot me a smile. "It's fine, I've got most of the curtains drawn so it's hard to tell. Besides, I'm sure somebody your age hasn't had many occasions to be here."

I sat up, confused and disoriented. "What happened?"

Father Andrews frowned, his expression growing grave. "That's what I was hoping you could tell me, Alex. You don't remember anything?"

"No, Father," I said, shaking my head. Memories flashed in my mind—of a belt, of Papa's angry face storming up the attic steps. "I remember being in a lot of trouble," I began. "I remember feeling…"

"Feeling what, Alex?"

The word I wanted to say was *afraid*, but I knew I'd get in worse trouble for saying that. It wasn't fair of me to make Mama and Papa look bad in front of the Father. "I remember feeling tired," I lied, before quickly changing the subject. "Why am I in the hospital, Father? Am I okay?"

"That depends. Do you feel okay?"

"I think so. I feel tired and I've got a headache but mostly I feel alright."

Father Andrews moved closer to me, and a gravity fell across his expression. When he spoke, it was in a quiet, measured tone. "Do you feel like yourself?"

My head spun. Memories lurched out of dark spots in my mind, memories of a voice, of a malevolent presence tempting me to admit I'd been crying during my prayers. Now I was here, in the hospital next to Father Andrews. A priest.

"What's going on?" I asked, more urgently. Even at six, I could connect the dots that something was very wrong. "Something happened, didn't it? And—"

"Easy, Alex," Father Andrews soothed. "The doctors have been in. You'll be happy to hear that, as far as they can tell, you're fine. A little worse for wear, but nothing that won't clear in a few days. And the doctors will be happy to hear you've woken from your coma."

"Coma?" The word was new to me, but I felt like I'd heard it before. It felt like something bad, like something you didn't want to have happen to you. Terror shot through me. "Are Mama and Papa mad at me?" I asked.

A sinking feeling formed in my gut. The voice had destroyed so much stuff in the attic, and now that Mama and Papa had gotten a good look at it, they were probably furious with me. I'd likely get a second-helping of discipline when I got home.

"Sharon and Joseph are dead," Father Andrews said.

My mouth fell open. The gravity of the word was almost beyond my understanding. "Dead?"

Father Andrews sighed, then pulled the rest of the curtain shut around my bed, shielding us from view. "Alex, this is difficult to say... but they're dead because of you. "

I blinked. The situation felt like a bad dream, like a scenario so awful that it couldn't possibly be true. "I killed them?" I said, my voice barely a whisper. "No... No I didn't I—"

"You burned away every ounce of blood in their bodies and seared crucifixes into their foreheads. When the police showed up, they were husks. You were comatose."

I swallowed, my mouth dry. "No, that's not right, I..." Horror wrapped itself around me as more memories unearthed themselves. This time, I remembered the attic and the voice. I remembered it tempting me to break my vows to God by speaking a word. If I just spoke the word, it said, it could make the pain go away. "I loved them," I said, my voice cracking with the onset of tears. "I wouldn't hurt them because I loved them. I promise!"

Father Andrews folded his arms. "That may be, but they're gone now." He reached into his robes and produced a small, clear vial. Unstopping it, he held it above my head. "Now that you're awake, let's try this again." He tilted the vial and doused me in the liquid.

I coughed and sputtered as it fell into my nose and eyes. "What are you doing?"

"Holy water," he explained. He gave the empty vial a gentle shake in front of me. "Over the past three days, I've poured various amounts onto you, but it's never had any effect. Do you know why that is?"

Holy Water. It was something I once learned about in Sunday School: water that had been blessed to protect against demons and other terrible things. If he had been pouring that on me, then it was because he suspected me of being a terrible thing too.

I gazed up at him, horrified. "It wasn't my fault!" I cried, shaking my head as though if I just denied it hard enough, then I could make it all go away. The demon. The dead parents. All of it. I just wanted a second chance.

"What wasn't your fault?" he replied.

Guilt twisted inside of me. "The demon in the attic!" I blurted out. "I didn't mean to talk to it, I swear! It just kept pressuring me and pressuring me and then I got so scared, and I accidentally said the word, but I didn't mean to, I didn't..." I broke off into a long sob.

Father Andrews grabbed me by my shoulders. "You said a word?"

I nodded, my lip curled up and snot leaking down my nose. "I didn't mean to."

"What word?"

The word sat on the tip of my tongue, but fear gripped me. What if the demon was waiting in here, unseen, just like it had been in the attic? What if when I said the word, the demon would crawl right back inside of me and start killing people all over again? I couldn't face that. I couldn't risk that. "I can't," I said.

Father Andrews brought his mouth next to my ear. When he spoke, his voice was quiet, deliberate. *"What was the word, Alex?"*

"If I say, then the demon might come back and hurt some-body."

"Say it!" he snapped. "Say the damn word!"

I slammed my eyes shut, pursing my lips and shaking my head. There was no way I could do it. No way. Not after what had happened last time.

The Father snarled and tore the crucifix from his necklace and pressed it against my forehead. He muttered words in a language I didn't understand. "Enough excuses!"

"Help," I whimpered.

"I'll help you once I'm sure—"

"No," I said. "That was the word. I asked for... help."

"Help?" He stared at me blankly, mouth hanging open as though processing something. "Did you say that you asked for... help?"

I nodded, shaken.

"Oh, Lord Almighty Above." He heaved a sigh, pocketing his crucifix and sitting down in the chair next to my bed. "Thank God."

The situation had only gotten more confusing. "Thank God?"

He took a breath, then another. Eventually, he stood up and approached my bedside, placing a hand on my arm. "Things aren't as bad as they seem."

"They're not? Does this mean I wasn't possessed? That it wasn't me that hurt Mama and Papa?"

Father Andrews' smile faltered. "I don't have much experi-ence with this, so you'll forgive my bluntness. But you deserve the truth." He paused. His next words came slowly. "It's clear to me that you really were possessed, Alex. And, for better or worse, that same force used you to commit violence against Joseph and Sharon. Through you, it killed them."

My heart fell.

In that moment, my world, small as it was, collapsed around me in slow motion. I shrank before Father Andrews. I wanted to keep shrinking—become tinier and tinier until there was nothing left of me and I wouldn't feel this horrible *guilt* and *shame.* My body quaked with the fresh onset of tears. "Will that demon keep possessing me?"

Father Andrews stared at me as though dumbstruck. "De-mon?"

I tried to respond, but it just came out as a torrent of ugly sobs.

A moment later, he seemed to have realized something. He shook his head as though chastising himself and then pulled me close, wrapping me in one of the warmest embraces I've ever felt. "You weren't possessed by a demon, Alex."

He squeezed me.

"You were possessed by an angel."

Made in the USA
Middletown, DE
07 July 2022

68767225R00118